Kissing Alice

Jacqueline Yallop

Atlantic Books
LONDON

First published in hardback in Great Britain in 2009 by
Atlantic Books, an imprint of Grove Atlantic Ltd.

Copyright © Jacqueline Yallop, 2009

1 3 5 7 9 10 8 6 4 2

A CIP catalogue record for this book is available
from the British Library.

978 1 84887 033 8

Printed in Great Britain
by the MPG Books Group

Atlantic Books
An imprint of Grove Atlantic Ltd
Ormond House
26–27 Boswell Street
London WC1N 3JZ

www.atlantic-books.co.uk

i. Arthur

ARTHUR SCRATCHED BRISKLY at stubborn patches of paper pasted thick to the wall, a skin of interweaving pink flowers, half grown and faded. The scrape of his trowel was sharp in the quiet. The sun, pouring in through the library windows, latticed the floor. Sweating underneath his overall, he paused to take off his cardigan, stretching out the pain in his fingers. It was his nineteenth birthday, and it seemed to him as though something might happen.

In order to pull out the shelves and strip the paper behind, Arthur had to move the books. He eased them loose and carried them in piles of two or three to a clean patch of floor where he stacked them and covered them with sheeting. They breathed a floury dust. Flakes of rotten leather binding and tiny scraps of spoilt paper floated around him, catching in the wool of his trousers as he went to and fro across the library. At the end he brushed himself down, releasing the heady smell of the past. His stomach rumbled.

Weary now, and bored by the routine of the long morning, Arthur paused, his feet in a square of fretted sunshine. Without much thought, he peeled off a corner of the loose sheeting and opened the book on the top of the pile. Church bells pealed further down the cathedral close, and Arthur felt his breath falter.

The pages alarmed him, the gusts of colour, summer-blue

flashes, swirls of pinks and reds bleeding together; taut figures, a half-dog beast, a fan-tailed bird coasting into heaven on pale breezes. Nothing was quite clear. It was light bursting through the darkness, the moon or fire; swirling branches of shadowy trees or grasping vines or fire, again, in tongues. It was serpents curled into roses; infants crouching; figures, almost human, but with wings sometimes, or haloes or auras of light, not quite man and not quite woman, but brimfull with the promise of sex. Arthur could not shift the blunt craving that made him look again and again, that made him forget himself. It frightened and sickened him. But still he fingered the pages to ease the sense of them into his skin and his greed for them was overwhelming.

The theft was easy. He had with him, as always, a wide, floppy cloth bag, immaculately clean, in which he kept the brushes, rags and bottles of his trade. He took the book from the top of the pile, wrapped it in a piece of heavy tarpaulin that better obscured its shape, slipped it into the bottom of his bag and stacked the rest of his things on top of it, covering it lastly with his folded cardigan. He then wrapped the remaining pile of books with the dust sheet before continuing his work. At the end of the day, as the other workmen chimed saucy jokes through the open doors, he carried the bag back to his lodgings, where he sat through the dusky hours looking at the plates one by one, slowly, his face bending closer and closer to the pages as the spring light faded.

Through the long hot summer of 1913, and the soft autumn that followed it, while other young men were swimming in the Wear under the shadow of the cathedral, jumping from stone bridges into the green water or lolling through the long evenings on the cobbled Durham walks, Arthur Craythorne preferred the quiet of his lodging room, airless though it was, hung with the stench of burnt mince, the backstreet damp creeping through the cracked window frames. He gave himself up to the pleasures of the book, blurring the edges of himself and imagining new margins.

When the refurbishment of the library was finished, his work took him southwards, with a distinctly ecclesiastical feel, through the holy precincts of Ripon and York. Arthur was not curious about places. He did not notice the change from flood plain to limestone outcrop; from sand and clay to iron-red earth. He was not one for watching the sky, whether hanging vast beyond the coast or squeezed between the breasts of hills. He did not fly kites, wade through rapids after fish or kneel in the wet soil to turn up the caps of mushrooms. He disliked the way nature clung to him, mud to his shoes, drizzle to his hair, seeds and leaves and burrs. What mattered to him was his work. And when war broke out, the urge for redecoration had to be suppressed even among the clergy. Arthur had no choice but to go home. He began the long journey to the West Country with a new suit of clothes, a substantial sheaf of bank notes clipped to his pocket and his book safely wrapped at the bottom of his bag.

Back in Plymouth, Arthur tried telling them about the book, about the things he had sensed emerging flutteringly from the painted pages, but there were other distractions. His family bought him beer and made him cakes, reinventing the man they remembered, and he began work with his older brother, George, lifting and carrying for the railways that smoked to the dockyard. Ships peeled out of the harbour; more and more soldiers folded in and out of lines on the quay. Urgency was everywhere, unspoken, and even the simplest tasks were rushed.

'I could show you, if you like,' he said to his sister Annie.

She was tipped out of the open window trying to see what was happening in the waters of the Sound.

'It's worth a look. The pictures. I could get it out later. We could show the children.'

But with the noise from the street and the soft brush of the breeze against her face, Annie heard his offer only vaguely.

'I think it's some kind of convoy,' she said. 'There're ships as far as you can see, banking up, way beyond the breakwater and round Drake's Island. Come here, Arthur, come and have a look.'

And Arthur, edging up behind his sister, kept the secret of the book to himself.

Even when he met Queenie May he didn't mention it. It didn't seem the sort of thing she would understand. He tried it once, walking with her where the banks of the Tamar became grassy, holding her hand, but it didn't come out right.

'It's not what I thought, being back,' he said as they headed towards the shade. 'It's not quite as it should be – it feels strange.'

He took off his jacket and spread it carefully on the short grass. She sat with her feet tucked under her and her hands wrapped around her knees.

'You'll get used to it,' she said, looking away to the other bank where some boys splashed in the shallows, a dog swimming out beyond them into the still water.

'But what if I don't?'

She shrugged.

'What if I don't, Queen?' He put his arms too tightly across her shoulders. 'What if it's always like this, and I keep thinking of it – the things I could be doing, the decorating and such?'

Though he did not want to, there was a girl he pictured then, smiling: a callous-handed Cheshire girl who had promised to wait for him.

'Tide's changing,' said Queenie May, leaning back against him. His arms weighed heavy still, pinning her, so she flicked just a hand out towards the gathering swell. 'It'll bring the clouds in, I warrant.'

'I do think of it though, Queen. All the time. I wish I didn't but I do.'

She squeezed around under his arms, kneeling to face him. 'You're just up and down at the moment, Arthur, with every-thing. Everyone is. It's like that. It's not rightly normal, with the war and such.' She breathed a soft laugh against his mouth. 'I'll take your mind off it,' she offered.

He looked past her to the water and the birds skimming low and fast across it.

'I don't know, Queen. I…'

But she sprang at him, bright-eyed, laying claim to him with a flush of kisses, and he could not tell her then about the book.

They were married quickly and went to live in two rooms above Annie's family, in a low, recently built brick house, ten minutes' brisk walk from the dockyard. The house was entirely plain except for three panels of coloured glass above the shared front door, which, for a few minutes each morning on a fine day, sent spangled reflections across the brown-tiled hall. This was what Queenie May held on to when she thought of their first home.

Queenie May sat with the windows open, listening to the world beyond. She could hear the trains screeching in and out of the yard, and tried to imagine Arthur then, although she couldn't quite picture him. So she was saved from the sight of her new husband cowering under the noise and the steam, struggling with the weight of his loads, spitting smut, wishing he was back in the serene drawing rooms of the wealthy, putting down layers of paint with such careful skill that they shone. And she did not understand why he was prickly with her when he came home. She could see no reason for his anger when she was light and playful and irresponsibly warm, as though there were no war and no dockyard and no incessant rumbling of trains.

She felt his inexplicable disappointment settling on her like wet linen.

'Come on Arthur. Let's walk somewhere.' She smiled at him, flirting.

'Not now, Queen, I'm tired.'

'I know, but when you're working always. We never get out.'

'You go, then.'

'I can't go on my own, Arthur. Go on, come with me.'

She stepped up close to him, stroking his pale face, brushing ash from the contours of his stubble. He smelt industrial.

'Go on, Arthur,' she wheedled, her body against his now. 'Go on.'

'Let me be, Queen,' he said softly, kissing her lightly.

And so she sat with him, many evenings, waiting for his weariness to lift, and at the first signs of her pregnancy she smoothed her stomach with tireless hands, showing him what they were doing together.

They hung, moon-faced, over the new baby, the cradle swinging erratically between them. Queenie May saw the way her husband watched her, as she manoeuvred her daughter deftly under the blanket, something like approval in his eyes. She smiled at him, still believing they would get used to the surprising weight of each other. But they had very little time. Arthur was conscripted.

'You'll be fine, you and Florrie, till I get back,' he said to Queenie May in the week before he left, blowing out the smoke from his cigarette, watching it swirl away ahead of them. Florrie dangled on her mother's arm.

'And when you come home, you'll set your mind to decorating again, won't you, Arthur?' Queenie May said.

'I will,' said Arthur, certain.

And that evening, he got out his bag of tools and brushes, cleaned each clean piece carefully with a cloth, turned them over in his hand, weighed them, checked them, and spoke to Queenie May about them, drawing her close to him in a new way as he explained what everything was for. Queenie May was quiet as he showed her the bag. His voice was steady and sure, his hands deft as they threaded through the hairs of the brushes and Queenie May saw how he could be, if things all came right. She kissed him fondly and gently on the curve of his ear, slowly, so that the shiver of it prickled them both. It seemed as if they were summoning a future.

It was then that Arthur got out the book. He opened it slowly, and felt such a jolt when he saw the familiar colours that he looked a long time at the page before speaking.

'Are you coming to see?'

Wrapped in tarpaulin, slipped in at the back of the shelves where they stored the odds and ends of bedding, the book had always seemed unnecessary to Queenie May, ballast from her husband's past. She bent away from him to fold the covers over Florrie, murmuring nonsense to their daughter, cheerful and rhythmic.

'She's dribbled,' she said. 'She's made her covers proper damp.'

Arthur stood for a moment watching her. He saw the top button of her skirt undone for comfort and the folds of her belly pushing over the waistband. He caught himself wishing for something else.

'Haven't you wondered about it, Queen? Don't you want to see?' But he could not be sure, even then, that she deserved to see it, and his questions kept her away. She fiddled with Florrie's covers a while longer.

Arthur hardly sighed. 'Forget it then.'

He began to turn the pages without her. He did not invite her again. And although she wanted to move across to him, to take his hand and be part of it, something in the bristling quiet stopped her.

For several hours, Arthur looked at the book and Queenie May found things she could do, sweeping around his feet and along the length of the house, washing baby clothes in the sink. She hummed while she worked. They did not look at each other. But nonetheless they seemed strung together in a kind of rite, the flick of their movements tugging between them. Every sudden gesture landed like a slap. Arthur's going away to war had a momentousness that had to be marked somehow, they knew that, and the book was the only thing they owned that could act as some kind of token. So in the end, because she could not think of anything else to do, Queenie May went to stand behind him, her hands hanging still over the back of his chair, her eyes straining to see the details on the paper. She was not sure what she should be looking at. She tried to make a story from the pictures on the pages, but it didn't make sense. She waited for a clue from Arthur.

'Isn't it beautiful, Queen?' was what came. She didn't like the soft reverence she heard in his voice.

'It's muddled,' she said, her West Country vowels yawning. 'It don't make sense. Not to me. P'raps it's put together wrong.'

She moved away from him and went to sit on the bed. Arthur took it as a rejection, and did not look at her. They could hear Annie's children playing a noisy game below. One of them screeched and there was a clatter on the stairs.

'They'll wake the maid,' Queenie May said, glancing at the cot, but knowing Florrie was used to the noise and wouldn't hear it. Still Arthur didn't speak and she watched him again with his book. It was getting quickly dark and he held it up at an angle to the window to catch the last of the light, his face turned away from her. She wished she hadn't been so quick with him. She wanted another chance. Looking across at him in the dim light, he seemed already to be floating away, the essence of him drifting apart, the familiar fall of his hair, the worn threads of his collar, the form of him, dissolving. It was then that Queenie May had a glimpse of what the war might mean to them. She put the thought aside.

Arthur was intent on the book. He did not look up. Just a glance from him then, just the slightest of smiles, would have been enough for Queenie May to go to him again and hold him. But Arthur kept apart and she spoke to him from across the room, the words sharper than she had meant in the velvet of the dusk that hung between them.

'Where d'you get it, any road, something like that?'

Arthur did not look at Queenie May as he answered her. 'It was in a house that I was working on. Way up north,' he said. Then, as if that was not provenance enough, 'It was a Church house.'

Queenie May pulled her feet up on to the counterpane. 'They gave it you?' she said.

'I took it,' said Arthur quietly, without a pause.

He raised his face to her, but in the almost dark Queenie May could not see what he meant. 'Is it a Church book?'

'No. It's poems,' said Arthur, forced now to put the book down, either by the fading light or by Queenie May's persistence. 'Rhymes,' he added, not wanting to puzzle his wife unnecessarily.

Queenie May thought about this. 'Have you read them, then?' she asked. 'How do you know, Arthur?'

''Course I've not read them. You know I can't read them. I just know. By the shape. It's what rhymes look like.'

'Like what?' Queenie May thought of the pictures she had seen over Arthur's shoulder.

'Like – this.' He gestured at the book on his lap.

And then they were quiet for a minute. It was Queenie May who began again.

'What was it doing in a Church house? Are they religious, the rhymes, like hymns?'

That the pictures might be in some way religious had never crossed Arthur's mind; he would never have dared steal a sacred book. The thought of it now sent a shock of heat to his face.

'No,' he said sharply. 'Nothing like that. It's not about God.'

'But if it's a Church book?'

'I didn't say that. I didn't say it was a Church book. I said it was in a Church house. It's not the same thing. They have all sorts, those people. It's not holy. It's not like that.'

Queenie May giggled. 'That's what I thought, seeing it. It couldn't be a Church thing, could it, looking like that? With them in the nuddy almost. That's what I thought.'

The children downstairs burst into noise again although they should long ago have been in bed.

'You'd better see to Florrie,' said Arthur, although the child had not stirred. His voice was gentle. 'We'll leave the book. We'll do it another time.'

And it was as Queenie May bent away to brush hair from her daughter's face that Arthur finally looked at her as she had hoped, smiling at the warmth of her in the dim room. But Queenie May, turned aside, saw nothing of this. And for the rest of the evening the book lay on the floor between them, apparently unnoticed, and through the night it was Florrie who kept them apart in the bed, writhing slightly with her baby dreams.

Arthur packed the few things he was planning to carry to

France and shook hands solemnly with those left at the railway. He rolled a stock of cigarettes and stored them in a tin. He watched Queenie May as she did the simplest of chores, trying to fix the idea of her in his head. But in the end it was still not as he wanted it to be. It was muddled and unsatisfactory, a surge of noise in the hallway with Annie and her children crying over him, and Florrie slipping from his grasp as he tried to balance her with his bundle, and Queenie May hanging back, staring at him as though he were new to her, and someone outside on the street calling to him, and nothing noble about it, just terror overtaking him at the last, so that he could not suppress the trembling in his legs. It was the irresistible sense of things being ripped away. And in all of it, Arthur had no choice but to leave the book with Queenie May without explaining, or showing her what it could mean.

'Look after the book, Queen,' he said under his breath as she was pushed to him.

It was not all he said to her, but it was the words he remembered. Then he was gone.

It was very quiet afterwards. Annie's children were too frightened to make a noise, and the hum of the street retreated. Florrie slept. The fire smoked but did not crackle. Queenie May, sitting still, did not cause the floorboards to creak nor the bed to groan. Her tears were absolutely silent.

For several days, Queenie May stepped around the book, ignoring it. Then she picked it up, wiped it quickly with the flap of her apron and, without looking inside it, rewrapped it in the length of tarpaulin. She covered it neatly and folded the edges tight. She tied it around with a piece of thick string. Then she tucked the book on the highest shelf in the room, as far up and back as she could reach, away from her. It stayed there for the duration of the war.

Lying back against the damp banks, his feet lodged in the bend of another man's leg, his hands quivering, Arthur would close his eyes and think sometimes of Queenie May, or of Florrie. And in time, someone wrote to him about a new baby, another girl whom they had called Alice, and the note was read to him in the birdless quiet of a spring evening. He tried to imagine his new daughter. He had the flush of her skin in his head, the softness of her, and he found himself slinking through the trenches with the thought of her hand in his, tiny and tight. He cherished the idea of her, holding her away from the devastation around him and at night sometimes, under thick stars, he thought he could hear her soft cries calling him home.

But most often, shivering in the skeletal cold, Arthur found his mind would drift from the mud back to the dense colours of the book. This was the greatest comfort.

'I wish I'd brought it with me,' he said in the blinking fury of a battle night, leaning close to the man next to him, an Irish soldier. His battalion was re-digging skeins of trenches with the Irish, the soft sweep of their accent and their quiet mournful songs emphasizing the wretchedness of things.

'Here? It's no place for it here.'

The ground trembled.

'To look at it though, when it's quiet. I'd have liked that,' said Arthur.

'Can you not say the words over in your head? Like prayers?' said the soldier, sinking lower. An explosion broke, not far away, stopping time. Then the sound passed and they breathed again.

'I don't know the words,' said Arthur.

Later, another night, the same man found him out, sliding along to him, purposeful. That day they had stood together on a gloriously sunny afternoon shovelling the leaking body parts of their comrades into pits.

'You can borrow this, if you like, instead,' he said. 'It'd be something for you.'

He handed Arthur a small Bible, dirty and worn. Smoke blew thick above their heads.

'Oh no, I can't,' said Arthur.

The soldier did not understand. 'Just now, for a few minutes. That's all. It's not a gift. It's my Bible; my mother's Bible. I'm not going to give it away.'

'No, I mean it's no good. I can't read,' said Arthur. 'It would do no good.'

'Sure it would. Look.'

The soldier opened the pages and began to read. He pressed his finger hard along the lines of words. Arthur watched it, the bitten black nail sloping from the ruptured skin. He heard little of what was said, but the steady rhythm of the finger transfixed him. A long time passed while the Irishman read.

'You see now, is that not better?' said the soldier when he'd finished. 'Is that not a comfort to you, like your great book?'

Arthur nodded and gently touched the hand that had held

up the lines of reading. 'Yes,' he said.

That night, for the first time, Arthur prayed with the Irish soldiers. He did not know the words of their prayers, but he bowed his head with them and said the closing Amen. He did not, just then, cross himself like they did although in time, too, this became a habit, a way of warding off disaster. And as the rain and the men fell, and the screech of battle persisted, Arthur came to rely on the intense, confident faith of the Catholic men, and to long for the comfort of their God. He looked over their shoulders at the tight-packed verses of their Bibles and in the lull of war they dragged their fingers for him beneath the words until the jumble of letters began to straighten.

When the soldier's chest and neck were torn apart by fragments from an exploding shell, Arthur was several yards away, tucked into a bend in the trench. He was lying still and small. But he heard the man's cries, above the terrible noise, and in his single act of valour, or something like it, he hustled through the mud to hold the soldier in his arms. He slid the Bible from the Irishman's pocket, and with the terror of death sticking in his voice and the thunder of the enemy pressing around him, he read three verses of the Psalms in the budding light of an unwelcome dawn. By the time he had finished reading, the man was dead. Later, Arthur found his name written neatly inside the front cover of the book.

Arthur walked up the street slowly, with two sticks, trying not to see the black-edged cards wedged in the windows. While he was away, his family had taken different rooms. They were smaller and cheaper to keep. He noticed the tightness of the houses and waited by the door without knocking. It was only when Queenie May pushed open an upstairs window to flick out a duster that she saw him below. The shape of him was unfamiliar.

'Yes?' she said. 'Yes, sir, can I help you?'

He looked up then. And seeing her face so close and unremembered loosened something in him. He crumpled on the doorstep.

'Arthur,' she murmured, not moving.

It was two men from down the road who, in the end, helped him into the house. He had a stinking, thickening gash that revealed the glint of his shin bone and he hissed at them when they hurt him.

Despite the warmth of the late summer, Arthur shivered continually, his limbs twitching. At first Queenie May sat with him, trying to understand, but it seemed to make no difference and so she went back to her work. She did not ask him about the war and Arthur watched her, bewildered, surprised at how the familiar pattern of things had kaleidoscoped out of shape while he was away. He was silent and pale and tight and Queenie May could only imagine what it was that haunted him.

'Is it like they say?' was all she asked, once, when they lay in bed together.

Arthur pretended he was asleep.

His secret nagged at him. Waiting for it to be discovered made all his pains worse. He tried to find the right day to tell them, but it was never quite as it should be, the time, the light, the look on his wife's face. There was never the quiet he needed.

But it went on gnawing at him, fidgeting in his gut, and in the end it spilled out unspectacularly, without the fanfare he had envisaged.

The girls, shy of their new father, were out in the street. There was a cold wind from the sea and the windows rattled in their frames. Queenie May cleaned Arthur's wound and was folding the blanket over his knees so he would not feel the chill. In all this, she hardly touched him.

'Can you find me the book, Queen?' he asked.

She reached it down from its shelf, unwrapped it, and placed it gently on his lap. He put a hand on her arm to stop her moving away.

'Listen,' he said, opening the pages. 'Listen, Queen.' With care he began to read. '"Little Lamb, who made thee? Dost thou know who made thee, Gave thee life and bid thee feed."' He read haltingly but correctly, with the rhythms of the verse intact. Then he closed the book and looked up at Queenie May and smiled at her. It took her a moment to realize what had happened.

'Well,' she said at last. 'Who'd have thought.'

He felt further away from her than ever.

'Oh, but Queen, I can read almost anything. Not just this. Newspapers, letters, anything. It all comes the same in the end. And you see what we can do, once my leg has healed, now I can read? You see what chances there'll be?'

Queenie May did not quite see. It was too new a phenomenon for that. But she liked the way he put his arms around her waist and pulled her to him, breathing in the clean cotton smell of her housecoat and glowing with what might have been love. She was happy to sit with him while he read through the book, even though mostly he was quiet, reading to himself, absorbed.

Now he could decipher them, the words surprised him. The sense of them was startling. So once or twice, just to be sure, he tried things out on her.

'Look here – about a chimney sweep, a little chimney sweep.' He read more. 'And here, Queen, it's flowers, roses and sunflowers – and lilies. You like lilies, Queen; you'd like it.'

There was so much of it, clamouring.

'*Songs*, they're called. *Songs of Innocence and Experience*,' he said at the end, as though this might help fathom things.

'To sing? With music?'

Arthur felt he should know. 'Ah, no,' he said. 'Not like that. Different.'

And then Florrie came in holding out grazed hands, barely bloodied, and Queenie May was never to know that he couldn't explain.

'Go to your father,' she said, having examined the damaged hands. 'He'll kiss them better.'

And although it was not much – two tiny hands held sheepishly towards him – it was something. Arthur placed his lips on Florrie's cold skin with extravagant ceremony.

'Good girl,' he said, looking over her head to Queenie May.

Despite his new reading skills and an unshakeable belief in a Catholic God – two things that he believed would save him – Arthur woke many times in the long nights, dripping with sweat, his teeth clenched and a taste of blood bitter in his mouth. He smoked determinedly and his speech stumbled and stuttered, tormented. He had moments, in plain daylight, in the middle of the street, when he wanted to sit on the kerb and weep. His prayers were desperate.

'I don't understand. I don't understand, Queen. I thought it would be better. I thought it would be all right now I can read.'

'I don't see how.'

'But with knowing the words like that.'

'I can't see it's such a good thing, Arthur,' she said firmly. 'Look at you.'

There was nothing much to see. His leg was slowly healing and he had put on weight. Arthur looked down at his bandages thinking it was that.

'I've prayed for it, Queen. I've prayed for everything. But still…' He could not explain. He put a hand out to her. 'It just takes time. That'll be all it is, I warrant,' he said.

But Queenie May could not get used to Arthur's strangeness. And she could not hide her prejudice of his embarrassing faith; when he said he wanted to continue with the Roman form of prayer, and to attend the chapel daubed on the end of the dock-yard buildings, she knew it would wedge between them.

'You'll be like them, like the Irish,' she said.

'Don't be stupid, Queen. There's people all over the world as is Catholic.'

'But the ones you know, the ones at the yard, they're all Irish, aren't they?'

Arthur didn't answer.

'And you should stay apart from them now, now you're home. Like before. It's not… it's not decent.'

Arthur understood, for the first time, the settled strength of her. 'It'll do no harm, Queen. It's just a way of praying.'

But Queenie May never prayed. 'You don't belong to them, Arthur,' she said.

'It's new to you, Queenie May, that's all. Like it was to me. That's all. Take a week or two to get used to it. Come with me, if you like. See it for yourself.'

'I'm not going to no ruddy Irish circus.'

Arthur slapped his hand against the glass of the window. The pane shivered. 'For pity's sake, Queenie May. You don't understand. It's made something of me. I can read now. I go to church. I'm a better man – I can see how things should be.' He struck the window again, and a cobwebbed crack appeared. He turned away from it, defeated. 'They're good soldiers, Queen,' he said softly.

Queenie May shook her head at him. 'That's as may be. I don't say they're not. But you're back with us now, with me and Florrie and Alice. And what'll everyone say? Think of that, Arthur.'

'I'm a respectable man, Queen. I'm good at my trade. That'll not change.'

It was the first time since coming back that Arthur had touched on his decorating. It crumpled Queenie May's resistance.

She sighed. 'Leave it then, till after you're back at it; till after you've begun again on the decorating,' she said.

Arthur nodded, grateful for the concession. He pressed his finger on the broken window, leaving a smear of blood on the glass.

In the evenings, after tea was done, they read the poems.

Arthur sat with his damaged leg high on a chair in front of him and the children piled as best as they could on his lap; Queenie May always stopped what she was doing to listen. They imagined the pictures of the book together, lulled by the rhythms of Arthur's monotone reading, preferring it to the torn-backed Bible he had brought home from the front. It was because of this that Florrie, when she remembered her childhood, always thought about the readings in the long dusk, the slight smell of pus and disinfectant, and the way the book sat so securely in her father's hands.

When Arthur tried to go back to decorating it didn't suit him. The fumes of the paints and solvents sickened him, the rawness of his hands depressed him, and the slight shift of the wooden ladder in the gusting wind made him tight and frightened. After barely two months he screwed up his overalls into a bundle and threw them into a hedge. They caught on a branch of reddening hawthorn and half unravelled, but he did not bother to untangle them. When he got home, he emptied everything out of his floppy kitbag, flapped it inside out to make sure it was clean, replaced his brushes and jars carefully, wiping each with a thick cloth, closed it up, and left it on the front doorstep. Queenie May brought it in out of the autumn drizzle.

'Leave it, Queen,' he said. 'It's for someone to have. I'm going back to the railways.'

'But Arthur, I thought you promised.'

This pricked him. He missed more than anything the feeling that there was a meaning to life, and that it had something to do with wallpaper well hung and paint well applied. He couldn't understand why things had changed.

'It's not the same, Queen,' he said. 'It's not what I thought. It's, I don't know – brittle.'

'It'll just take getting used to, Arthur, that's all. I'm sure that's all,' said Queenie May, but he made her put the bag back on the step.

It was still there, untouched, on Sunday when Arthur went for the first time to the Catholic chapel at the dockyard, and introduced himself to the priest there. When he came home, his face glowing, he stepped neatly over it, and Queenie May, watching from the window, was more angry than she could ever remember.

'What d'you do then?' she asked, trying to control the way she spoke to him.

'Not much.'

'You walk all that way, on a Sunday, for not much?'

Arthur was cold from the stiff sea wind, his cap and coat were damp, and he pressed closer to the fire. Florrie and Alice watched him, wary.

'We pray, of course. And there was mass. It's sailors mostly, and men off the shift.'

'Irish?'

'Not all.'

'You can always tell a Sunday morning 'cause the Irish are sober. That's what they say,' said Queenie May.

'You're set against them for no good reason, Queen. You don't know.'

'But you're one of them now, are you, saying their prayers,

labouring at the yard like a navvy for a few ruddy sous when you've a perfectly good trade of your own?'

Arthur hung his coat behind the door so that he could turn his back to her. Still, though, she talked.

'You're going back on your word, Arthur. You promised. You were going to be a decorator. Once you were fit again, that's what you said, you were going to go back to it.'

'It makes no difference, Queen,' he said quietly. 'It makes no difference. It's just the same – one thing or another.'

'I don't understand,' said Queenie May, meaning everything. 'Now there's another baby coming, I thought you'd set to it. You promised, Arthur.'

'I'm going to be a Catholic,' said Arthur.

He had not thought about it as clearly as it sounded to them both then, but he was excited from having been clasped around the shoulder by the priest as he left the chapel and Queenie May's indignation provoked him.

'You can't just do that, can you, just change?' said Queenie May, who had never heard of anyone choosing a God. 'It's something you're born, Arthur. It's decided for you. You can't just go changing.'

Arthur turned to her at least, but kept his hands flat behind him, warming them at the fire.

'You can change,' he said. 'They told me. You can convert. It's called converting. They can make me a Catholic, if I want.'

'How?'

'It's an oath,' said Arthur, and then he remembered. 'And they baptize you. With water.'

Queenie May huffed. 'That's what they do to babies.'

'No, to everyone. It's what they do.'

'But you're already baptized, aren't you? You have to be baptized, everyone does.'

'Well, this would be different. New.'

'And what happens to the old baptism?'

'It doesn't count any more. The Catholic one would count.'

There was a pause.

'And that's it? That's all it takes?' asked Queenie May.

Arthur did not know. He had not asked. That morning he had sat quietly in a pew towards the back of the chapel, unable to follow much of what was going on and baffled by the elegant sounds of the Latin being intoned obediently around him. He had been intimidated by the heavy canopy above the altar and the shine of the gilt. He could not see what the priest was doing, he had not sung, nor had he taken communion. Mostly, he had watched the men around him, trying to measure himself against them.

'It's a question of vocation,' he said, wondering where the word had come from.

Queenie May rested her arms on the bump of her pregnancy and looked out of the window, down the slope through the close houses of the alley. She could see the choppy water opening up beyond, whipped up and swirling in the cold, the snappy edges of a vast dispiriting sea. This was how, for the rest of her life, she pictured the faith Arthur was choosing.

'But Arthur, what about us? What about the girls? You can't just do that, you can't just make us.' She was almost shrill now. 'And the new baby, Arthur. What are you going to do when it comes? Will you have it different?'

Arthur tried to calm her by keeping his voice flat. 'It'll take a long time, Queen. It's not sudden. It's not to worry about now.'

'But… but if we don't want it, Arthur, what then?'

'Well then, don't do it. It's me, that's all,' he said.

Queenie May trembled with the anger of it. Arthur had closed his eyes.

'And that's what you want? To be different from us? Like them grubby navvies?'

He did not move. 'It's not like that,' he said.

That evening, for the first time, Arthur insisted on reading the Bible instead of the *Songs*.

'It's only right, on a Sunday,' he said.

Queenie May said nothing. It was Florrie who tried to change his mind.

'I like the other,' she said definitely. 'Your book.'

'This *is* my book,' said Arthur, holding out the Bible.

'But I want to see the pictures. I like it when you show me the pictures. It's a better book, Da.'

But Arthur ignored her. He read out loud instead a letter from St Paul, which he had read several times before. He did not understand it; the words flapped loose. Queenie May sat in silence, the cadenced click of her knitting needles upsetting the rhythm of the reading as she worked on a jacket for the baby. Florrie sulked, refusing to sit on her father's knee and squatting uncomfortably instead to one side of his chair.

Arthur read on, beyond the first letter to the next, hardly pausing at the break of a verse or the turn of a page, because he was afraid of what might happen when he stopped. Queenie May continued with her knitting, even when she dropped a stitch, fingering the reducing ball of wool on her lap at the turn of each row. But the stitching would have to be unripped next day, all the rows unpicked and redone; and no matter how hard Arthur concentrated on the shape and sound of the letters in front of him, he could not get them to mean anything: the exhortations of St Paul splintered into nonsense. When he closed his Bible he looked down at Florrie, pouting back at him, still resentful, and he burst into tears.

By the middle of the following week Arthur's kitbag had been taken from the doorstep, and he felt a relief and an immense sadness at the passing of the man he had once hoped to be. Nothing more was said about his conversion. He continued to go to the Catholic chapel every Sunday morning, but the habit was so entangled with his starting work back in the ashy steam of the trains, the clatter of the yard in his ears, in the dark, that it seemed painful, even to him. No one talked about it. Arthur did not read again to his family from the Bible, but nor could he bear to open the stolen book. Instead, to keep up his reading, he brought home a heavy directory that had been thrown out at work. It listed railway stock in a tiny practical print. It was not conducive to family recitals and Arthur read alone, practising the sounds over and over. Queenie May and the girls got used to him being there, in the corner by the window, resting the heavy blue book half against the wall as he read; they found other things to do and did not disturb him.

The girls, eager for the bright colours of the *Songs* and the peculiar figures that frightened them, learned to stand on a chair so they could reach it down from its shelf. They took turns to hold it, because it was heavy, and as soon as they heard a noise on the stairs or in the hall below they stuffed the book back on to the shelf, half wrapped in its tarpaulin. It was an adventure. In their own minds it was the naughtiest thing they had ever done. So when Queenie May caught them at it, she surprised them by putting down the bundle of washing she was carrying, and sitting with them, holding the book firmly on her knees and turning the pages slowly. They squealed at some of the pictures, drawing back from the stretched shapes and strange landscapes even as they fingered them, laughing, wriggling close to their mother. And afterwards the girls would get the book down even when Queenie May was there. Puffing with the heaviness of her pregnancy and shuffling through the preparations for the new baby, she rarely stopped her work to sit with them again, but she liked to see them together, huddled around the pictures, pointing and giggling and making stories, and she smiled at them, encouraging.

The birth of Arthur's first son was raw and exhausting, and the baby whimpered for many weeks afterwards.

'Is he supposed to be like that, Queen? Red like that?' Arthur asked, but his wife just shook her head at him.

Arthur poked a long finger at his son, speculatively, and turned away. Queenie May picked up the baby and pressed him close, but he would not hold still for her. She felt his wriggling as evidence of discontent and she pinched his tiny ear, making him squirm even more.

The baby remained red and somehow unfinished, demanding something that Queenie May could not fathom. She felt the shakiness of things and when another boy came, barely a year later, she was ferocious with her husband.

'You can't keep getting laid off, Arthur. You'll have to get other work. Look at this house, now. Look at where we are.'

'I'm trying, Queen,' he said. 'It's not just me, you know.'

'Well, try ruddy harder. If you'd still had a trade—'

The babies howled and he did not hear her finish.

The girls were delighted with their brothers, spinning scraps of cloth to catch the light for them, but Queenie May could not love the crimson ridges of the boys' skin. The turn of their mouths accused her and their feeble unremitting wail shut out the world from her. Arthur was nagged by their resolute frailty.

'I want them baptized,' he said at last. 'I want both the boys baptized.' He tried to find a way of explaining how uncertain life had become. 'It's no good, going on like this, with everything muddled.'

They were pushing the pram out in the weak sun of an early spring afternoon. Queenie May had her mind on shoes for Alice who was clattering ahead over the metal bridge that crossed the railway. She did not answer.

'All of them. All the children. They should be coming to church with me now, Queen,' pressed Arthur. 'Do you hear? We can't have them going on like this, like everyone, ordinary. We've got to do something. Otherwise what'll it be, what'll happen?'

'Oh Arthur,' she said, as if he were being eccentric. It irritated him.

'I mean I want them coming to mass with me, being baptized properly, being brought up properly, Catholic,' he said. 'That's something, at least.'

'Sssh, Arthur. Not here, out loud, in the street,' said Queenie May, flapping her hands at him.

But Arthur wasn't going to be put off. 'Where then? Home? All right, then let's go home. Come on, Queen. I want to have my say out. Let's go home, talk about it there.'

'But we've only just started, Arthur. I thought we were walking. I wanted to see the primroses,' said Queenie May, but Arthur had already turned, setting off hard through the twists of lanes and alleys as though the sea were flooding up across the dockyard towards them. Queenie May thought about letting him go, but did not quite have the courage. So she called the girls to her, and they followed him, more slowly, sorry to be turning back. They made no effort to catch him.

Standing on the pavement, waiting, Arthur was struck by the shabbiness of the house. He looked at it for a moment with a decorator's eye, noticing the brutal wear to the window frames, the gaps where they needed filling, the thin flakes of paint. He noticed the dark rot bleeding upwards on the front door, a stain spilling from under the roof tiles where the gutter was split. He blew a sigh through his nose, kicking a loose stone hard against the wall so that a tiny puff of brick dust hung scarlet for a moment in the air. He wondered how he had come to live here, in such a house. He remembered other houses, other rooms, places he had lodged and worked in, long ago and far away. The details came back to him: the neat set of a door, the hue of a slip of paint, floor planks crossed at an odd angle, the twist in a tiled fireplace, the scent of polish. He had not thought about these things for a long time. He had not known he could. And even now, as they came tumbling from his past, breaking upon him like a sudden rainstorm, it was a physical pain to tweeze the images from somewhere deep inside him. He felt himself splitting, his old wound reopening, his flesh smarting. He wanted to cry out. Perhaps he did. And once the pictures were there, plain and new and clear in his eye, he could not bear to put them aside, even though they throbbed with the weight of loss. He lost himself in the swirl of them.

When Queenie May arrived he could not see her. But she spoke to him, to bring him back, and would have slapped him too if she had not had her hands full yanking the pram over the front doorstep. The blankness of his face annoyed her.

'Well then, Arthur, here we are. You can tell them,' she said from somewhere in the dark hall.

Arthur heard her and his past dissolved. He was left with only his grief. He wanted to run, but Queenie May had parked the pram and was at the open door again, watching him, her arms folded hard. Her voice was edgy.

'You made us come back, Arthur. You've made the children come back. What is it you want to say?'

And it was something in her tone that hardened him, and something in how small he was feeling, and how sad. So that his argument for the baptism of the children was stiff and dark and terrifying. He followed his wife into the corridor, picking Alice up from where she was loitering on the step, half in and half out of the house, uncertain. He held her tight in his arms.

'We're going to be baptized,' he said. 'As Catholics. All of us. We're going to go along to the church and let them put water on us and make them have us, as Catholics.' He spoke without breathing, clutching at his daughter. 'I know what it's like, I've read what it's like, the place you go to – the hell. It's fire, all the time, always at you, and everything dark except for the flames, everything burning, smoke in your eyes worse than ever at the yard, all around you, all the time, with the noise of the damned screeching and screeching till you go mad.'

His hand was in Alice's hair now, pulling through the tangles with long strokes. She tried to shake him off but he was too strong for her.

'It's for ever,' he went on, 'every minute of every day, for ever. There's a pain in you that you can't imagine, that'll never shift, knowing there's no way out, no use of repenting, and the flames at your feet and at your hair and crackling your skin, burning everything, over and over, for ever. For ever, Queenie May.'

He looked across at the blistered horror on his wife's face. There was the clatter of voices outside in the street.

'And it'll have to be us all. Every one of us. I can't do it on my own, or they'll never take my worship as true worship. It's important to me,' he said. 'The maids are too young to understand. But they'll see, one day. And you'll see, too – it's important, Queen.'

All Queenie May could do was raise her eyebrows at him, disbelieving. So he softened his voice to talk to his daughters.

'You'd like to be baptized with me, to come to church and see it all, wouldn't you?' Arthur held his hand flat now on Alice's head, unmoving. She leaned away towards her sister, and Florrie, being the elder, thought it must be her duty to answer.

'What will they do then, Da, if you take us to church? What will they do to us?'

'They'll baptize you,' said Arthur. 'With the Holy Spirit.'

Florrie thought about this, and didn't like it. 'I don't think that sounds very good,' she said, trying not to disappoint her father.

'It doesn't hurt. It's a good thing,' said Arthur. He looked for a way to explain. 'It makes you a child of God.'

This sounded worse. 'Can't I still be your child, and Ma's, instead?'

'Look, that's enough,' said Queenie May. 'Enough for now, Arthur. You'll frighten them.'

'It's nothing to be afraid of,' said Arthur. 'It's only—'

But Alice interrupted. 'Why are you doing this, Da?'

She did not mean to accuse him. She did not understand what had been said. But it sounded, even from a six-year-old, like an accusation, and she could feel his rage tightening in his arms even before he flipped her down on to the floor and, holding her hard by the shoulder, smacked her, over and over, taking no notice of her surprised and then her pained shrieks, whipping his cold hand against her legs, his face suddenly so furious that Alice thought he was going to bite her.

Arthur used all the strength he had built up in the dockyard to hit his daughter. He felt a joy in it, at first, a release, and the softness of her in his grip made something surge inside him. He did not see what he was doing. He looked over Alice's squirming head to Queenie May, and he met her eyes, and his blows came harder and stronger. And they looked at each other, the two of them, without once dropping their gaze, and Arthur struck out the words they could not find on Alice's raw flesh. So that even when his daughter was cowering, curled on the floor, trembling, and Queenie May, eventually, had pulled her away, and the boys had begun to cry, Arthur sat on the stair and continued to wave his arm, as if beckoning her.

That night, with the children tucked around them at odd angles, Arthur lay very still alongside his wife. The night was bright and moonlight slashed squarely across the floor. They lay together, listening to each other's breathing, and neither of them slept. But just before dawn, when the moon had sunk away, Arthur reached across and laid a hand on Queenie May's stomach and the gentle pull of his fingers electrified them both. And as the days passed, they were fierce, engrossed, feeling the flicker of each other's presence on the stairs, the invitation of a glance. The girls could not work out what was making their parents so silent; they felt left out and unnecessary. Alice, nursing her bruises, was not at all sure that violence might not break out again. And when the passion finally erupted, coarse and brutal, with Arthur and Queenie May so furious in the bed that the children were piled, shivering, on to the floor; when Queenie May cried out with such ferocious exaltation that the dust showered through the dark from the shelves above them, the girls were afraid of whatever it was they were witnessing and huddled together in the long silence that followed, wrapped in a blanket and whispering in the corridor.

'It must be my fault,' said Alice. 'Do you think, Florrie – do you think it's my fault?'

Florrie held her sister tight, protective. 'I'll ask him. I'll find out about the baptism. It'll make things better,' she promised.

She chose a quiet morning as she walked with Arthur part of the way to the yard, to collect her mother's ring from the pawnbroker's. She asked him what it was like at his church.

'Peaceful,' said Arthur, checking his stride. 'Peaceful to hear them all, chanting and singing. It makes you think of – I don't know, Flor – coving or skirting boards, something clean. You wouldn't understand.'

Florrie tried again. 'But God, is *he* there, Da?'

'Oh no,' said Arthur, 'not God. Just ordinary people, like you and me. God is different.'

He tried to explain about the Holy Trinity but could see that it baffled her.

'But there's other things there, that God would like,' he offered, 'candles and incense from a big swaying urn. And everything in a special language, in Latin, that takes your breath away sometimes it's so strange.'

'Latin?'

Arthur quoted: '*Agnus Dei, qui tollis peccata mundi*. Like that, all the time, hanging loose in your head for days.'

Florrie was tempted. 'You could take me, Da, if you like,' she said.

They were at the corner by the pawnbroker's where they had to part. The streets were busy with men making their way to work. But Arthur, nonetheless, kissed her, bending to touch his lips to her hair.

'I think everything'll be better now,' she said to Alice later, holding her hand.

But Alice heard again the midnight screams her mother had made and was not at all comforted.

When Florrie and Arthur came home after church on Sunday, Florrie's eyes were dreamy, seeing something far away. Sitting around the kitchen table she brushed her hand against her father's arm, and Queenie May saw her tap him lightly across the knee when he spoke, feathering her fingers like wings. Later, she announced that she wanted to be a Catholic, like her father was going to be.

Queenie May was not surprised.

'It doesn't decide anything, for the others. They're too young. The boys are still babies,' was all she said, as Arthur lifted Florrie with a whoop of joy so that she banged her head on the ceiling.

The influenza went steadily from house to house along the road. Queenie May and Arthur crept, aching, to the bed and lay together without speaking, exhausted. Their skin was cold and clammy and Arthur's old wound throbbed. They did not want to touch each other and when Arthur moaned, soft and low, Queenie May turned aside, angry.

Florrie could not be sure that the disease was not some kind of visitation and she worked hard to repel it. She soaked cloths to cool her parents' faces and she toasted bread to tempt them. She got Alice ready for school and walked with her as far as the railway. She did everything she could for her brothers, holding and bathing them, kissing them over and over, singing to them, and praying, on her knees, that they would be saved.

'Ma, do you think I should get them something?' she asked, seeing how they struggled to breathe.

But Queenie May knew there was nothing to be done. 'Leave them be, Flor,' she whispered.

And the boys died without fuss, long before Arthur had resolved their religious affiliation.

The first Sunday, when Arthur could hardly raise his head from his drenched pillow, Florrie asked Alice to go with her to the dreary chapel.

But Alice shook her head firmly. 'I don't like the dockyard, Flor. Them men look at you funny,' she pointed out, and Florrie left her sister in charge of the nursing while she hurried down through the quiet streets.

She did not ask again. But while the sickness hung low over everything she went to mass every Sunday, and sometimes again in the week, saying out the responses as loudly as she could, with her head tipped back, as though she were calling into a storm wind. She became known. Other families beckoned to her to share their bench; the priest touched her head lightly.

'Is there no one to come with you?' they asked. It did not seem right that she should be alone, as if orphaned. And Florrie had to explain, many times, that neither her mother nor her sister believed in the same way she did; there was only her father.

So when Arthur was well enough to go with her to church again, he found he was welcomed with unexpected affection. He was pointed out in the dark-coated mêlée gathering outside the chapel. People came to shake his hand as he knelt to pray or queued for confession; they stopped to chat with him, never mentioning Queenie May. He heard other members of the congregation whispering about him in the chrysanthemum quiet of the lady chapel. His family became, for a short while, a novelty in the neighbourhood, unconventional and conspicuous, split by their allegiance to the different faces of God.

None of this consoled him.

'I should have done it before. I should have got it done, for the boys,' Arthur moaned.

Queenie May opened the doors and windows wide, spreading out the bedding on the windowsills, and felt the clean air rushing through the house.

'Let's forget it, Arthur, now,' she said. 'You've got Florrie with you. Leave it now, for the rest of us. Leave it.'

But Arthur changed his route to the dockyard so that he did not have to pass the bleak plot of land, shadow-walled and greening, where his unbaptized sons had been buried, unrecorded. And he sat clenched alongside Florrie during the majesty of the mass, screwing his nails tight into his palms, feeling it might be wrong to pray for them.

'Show me your reading, then, Ally,' Arthur said. He was sitting heavily on the bed, weary from his shift. He patted the blanket beside him in invitation, reaching for Alice with his other hand, cold from the outside air and hard from years of carrying. It surprised both of the girls.

'Oh Da,' Alice said, 'I don't know. I can't...'

Florrie, who was hanging up her father's coat to dry, watched closely. Her faith was unquestioning and indefatigable. The priest smelt to her of stale sweat and wet wool, but still she let him finger her hair and bend over her in blessing. She learned the meaningless music of the Latin responses and she tried not to fidget on the hard benches. Every evening, kneeling out in the corridor, she prayed for the release of her brothers' souls, begging God not to damn them, and when Queenie May fell pregnant again, pacing up and down during the damp nights, Florrie recited scraps of prayers to her in what she considered a reverent monotone. She refused to eat meat, if there was any, on Fridays and she went weekly to confession, scraping together a litany of sins that could be reasonably forgiven. So when Arthur began to show special interest in one of his daughters, she felt that, by rights, it should have been her.

But it was Alice he went to.

'Sit with me here, Ally, and read. Read to me.'

Ally let him pull her on to the bed.

'I can't, Da. There's nothing to read,' she said, but Arthur had his hand tight on her leg now, above the knee, and she could not move away.

Seeing her chance, Florrie took a step forward, wanting to show how much better she was than her sister at reading, so that Arthur would look at her instead, and make room for her next to him on the bed.

'I'll get the Bible, Da, shall I, for her to read? We can both read it. I can read more than her, the long names and everything.'

'The other one,' said Arthur, without looking at her. 'From the back shelf.'

He was clear about that. Florrie stood on the chair to fetch it down, careful not to catch the end of Arthur's coat with her ashy feet, and she held it in both hands to pass it to him ceremonially as she had seen the altar servers do with the great missal on a Sunday. Then, not wanting to turn her back on them, but not wanting either to sit with them on the bed, she remained standing, the toes of her right foot bent double and crumpled hard into the floorboard.

'Well then, go on,' said Arthur, opening the book carefully at the first page.

Alice tightened beside him. 'I can't, Da,' she said.

'I can, I'm sure. Let me, Da,' said Florrie.

But Arthur ignored her.

'Start here, with this.' Arthur wrapped his arm around Alice and pointed his finger beneath each of the words in turn. '"Piping down the valleys wild,"' he read slowly.

Alice began to sniff. She tried the next word, but it was 'piping' again, a word she had never seen written before and had no chance of recognizing. Only the p sounded.

Then, to save herself, she said, 'Ma lets us look at the pictures, that's all. We don't do the words.'

It took a moment for Arthur to realize what had been said. 'You read – this – with your mother?'

'Not read. I said, Da. Just look.'

Alice shuffled away from him slightly, wary of his tone. Arthur looked at Florrie now.

'When is this? When do you use my book?'

Florrie shrugged and pressed her toes harder into the floor. 'Not often, Da. Just sometimes. For the pictures. And we used to – sometimes – show them to the boys; play with them.'

They waited for him to say something, but he held tight on to the edges of the book and was quiet.

'But I could try and read again. I could try. If you like,' said Alice, frightened by his silence.

He turned and looked at her, pulling her back towards him, tightening his grip this time on her leg.

Florrie wanted to be part of it. 'No. Let me. Let me read, Da,' she said.

But it was Alice that Arthur wanted. He was short with his elder daughter. 'You'll just go sidling up to your mother. I'm better off with Ally.'

Florrie backed away at this, but she continued to watch them, waiting for the moment when she could step in and read. It didn't come. It didn't turn out that way, neither that afternoon, nor on the afternoons that followed. Instead, Arthur made Alice read. They practised the first two lines, over and over, until they were perfect and the word piping ran off her tongue. He did not realize that she was memorizing, nor that her understanding was so distorted and her sense of the words so distant, that the piping she envisaged was thick and rusted, riveted together in long sections like the duct that wound its way around the back of the school yard. He just heard the correctness of the sounds she made. And so they moved on, learning more lines, deciphering longer and longer words, turning the pages of the book from one poem to the next, becoming slowly more assured and fluent. And when Arthur rewarded Alice for her literacy by reaching his hand clumsily under her skirt and pushing her back hard on the bed while his fingers shivered at the feel of her, Alice was too breathless to disillusion him and Florrie was speechless with envy.

By the end of the year, Alice and Arthur had read the whole of the book together. Alice's reading was much improved. She had a sturdy confidence in her ability to decipher new words, however peculiar. Hurrying home from school ahead of Florrie, taking the hill too fast, ignoring the squeal of her breath, she would feel the pound of her heartbeat as she climbed the stairs, seeing her father sprawled on the bed, waiting, his eyes widening at the sight of her. It seemed to her, always, a time of sunlight, of moving shadows quick across the sky, of summer air. It never surprised her that Florrie always threw open the tattered windows as soon as she came home.

'You should tell Ma,' said Florrie on one of these afternoons, leaning out to catch sight of the sea as she let in the breeze.

Alice was sitting on the edge of the bed, quiet. 'Tell her what, Flor?'

There was a pause. Florrie looked at her sister.

'That you got moved up again, in class,' she said at last, flatly.

Alice was now by far the best reader in her school. She read everything she was given with certainty, and with a voice fluid with poetry, so that even the most ordinary things came out sounding special. She was quite a marvel, leapfrogging up the benches towards the front of the classroom, leaving Florrie languishing behind. Queenie May could not have guessed this.

'It doesn't matter,' said Alice, relieved, lying back on the counterpane as a gust reached her from the open window. It blew the ends of her hair across her face.

'She'd like it though, Ally. You could read to her even; show her.'

'I don't want to read to her,' said Alice.

Later that evening Florrie found a folded newspaper on the stone windowsill of a house in the next street. It was slightly damp. She took it home, flapping it hard in the air to dry it.

'I'll read to you, Ma,' she offered. 'To take your mind off the baby. To find out about things.'

But Queenie May was weary and fell asleep before Florrie had finished the first page, the words coming slow and stilted. Florrie went back outside, and the newspaper was used a few days later to clean the windows. On Sunday she tried again, saying out the prayers loudly next to Arthur in church, so that he would notice how well she sounded the words, and praise her. But he never did. And before long she became accustomed to the idea that she did not share Alice's precocious talent for words. She spent the smooth-tide summer evenings playing mechanical games of hop-scotch and she grew suddenly tall and spindly, which she took as further proof that she was somehow foolish and badly developed. She ceased to believe in the efficacy of prayer.

Queenie May did everything she could to stop the next baby, and her daughters helped her.

'We can't manage it, with another one,' she explained to them. 'Not now.'

So Florrie and Alice took turns to stand on their mother's stomach as she lay on the floor, stamping as hard as they dared, until they made her cry and they couldn't go on. They went instead then, together, to the chemist, investing in a large number of pills. They waited with Queenie May, encouraging her as she retched so that she would not vomit up the expensive medicine, and they discussed between themselves on the way home from school the reasons why nothing had happened. They boiled up soap and quinine over the stove and gave it to their mother to drink, to poison the baby, but Queenie May could not keep this mixture down, no matter how hard she tried. So that evening they made up the mixture again and with a stiff nozzle of newspaper Queenie May poured it inside herself.

Queenie May emptied the funnel of poison three times a day, for as long as she could bear, but still nothing happened. They expected some kind of sign when the baby died and were puzzled. They could not be sure that they had successfully killed it. If it would not come out, there was no way of knowing.

'It might be tiny. No bigger than a bean,' said Florrie hopefully. 'Perhaps you didn't notice, Ma.'

But Queenie May was certain. 'There's been nothing,' she said. Her head was thick, stuffed with wet feathers. Her thoughts could not get through. So she did not know what to do next, and it was Alice who went back to the chemist for sticks of slippery elm bark that Queenie May could thrust inside herself, deep. But the sticks did not work either.

Finally, Florrie said it would have to be something sharper.

'A needle, Ma; a knitting needle,' she said, having asked around. 'If you do it carefully, you'll be all right. It'll just be the baby that gets it.'

Queenie May had never gone so far before. The thought of it made her flinch.

'I don't know,' she said. 'Perhaps we've tried enough. I'll think about it.'

But she couldn't think about it; her thoughts were rattling around too loosely.

'Don't tell your father,' was all she said, in the end, before she lay back on the bed with a folded towel beneath her to catch the blood. But she did not have the courage to take the knitting needle herself and poke around. She did not want to feel the dense softness of her baby at the end of it, impaled. So it was Florrie who did it, while Queenie May stared hard at the damp rings on the ceiling.

Florrie herself was surprised at the feel of it, and at how deep the needle would go. She was cautious. She had heard about what could happen. She had heard of a woman whose insides had been pulled out to hang loose between her legs, almost to the floor, dragging low like sodden stockings. She did not want that. So although she made a show of things, she could not in the end stab as hard as perhaps she should. And so both Queenie May and her child came out of it unscathed.

After that they gave up, and nothing was ever said about not wanting the baby.

When Arthur's third daughter was born, two weeks overdue and squawking, Queenie May finally saw that there was nothing to be done. The things she had always believed would happen to her, had somehow happened elsewhere, to other women. What she was left with was repetition, and a sense that her life was being lived by someone else, somewhere out of sight. She sat wrapped around in Arthur's coat, despite the damp heat of late summer, with the baby across her lap, her hair untied and lank, wetting the cushion slightly each time she coughed. She stopped worrying about the rent, the cost of shoes, and the tightness of Alice's breathing. She refused to name the baby.

'Then I'll do it,' said Arthur, bending over the basin to wash his face. It was another morning when he did not have to go to work. 'We'll call her Mary.'

Queenie May looked down at the baby sleeping on her knees, pink with the heat around her ears and forehead. She did not want to argue, so she nodded. And Arthur offered a silent prayer of thanks, that at last he would be getting his own way with things, and one of his daughters would be blessed with a sanctified name.

'Will Mary come to church with me and Da, or not?' asked Florrie a few days later when she and Queenie May were alone together and the baby was sleeping.

Queenie May was idly tying threads into the back of a patch of darning. 'When she's older, she might, sometimes,' she said, breaking a thread with her teeth.

'I think she should, Ma,' said Florrie firmly.

'I s'pose your father will decide.'

Queenie May heard the torpor in her voice as though from afar.

'But she should come, from the start, Ma, really,' kept on Florrie. 'I've seen babies at church before, little babbies still in arms.'

Queenie May was surprised. 'I thought you were fed up of it, going on a Sunday now. All that fuss you make about having your hair neat, my girl, and getting your clothes brushed. You're going on eleven now, Florrie – I thought you were growing out of it.'

'Yeah, well, it's not that, is it,' said Florrie, not making sense. 'And I like the walk.'

Queenie May had caught a glimpse of her daughter, close to Arthur in the smoke-thick streets, talking, their heads down, hurrying to the church. She could see why Florrie would not want to give this up.

'You wouldn't mind,' she said, 'if you had to take Mary along too?'

Florrie couldn't look at her mother, but she said it nonetheless. 'I wouldn't mind.'

Queenie May shrugged. She fingered the threads distractedly, glancing occasionally at Mary, out of habit, but not seeing her. And it took such a long time for Florrie to say something more, that it might have been a different conversation.

'And if she comes to church with us, and Da gets her baptized, and the priest holds her head over the water and splashes it on her, and we all have candles, then she'll be a child of God, won't she, Ma?'

'She will. I suppose.'

'Good,' said Florrie.

Mary stirred slightly, gurgling, and Queenie May got up with a sigh and went over to her baby but did not pick her up. She looked at Florrie, noticing she had grown out of her skirt again.

'Well, don't set your heart on it, my girl. It might change. We'll see. It might just be you and your father, as before.'

'Oh no, you must let her come, Ma, you must. And let the priest pour water on her and hold the candles. No one'll touch her if she's a child of God.'

Queenie May saw the tears in Florrie's eyes. She looked at her daughter, wicker thin before her, her weight shifted on to one leg with the other pressed into the floor on curled toes, the new rise of her slight breasts pushing at the buttons across the chest of her blouse, her long hair tucked behind her ears, her eyes wet still with the passion of fear and her grubby fingers in her mouth. Queenie May looked at the child who looked back at her, waiting, and she wished she could feel some of what Florrie felt, some spark of life. She did not, of course, come close to understanding what it was that Florrie was trying to say. And when Mary let out a sudden, full-blooded screech, she turned away to the baby. She did not want to look at Florrie any more.

The only thing Queenie May could think of, at that moment, to take their mind off things, was Arthur's book. There was nothing else in the room that would not just remind them of where they were. It was something she remembered Florrie liked. She dandled Mary over her shoulder to quieten her.

'I know, Florrie, my love. Let's have a look at them pictures. Get the book down, will you? It'll do us good, a bit of something different,' she said, hoping it sounded the most natural thing in the world. 'We can show Mary.'

Florrie didn't know what to say. 'There's no time, Ma,' she settled on. 'Da'll be home soon. And Ally.'

'Well, that's all right. Ally can see too, if she comes.'

Florrie could not quite imagine this.

'Come on, Flor. Reach it down.' Queenie May was impatient. She didn't want the effort she was making going to waste. But Florrie was not stirring herself. She was scraping grease from the floorboards with her toe and wouldn't look up.

'Get it, Florrie, my girl,' said Queenie May sharply.

So Florrie did as she was told, because she had not yet found a way of resisting. She no longer needed to stand on a chair, and when she reached to the back of the shelf the book was naked; there was no sign of the old tarpaulin. This surprised her. And the cover, she noticed, was paler now at the corners and along the top edge, where the clutch of Alice's fingers had worn the soft leather. Looking at the tones of it, the contours of its shade, she had the sudden, lurching sense of the world having changed, leaving her stranded with her mother in their close, dark room. She could not bear to hold the book, to slide her fingers on to the worn skin where her sister's had been, to be still with it, marooned, while things whirled around her, warping. She dropped it with a dull thud to the floor.

Queenie May would not be so easily defeated. With a sniff, and a sidelong glare at Florrie, she put Mary down and picked up the book. She held it for a while without opening it. She was waiting for Florrie to come next to her, but Florrie didn't move and Queenie May could not press her point. She was suddenly tired. So she let Florrie stay apart. She sat heavily on a chair and opened the book on her knee. But it wasn't what she'd hoped. Florrie was not won back. She was stiff and watchful, accusing her mother of something Queenie May did not understand, and the pictures had no allure in them. They were colours, that was all, too bright and squalid for the dense summer daylight.

'There should be something else,' said Queenie May, putting the book down beside her. Mary started to whimper. And then Florrie came to her mother, holding so tightly that they could feel the pinch of each other's bones. The world continued to pitch and sway around Florrie, to sicken and disorientate her, but she held on for as long as she could to Queenie May, her eyes closed and her head burning.

Arthur waited outside the school for Alice. He sat on a low wall across the road, half obscured by the thick trunk of an old elm, pushing the gravel into patterns with the heel of his shoe, smoking. He waited a long time. He saw Florrie first, walking slowly with two other girls, bending together over something on a scrap of paper. He saw one of the teachers come to the gate and look down the road, away from him. And then he saw Alice, alone, as he knew she would be. He did not call to her. He got up as she turned out of school, walking with her but on the other side of the road, waiting for her to notice him. When she did, he beckoned her and she came.

'What are you doing here?' Alice was whispering, although there was no one close to them.

'It's a lovely day, Ally,' he said, flicking his eyes at the clear blue sky. 'I walked out, to see you. I could carry your books.'

Alice had brought two schoolbooks home to read but this was special dispensation from the teacher, and she held on to them, not trusting her father with them.

'I'm all right, Da.'

They took the usual path, cutting through the scrubland by the side of the railway. The summer plants were high, great heads of hogweed floating above Alice and crickets chirping industrially.

'If you like, Ally, we could take a bus,' said Arthur, flinging a bramble from across their path with pinched fingers.

'The bus? Where? What for?'

'We could go up on the Hoe, have an ice cream. If you like.'

'Have you got money for that, Da?'

Arthur, grinning, flicked the change in his pocket so that Alice could hear it rattle. 'Plenty,' he said.

'For ice cream?'

'For everything.'

Alice wanted to walk. She liked the looseness of the hot day. But Arthur knew there was more chance of them being seen that way.

'We shouldn't risk your chest getting bad, Ally,' he argued. 'We don't want to start it off.'

And so they took the bus, together, for the first time, and rode all the way to the end of the Hoe where they could see the sea stretching evenly to the horizon. Then, as he had promised, Arthur bought his daughter an ice cream.

'Oh my,' she said, licking the drips from her wrist and running her tongue hard between the wafers until she had bored out a vanilla groove. With her free hand she held her schoolbooks away from her, her arm far outstretched, so they wouldn't get spoilt. 'Oh Da. Whatever'll Florrie say?'

'Best keep it to ourselves,' said Arthur, bending down across her to lick the ice cream himself.

They went to the park then, grateful for the shade of the trees. Alice took her shoes off and ran a little way on the hard grass. When she stopped, Arthur caught up. They sat down, the ground around them worn away by feet and tree roots and the long summer.

'Do you want to read, Ally?'

Alice shook her head and moved the books behind her. 'They're for something else,' she said.

Arthur nodded. His face was red, shiny with sweat, his mouth restless. 'Lie back then,' he said.

Alice was surprised. 'What? Here?'

She looked around. Two young boys were playing with a ball

beyond the trees. A dog ran hard across the open ground.

'Yes, Ally. Here.' There was a threat in it.

'But what if someone… what if… ?'

Arthur pushed her then, hard enough to crush the rest of the words out of her, and he lay beside her, propped on an elbow, leaning across her, blocking the stippled light from the trees.

Alice waited. Arthur caught the cotton of her blouse through his fingers, pressing. They were very still, just the heat of his hand seeping into her. Then he smoothed the ridges of her skirt, taking time to even out the creases. He rested his fingers on her knee, and Alice felt the slide of them, damp against the hot skin of her thigh. She closed her eyes. But still his fingers hovered, uncertain. She could hardly feel the weight of them. It was not what she was used to. Then, for a moment, she felt the scratch of a nail, something grazing against her skin, and Arthur had peeled away from her, flopping back, his head resting against the low pile of her schoolbooks. Alice sat up.

'Da? Are you all right?'

Arthur had his eyes tight closed, but from the corners of them Alice could see the squeeze of tears.

'It's all right, Da. It doesn't matter. It's too open that's all, out here. It's too different. Da?'

Still Arthur didn't say anything.

'It doesn't matter,' said Alice again.

Arthur opened his eyes and the trapped tears slipped on to the bulge of his cheeks. 'Will you read to me, Ally, when we get home?'

'Of course I will,' said Alice, relieved. 'But I think it has to be at home, that's all.'

They walked all the way back, the bus money spent. Florrie watched them climb the hill to the house. The afternoon light made them bright, like puppets, and she picked them out easily as they made their way up through the knitted streets.

'I stayed late, to collect the books,' Alice tried to explain, but she could see that Florrie didn't believe it. Queenie May and Mary were asleep together on the bed.

Arthur patted Florrie briskly on the head and went to sit apart in the kitchen. Alice put her schoolbooks safely on top of a box by the window and then turned to her sister. The sun streamed in across her shoulders, lighting her hair.

'He bought me ice cream,' she said, flushed.

Florrie moved towards her and hissed. 'I'll tell someone,' she said.

'Tell them what?'

'Tell the truth and shame the devil.'

Alice laughed. 'I'm going to go and read to him,' she said.

But Florrie stopped her, putting a hand hard on her arm.

Alice squealed. 'Ow!'

'If you came to church with me… if he thought… ' She had to let Alice loose to brush the sudden tears from her eyes. 'It's because he thinks you're, you know, like the boys; he thinks you're going to hell.'

Alice laughed again. She picked up the book from its storage place on the shelf and brushed it quickly with her sleeve. 'I'm not going to hell, Flor,' she said, and she went through to her father. Florrie heard the ripple of his voice.

★

Florrie brushed her hair and sat for a long time by the window. She watched a beetle lumber up the frame, disappearing finally into a crumbling split in the wood. She could hear sounds from the kitchen, but she flicked her eyes away to the bleached blue of the sky and listened only to the soft rhythms of her mother's breathing as she slept, her face limp. When Mary woke, Florrie spooned mashed potatoes through her baby sister's creased lips, wiping trickles of spit-sick from her chin. Then she went out into the hot streets.

It was still brilliantly light. The damp gutters buzzed with flies, and there was nothing left of the smell of the sea. There were girls playing hopscotch on the corner by the butcher's, their grid drawn out across the pavement. Florrie stopped for a while, because they asked her to, but she did not want to play. She felt too tall for it. Her breasts slid up and down loosely in her blouse as she hopped, and she thought she saw people looking at her. She stepped on a line on purpose and moved out of the grid, setting off again without saying anything. The game continued behind her and she could hear the squeals. There were boys, too, chasing down to the dockyard, but she ignored them. In the still hot sun, a group of men stood outside the pub. They all knew her. Some of them sat close to her at church on Sunday.

In the end, without hurrying, Florrie made her way to her Aunt Annie's house, the same house they had once all shared. Annie's husband was an overseer now at the yard, and had never been without work. Another family had long ago moved in on the second floor, and, being regular with the rent, had stayed. It was a house now for seventeen children, one way or another, its doors and windows open to any cooling breeze and two small tight-haired dogs wrestling in the hallway. So Florrie, as she expected, simply blended into the crowd. She was patted on the head by someone. She stopped to tie one cousin's shoelace and to kiss another. She was offered a suck on a diminishing gobstopper. And she passed quite unnoticed through the kitchen, pulling out the drawer at the end of the scrubbed table where she knew Annie kept her housekeeping purse, and taking out all the coins she found inside.

Florrie apologized quickly to God as she slipped the purse back into the drawer. She did not dare take the neatly folded notes. She would have preferred not to steal the money at all, if it could have been helped, and she hardly looked about her as she left her aunt's house, moving quickly now through the streets, shaking off greetings, aware only of the coins bouncing slightly in her loose pocket. She was relieved to find the hopscotch game was finished, the chalk lines scuffed and already disappearing. Anxious not to be spotted, she skirted behind the house, ducking through the weedy alleys, turning away from the sea. She began to run, clipping into a skip sometimes to save her breath, keeping her hand tight over the coins. When she arrived at the pawnbroker's, sweating slightly, her heartbeat was stuttering.

The shop was cluttered with things she knew her mother would like, neatly arranged, stacked on shelves and hanging from hooks set in lines from the rafters. Even in the late light there was the gleam of glass-bead necklaces, the twinkle of buttons and buckles, the soft silk glisten of pale china, promises everywhere, waiting. But standing now in the midst of it all, feeling the pawnbroker watching her and the coins hard against her skin and the evening heat heavy across her shoulders, nothing was quite right. All Florrie could think of was her father's book, the thick thud of it as it fell and something she did not understand in the way Queenie May had held it. She sighed a long sigh.

'I don't know what to buy,' she said, out loud, but not expecting an answer.

The pawnbroker looked around and dusted the top of the counter with his hand, as though preparing to make a display.

'Well, my dear, there're all kinds. Something for all tastes. That's the joy of it. If it's something modern you're after…'

'It's for my ma,' said Florrie.

The pawnbroker could picture Queenie May, her hair tightly curled beneath her scarf, her face shining, the good-natured way she bantered with him as he wrote out his tickets. They had known each other, in a way, for many years. He looked again at Florrie.

'Then something useful, that'll be best,' he said. 'How much do you have?' Florrie put the coins on his counter and he slid them into piles. It was only slightly more than he had expected.

'Here then,' he said. He did not move from behind the counter because that was too much trouble in the airless heat. Instead he reached to the low shelves to his side and held out what was within reach. It was a flour jar, plain and bulbous, a thin blue line doubling around its waist. 'Keeps flies and maggots and what have you right out. Pretty too. She'll like that, your ma.'

Florrie fixed her eyes on a line of wedding rings pinned on a card. 'Is there nothing else?' she asked.

The shopkeeper shrugged and slid the jar towards her across the counter. 'It's handsome, this,' he said.

But Florrie wanted something with a story. She looked around. There were baby clothes, washed and folded, hardly used; heavy coats, blankets and hats with dusty crowns; a flute propped upright in the corner, a selection of buckets. There was a black and gold sewing machine with a carved wooden box and a wheel that Florrie could tell, just by looking, would turn without effort. But none of these things was what she wanted.

'That. What about that? Could I have that, do you think?'

It was the disc for a gramophone. The paper cover was glossy, a man in black hardly visible behind a pink-dressed woman, twirling. Florrie picked it up and laid it reverently on the counter.

The shopkeeper laughed. 'What you be wanting that for, my love? What're you going to do with it? You can't play it, you know. You need a machine to play it on.'

Florrie wanted to cry. 'But she'd like it,' she said. 'It's the kind of thing she'd like. If only she could see it.'

There was something of Queenie May in the way the dancer held herself, in the litheness of her.

'You don't see it, my love, you play it. It's music. You mark my words, you'll be better off with the jar.'

Florrie touched the record one more time. 'But I think,' she said, 'I think, if I could just…'

He shook his head and waited for her to change her mind.

'What's it like?' she asked him. 'The music? What's it like?'

'Oh, I don't know.' The shopkeeper turned the cover so that it faced him. He looked hard at the picture. 'Something lively I would say, wouldn't you; something flighty. That's what it looks like.'

'I'd like to hear it,' said Florrie.

'Then you'll have to save up. For the gramophone.' The shop-keeper snorted a laugh. 'You can come back for it then.' He looked at her hard. 'Here. I'll give you a halfpenny discount.'

He pushed the jar until it rested against Florrie's tight hand. She did not move.

'Come on, missy,' he said, suddenly brisk. 'I haven't got all day.'

'But my ma,' she said. 'If she could see the dancer...' Her words faded.

The shopkeeper slid the stolen coins off the counter. Florrie reached across, as though to stop him but he was too practised for her, patting her lightly on the arm. This appeared to seal the deal. She took the jar without looking at it, not able to tell him that her mother was, or could be, curious and funny and flighty, beautiful in the way she swayed and twirled, dancing in an unswept, unlaundered house.

Florrie turned the first corner after she left the shop, into a narrow street with a high wall blocking its far end. It was a quiet street, shaded. The blunt noise of the breaking jar ricocheted from the brick-fronted houses as she threw it to the ground. Someone leaned out of a window to find out what was going on, but seeing it was nothing, slipped back into the dark. Florrie stood for a moment, looking at the shards of china in the gutter. The plain blue tramlines that had run around the thick waist were wedged and truncated, like the threads of minerals in the winter cliffs. She wondered who the jar had belonged to, properly, before it had been hocked, and the thought of this, of someone being proud of it, loving it, filled her with such panic that she hurried back out on to the main street. And there she stood, stranded on the scrap of pavement, completely still. Only when a woman passed, pushing a pram and holding another child by the hand did Florrie move, stepping back out of their way, but it was almost ten minutes before she went back into the street. She picked up one of the scraps of cream china and put it in her pocket, an amulet.

A week later, when Queenie May came to wash Florrie's skirt, she found the broken shard of china and smiled at her daughter's odd taste in keepsakes, then threw it over the yard fence into the brambles beyond.

Arthur borrowed a spotless veil for Florrie to wear when she took her first communion, he tested her on her catechism as they walked to mass, and, occasionally, he prayed for her. But he was not bothered about Mary.

'I'll take her when she's older,' was all he said. 'When she's ready.'

But even when she began to walk confidently and was able to trot alongside, even when she clung to his trousers on a Sunday morning and cried to be part of the expedition, he resisted.

'Not old enough yet,' he maintained.

Florrie could not persuade him to change his mind, but she would take Mary aside sometimes, into a shadowy corner of a quiet room and make the sign of the cross for her, looping her arm around Mary's body, touching the four points with a jab of her finger, making her sister bow her head. Sometimes she would repeat it over once or twice, to be sure, slapping Mary if she fidgeted. She taught her the mantra, *'In the name of the Father and of the Son…'* and Mary lisped it after her. Then, as though it were part of the rite, they would go through to the kitchen together and Florrie would lift her sister to wash her hands in the sink, making her hold them a long time under the cold water.

They settled into a routine. When Arthur and Florrie set off down the hill to church, Queenie May and Mary crossed through the tilt-fenced back alleys to the square of park where there were two uneven swings. There were other families there, and Queenie May clustered with the mothers, whooping laughs, while Mary took her turn to ride, her hands stinging cold on the chains. They were high up, exposed, and even on fine days it was windy. But Queenie May liked to go. Alice always stayed at home. She sat at the front window watching for Florrie and her father, long before they were due to appear. When she finally saw them turn the corner by the derelict warehouse, she brushed her hair, put on her coat and hat with great care, and let herself quietly out through the front door. She always met them before they turned into their street, and Florrie always peeled away then, unsmiling.

'We'll just have a stroll before lunch,' Arthur said, but Florrie had already turned from them.

Arthur and Alice varied their route. They had nowhere particular to go. They dropped down into unfamiliar streets, exploring, until they found somewhere quiet and sheltered. There they would stand or sit together, depending on the weather. Alice was always very still, but Arthur was agitated on these mornings, more than ever, trembling sometimes, his face fretful. He pushed his hands against her at first at awkward angles, pinching her skin, bruising, and even though Alice knew to be quiet she whimpered sometimes into the wool of his coat. He would mutter then, tangled in his words, and only when he had finally forced the fist of his fingers hard into her, making her suddenly stiff, would she sense the hushed softness of him flooding over them. It was always a relief. On the way back, they would walk apart, and Arthur would sometimes stop alone at the street-end pub.

On one of these outings Arthur felt the first twinges of an unwieldy pain shifting in his gut. He rested for a moment as it took his breath, leaning on Alice and pale.

'Must have twisted myself somehow,' he said, blinking, and for a while it was forgotten.

But he felt it again once or twice in the following days, unexpectedly sharp, and before long it had become part of him, growing. At night especially, it would bulge, waking him many times, but he did not want it to mean anything and he kept it to himself. He was unusually secure in work and they had chosen rooms in a different building, taller than the last, set high on the mount behind the barracks, with a view across the squatting town to the open sea. There was a freshness to things. So he ignored the bloating ache, presuming it would pass, or that he would get used to it.

When Florrie came home from school for the first time to the new house he was on his knees propping up the bed in a corner with the help of two bricks. He seemed cheerful.

'Give us a hand, Flor,' he said, looking up with a smile and handing her one of the bricks. He held the bed high off the ground for her and she slipped the support in underneath. 'And the other one,' he said. 'Put that in too.'

He let the bed drop and sat hard on it to try it out. But the floor was rutted, and even with the wedge, the bed rocked noisily from side to side, slapping on the bricks as it fell back.

'It needs something else,' he said, 'something with a bit of give.'

And from the sack of things they had brought with them he took out his book. It was the right size to block the remaining gap. Its soft cover would deaden the rocking.

Florrie could not see his face, just the back of him, straining forward with his feet pressed out at odd angles, fragile and slightly ridiculous, clumsy. She didn't know what to make of him. Without pausing, he slipped the book between the bricks and the broken stump of bed leg, nudging it fully into place with his knee. Then he got up and sat on the bed again, swaying to and fro hard to test out its stability.

'Solid as a rock,' he said to Florrie, grinning. 'Come and try?'

'Won't you need it?' Florrie asked, not moving, but nodding slightly at the book. 'Won't you want to read it, with Ally?' Her mouth was suddenly dry. She found the words sticking.

'That maid could read the Bible backwards,' Arthur said, leaning back, proud. 'I don't need to bother with that. She's learned it all.'

Queenie May did not notice what Arthur had done to the bed and did not know that the pain in his stomach was starting to throb, but she noticed his cheerfulness. And when it was quiet that evening, Mary stretched out asleep under the patched blanket, she spent a long time at the window, listening to the sounds her family made and watching the lights blink across the town.

'It'll be nice here, Arthur,' she said quietly. 'Don't you think it'll be nice?'

Arthur was surprised by the lightness of her tone. Against the glow outside the window, with that spring to her sentence, she should have looked younger, like the girl she was when they began.

'It's better,' Queenie May went on. 'Being high up. I like being able to see across.'

'It'll be windy,' said Arthur.

'It'll blow things clean. And we can batten down when it's wild,' she said. 'We'll see it coming at least, from over past the breakwater.'

'See what?'

'The wind.'

Arthur sucked in his cheeks. 'It's cheaper here, anyway,' he said, and started to roll himself a cigarette.

'Cheaper, and cleaner. No soot to speak of. It couldn't be better,' said Queenie May, looking across at her husband, wanting to touch him. It was a feeling she remembered, a surge of possibility that burst on her like light.

But the next morning, Arthur woke with the pain rumbling in his stomach and he could no longer keep it secret.

'You've given your father indigestion, my girl,' Queenie May said sharply to Florrie as she braided her hair for school. 'It's all your talk of leaving. Fathers miss their daughters, that's how it goes.'

Florrie, coming up to fifteen, had been offered a place in service on the Hoe. It was something she was proud of.

'She's not going far,' said Alice, who was helping Mary with the fastening to her skirt.

'Far enough, though. Growing up,' said Queenie May. She

remembered the bitter morning smell of the first days away from home. But she wanted to be cheerful, now more than ever, with the sun streaming in the window and the breeze blowing cloud-shadows fast across the docks, and the promise of being high above the town, away from things. 'But it'll be nice, Flor, too,' she added.

'I'm only on trial, to begin with,' said Florrie. 'They might not like me.'

Arthur sat on the bed and groaned. The pain in his stomach was sharp for a moment. He tried to burp to relieve it, but nothing would come. He was working that day and could not afford to be late.

'Here, I'll rub it, Da,' said Alice and she stepped towards the bed, twirling Mary in her newly secured skirt as she did so. Mary giggled and put her arms out wide better to feel the spin. No one else moved.

'Where?' said Alice, and she sounded matter-of-fact, like a nurse.

Arthur lifted his work shirt and laid his hand on the pain. Alice bent towards him and laid her hand there too, circling it, pushing out with her fingers against the folds of skin. Her father's stomach was loose now, and paunchy. Queenie May noticed that, as though for the first time. She noticed too how pale his face was. She did not look at Alice.

Alice slid her fingers under the belt of Arthur's trousers, still circling with the pain. She looked up at Florrie, her head at an awkward angle as she continued to rub.

'Tell them at school I'll be late,' she said. 'Tell them what's happened.'

Florrie watched the fingers caressing her father's skin.

Arthur was breathing hard. 'You go on too, Ally. We can't be late, either of us,' he said, but he did not move from the bed and Alice did not stop the swirl of her hand.

Queenie May wished there was something to be done. 'P'rhaps it was bad meat,' she said.

'What meat? When did I have bad meat?'

'Not at the yard?'

'What ruddy nonsense.' But the anger in it was slack, and Arthur looked across at Queenie May for a moment as though they were alone, the two of them. He put out an arm, perhaps to draw her close, and their gaze was steady, unblinking.

The crawl of Alice's fingers distracted them, and Queenie May stepped away from him. She looked at Florrie who was standing awkwardly by the door, unable to bring herself to leave.

'Take Mary, will you, my dear,' she said.

Florrie bit her lip but by the time she had found something to say the others were all crowded around Arthur, bending close to him. She pulled Mary out of the room.

'I'll be leaving in three days,' she said fiercely as they turned into the street. 'I'll have finished with school, and left them; gone up on the Hoe. I'll be grown then, doing things myself.'

Mary held tight to her sister's hand and the wind spat rain at them from the sea.

Florrie took Mary to her class, and then she sat at her desk and watched the school-yard gate for Alice. She watched until her eyes were sore and she had to blink them hard. She did not mark her slate, nor recite tables. She hardly breathed. She just watched, seeing the clouds pull across and the morning darken.

Two horses passed by, held on a leash by a man in leggings; a paper bag lifted in the wind from the corner of the school yard and tumbled across until it got wedged in the wall. She watched two small boys come late, scampering in from the cold with their faces drawn, and she watched the hands on the church clock opposite as they slipped through the hour. And when Alice finally came Florrie sat back in her chair, her hands damp with sweat but tense with cold, her stomach swirling sick. The teacher took her long sigh to be nostalgia for the school life she was leaving. And because Florrie had said nothing about what might have been detaining her sister, Alice was smacked hard on her bare legs with the heavy wooden ruler propped by the door for just that purpose. She went to her desk without crying.

Queenie May, too, had been watching, but she had seen nothing to worry her. The mesmeric stroke of Alice's hand had brought some colour back to Arthur's face and it did not look as though he were dying. And so Queenie May, still cheerful, whistled as she spread out the laundry to wash. She waved high at Alice and Arthur as they left the house, and later, wringing the washing through the mangle in the yard, she enjoyed the way the wooden barrels clicked in the sun as they marshalled the cloth. Even the yard itself looked charming to her, sheltered as it was by the high walls around and hung with a line for drying the washing away from the dirt of the street. In her head she was singing. There was something clear about the day. She could not have known that Arthur was making his way very slowly up the hill home again, long before his shift was due to finish, the wind pushing hard against his back, his trousers loosened around his waist and the pain pulsing in his stomach like some kind of animal.

The first Queenie May knew of it was a knocking at the window, an offbeat rapping that broke the steady rhythm of the mangle. She looked up to see Arthur's pale face hung there, mouthing something impenetrable. She knew at once he had not been laid off again. And when she rushed up the stairs to reach him, his feet were trailing a thick phlegm of yellow vomit across their room. She stood for a moment at the door, one of Mary's wet blouses in her hand and another, she knew, half squeezed and left dangling in the yard. She watched him, remembering again the day he had come home from the war, his leg dripping and rotten, his cheekbones sharp and his eyes fixed on a point many miles distant from her, the anger of it, and the disappointment. And as he stretched for the bed, his body taut, stumbling, Queenie May dropped the blouse and hurried towards him, clutching him in her damp arms. She did not know if he would have fallen, but anyway she held him tight. And for that moment, a short moment before he spewed a hot dribble of sick across her chest, Arthur and Queenie May were bearing the weight of each other with young arms, their heads touching, and Queenie May knowing he was the only man she would ever have the chance to love.

Florrie was the only girl to leave school that week, and she got special attention. The very young girls wanted to hold her hand, or, better, have her pick them up. The older girls, her friends, touched her too, as if to make certain that she had existed. She was happy in the chattering tumble and she delayed the moment when she would have to step beyond it. Alice hung back through it all, watching, and when Florrie had finally made it to the gate she appeared at her sister's side. They walked home together for the last time.

'Ma's made you something, for going away,' said Alice.

It was supposed to be a secret. Florrie couldn't bear to spoil it and pretended she hadn't heard.

But Alice persisted. 'It's a little case,' she said. 'A purse. It's pretty.'

'I'll need to pack my things tonight. I'm allowed to take a bag,' said Florrie, listening to Alice's squeaky breathing. 'Still, I'll be home sometimes. When I'm given a day off.' She pulled ahead of her sister so that she could hear nothing more of her going-away present. But at the top of the hill, she waited, watching a ship moving slowly past the breakwater.

'It's tomorrow I go, Ally,' she said when they were together again.

Alice concentrated on her breathing and said nothing.

They stopped again at a bend in the road before the final climb up to the house. Florrie was desperate for her sister to speak. She waited longer than was necessary, watching the ship, which had now pulled into the open water and was turning. Alice looked out too, seeing a seagull circling closer to hand. It dropped on to the dark slates of a roof.

'What has she made then, Ally?' asked Florrie at last, not quite meaning to.

Alice caught her breath to speak. It made what she said next seem hushed and reverent. 'It's a case,' she said. 'Embroidered. The prettiest flowers.'

'A case for what?'

Alice had to guess. 'Hairpins, I should think.'

'Oh,' said Florrie. 'Well, I'll have to be neat, I suppose, if they're to like me.' It got her thinking of things. 'And Da? Has he said anything?'

Alice shrugged. 'I don't think so.'

The gull lifted suddenly from the slates, squawking.

'But you'll be all right, with me gone? You don't want to come with me? I could keep us both,' said Florrie, quite suddenly.

Alice laughed. 'On a housemaid's wage? Don't be stupid, Flor.' She wanted an end to it. 'I'm fine, I'm not ready to go.'

Florrie couldn't look at her. She felt her face burning. 'But you're his daughter, Ally. Like me.'

Alice shrugged again and looked hard into her sister's face. She let her words sway in the air. 'But it's not you he wants, is it, Flor?'

The girls arrived home ten minutes apart and busied themselves with things. Arthur was well enough, that final evening with Florrie, to sit up while they had their tea. He even thought about taking a slice of the fruit bread Queenie May had made in celebration but something about the sheen of it turned his stomach. The girls were not put off, however, and Mary danced around the table with her mouth crumby and her sticky hands swishing through the warm air.

'It's the best day ever,' she said, but no one agreed with her and so she didn't repeat it.

Instead, later, when she was finally asleep and Arthur was sitting pale by the empty fireplace, Queenie May sat with her oldest daughter looking out at the lights on the hump-backed rail bridge. When Florrie started crying, Queenie May held her tight for a long while.

'I've something for you to take,' she said at last, pushing Florrie's head gently off her chest so that she could reach in her pocket for the embroidered case.

It was, even by the dull light in the room, as pretty as Alice had said it would be. The knotted, curling petals were laid in pink satin thread over a piece of brown velvet cloth that, Florrie knew, was not a scrap from any piece of clothing ever owned by the family. And even though it had been made with Florrie always in mind, Queenie May was sorry to let it go.

'It's beautiful, Ma,' said Florrie.

'It'll be something nice for you, when you're on your own.'

Florrie traced the forms of the flowers with her fingers and felt something hard and ridged within the case. The thought of hairpins in such a beautiful bag was sad, and she did not want to look inside.

'Well, go on,' prompted Queenie May, and Florrie noticed the excitement in her voice. Alice, too, must have heard it. She got up from where she had been lying with her eyes closed on top of the counterpane and leaned over her mother's shoulder while they watched Florrie reach inside the drawstring opening of the velvet pouch.

It was Alice who spoke first. 'What's that?' she said, as Florrie held in her palm the twisted green glass beads, looped on a brass chain. 'She'll not be able to wear that, not with her uniform. They'll not let her.'

'It's not a necklace, Ally, my love.'

Florrie held up the beads by one end, and Alice could see the careful, symmetrical arrangement of them.

'It's a rosary,' Florrie said, amazed.

She tried to look into Queenie May's face, but her mother was embarrassed and was fiddling with the button on Alice's pinafore.

'Ma? A rosary?' Florrie said again.

Alice went to speak, but Queenie May wouldn't let her.

'It's like a prayer card,' she explained. 'For Catholics. Isn't that right, Florrie?'

'Where did you get it, Ma?' was all Florrie could think.

'From Mrs O'Malley.'

Alice went back to the bed.

'Do you see that, Pa? I've got a rosary,' said Florrie, reaching with her arm across the room and dangling the beads in his direction. He did not raise his head.

'Best not to bother your father with it,' said Queenie May.

The doctor tried to help Arthur, first with a thick black mixture and then with pills, but everything was vomited up within minutes, which struck them all as a waste of expensive medicine. So they stopped the doctor coming, presuming things would calm down naturally. Queenie May held on to the idea that there was simply an errant strand of rotten meat slowly and spitefully making its way through her husband's gut, and no one quite discounted the possibility that he was grieving for Florrie. So that when, not long after Florrie left, Arthur woke feeling better and began to get himself dressed for work, it would have been right for things to be resolved. He asked Queenie May to make him some breakfast. He shaved carefully and he cleaned his shoes. But before he left the house he felt breathless and dizzy and sat for a moment on the bed, and by the time the siren sounded for the shift, he was kneeling on the bare floor retching into a bowl.

Alice stayed home from school to look after her father. To pass the time, she read to him from his Bible, and wrote lists, ordering and re-ordering all the little jobs that could be done and choosing the sparse groceries they could afford on Queenie May's part-time wages. With Arthur unable to raise his head from the bed, there was no one but Alice who could read the lists, but still she kept on writing them. At the end of each day she tore them up into tiny pieces and threw the paper on the fire, beginning again the next morning as soon as the dawn spilt enough light to see by.

'It's a waste of good paper, my girl,' complained Queenie May, but Alice just made her writing smaller so as to take up less space.

On the night of the spring hailstorm, Queenie May came home from the laundry smelling of wet soap and with her hands raw, her scarf moulded to her head by the fierce rain. Protecting her face from the sting of the hail, she did not see Alice watching for her from the front window.

'Is he all right, Ally?' she whispered, routinely, as she took off her coat by the door.

'Look at him,' was all Alice said. He was curled on his side, knotted within himself, his knees and arms wrapped tightly across his abdomen and his head buried. There was something so stiff about him, so concentrated, that even his skin seemed rigid. The tight greyness of him was enough for Queenie May to know.

'Get Mary back,' she said. 'I saw her at Dyson's corner just now. Tell her to go and find Dr Walters. And go for Florrie. Tell them they have to let her come. Tell them her father's dying.'

It was the first time any of them had said the word. Alice flinched. Queenie May gave her some coins for the fare.

'And be quick, my girl. Or you'll be too late,' she said.

But as Alice was going out of the door, Queenie May thought of something else. 'Wait,' she said. 'You'll have to go for Father Durphy, too.'

'I don't know where, Ma.'

'Well, I don't know. Go to the yard and ask them where the chapel is.'

'But he doesn't live there, does he, at the chapel? All the time?'

Queenie May was wetting a cloth for Arthur's face. Having Alice there seemed a distraction.

'Just ask, Ally. Find someone who knows. Ask the ruddy Irish.'

Alice pulled on her coat but still had not fastened it when she found Mary, trying to catch the drips from the baker's shop awning in her mouth. Together they rehearsed, out loud, the route to the doctor's and what Mary should say. The hail throbbed around them. Alice stuffed her hands in her pockets and ran as fast as she could down the hill and all the way to the yard, stopping only when her breath refused to come at all, and panting, when she had to wait for traffic to pass. She asked for the chapel and found it quickly, but although the door was open and a little red light burnt in the dark at the far end, it was empty. She had to ask three other men before someone could direct her to the presbytery. One of the men winked at her. And when she found the priest he had just boiled the kettle for a pot of tea, and was only half dressed. Alice did not cross the threshold. She gave her message briskly, shaking the water from her coat, and set off again to catch the bus to the city, the sky clearing above her, a shaft of sunlight pouring green-gold on to the railway bridge.

Father Durphy made an effort to be quick, putting a small jar of oil, a plastic bottle of holy water and a silver-cased communion host in his pocket before leaving. He arrived at the house barely half an hour after Alice had first roused him, and, seeing Arthur coiled on the bed, smiled wanly at Queenie May and began at once with the prayers.

'You'd best wait outside,' he said to Queenie May, 'until I've heard his confession. I'll call you back.'

Arthur started at the priest's voice so close to his ear and turned his head. Queenie May heard him speak as she left the room, closing the door behind her, but his voice was strangled and strange.

'Father?'

The priest nodded, as if that were enough.

'I don't want it,' said Arthur.

Father Durphy was trying to loosen the cap on the bottle of holy water, and was not paying good attention. He had begun flicking the drops around the room, and particularly over the bed, before Arthur managed to speak again.

'I don't want extreme unction, Father.'

This time the priest heard. It did not surprise him. 'Be brave, man, and the Lord will comfort you. It's no good pretending.' He had learned to be strict about death. 'Take time now to listen to God, or it may be too late.'

'I don't want it.'

Father Durphy had his prayer book open, although he knew the rite by heart. He took a breath to begin, but before he could, Arthur, with unexpected strength, threw out an arm and swatted the missal to the floor. The bottle, which had been lying on the covers, was thrown too by the force of it, and spilt drops of holy water down the bedspread and on to the priest's worn shoes.

'You won't confess?'

Father Durphy picked up his missal to begin again. He expected Arthur to submit and sounded tired.

'I want none of it. Where's Queen?'

Arthur thought he was speaking loudly. He hoped his wife might hear him, but she was at the front door, on the lookout for the doctor and her daughters.

The priest tried again, because it was his duty. 'Confess to me, Arthur. Take communion and the oil of the sick. Make peace with God and yourself. Our help is in the name of the Lord.'

Arthur knew the priest would not understand. 'It's too much just now,' was all he said. 'I can't do it, Father.'

'But Arthur…' Father Durphy wanted to say the thing that would bring Arthur round, but he did not know much at all about the man in the bed. 'There's young Florrie to think of,' he said. 'She'll want to know her father made a good death.'

Arthur groaned.

'Let's begin, Arthur. Let us pray.'

Arthur let out a scream that Queenie May heard sharply and that woke the baby who had been sleeping in the attic room of the house next door. It exhausted him completely. Father Durphy, knowing he was beaten, slipped his missal back into his pocket, laid a hand briefly on the lump of body that sweated beneath the covers, and left quietly.

'God forgive me,' whispered Arthur to the empty room as he heard the priest shut the door.

Father Durphy passed Queenie May on his way out of the house and told her she could go back to her husband.

'That's it then, Father?' she said, thinking the scream had been part of the rite, some kind of purging, the exorcism of life.

'He did not want to confess,' he said.

Queenie May knew this to be a bad thing. She was cross with Arthur, after all the trouble of fetching the priest, until she got back to the bedroom and saw him again, crying, his head thrown back on the pillow and his fists tight. She damped her cloth in the cold water, and ran it over Arthur's forehead. He caught hold of her hand and held it. She did not pull away.

'It didn't seem right, in the end, not to die the same way you will,' he said, rasping.

She squeezed his hand. 'I knew you wouldn't want to be like that, apart from me. I knew you'd come back,' she said.

'I had to send him away,' said Arthur, very quietly. 'It's better that way. We'll both be sinners – the two of us – all of us. Like the boys. That's the thing, isn't it?'

Queenie May kissed him. His skin was sticky.

'Yes, Arthur,' she said.

The doctor who came with Mary did not stay a long time, and shook his head at Queenie May as he left. Mary saw this, and began to cry. Alice, who had been lucky with the run of the buses, was in time in the end, but the message she had left with the housekeeper where Florrie worked was not passed on until the evening duties were complete. So Florrie never saw Arthur's dying moments, and often wondered about them. She never quite thought it could be as they said.

Arthur made an effort to die well. He wanted to leave a mark somehow.

'Be proud of me, won't you?' he said, and of course Queenie May nodded. 'I won a war for you, you know.'

This was a surprise; she had forgotten. She touched the flaking skin of his cheek with gentle fingers, and then there was a long pause, when nothing was said. There were just the sounds of the house, uncomfortably loud, and the still, quiet passing of time, and Arthur's desperation. When he next stirred, his face was tighter than ever, his grip more anxious. He sat up to kiss Mary and he took Alice by the hand.

'You must have the book, Ally,' he said. 'To read.'

Alice thought he would say more. She waited.

'When I'm gone,' he said. 'Have it as yours.'

And that was all. There was nothing else he could have said. And they all heard him bequeath the book to her; they all accepted it as a dying man's wish. So that afterwards, when Florrie objected to the unfairness of the legacy, there was no room for vacillation.

Queenie May had seen several deaths, but Arthur's seemed strange to her and barren. She could not be sure that he had known each of them for who they were.

'I wanted so much to love him,' she said to Florrie, as they stood by the bed, the sheets pulled tight now, neat. They did not notice its slight lopsidedness, even when Queenie May leaned over to touch Arthur's forehead gently, and the bed tipped. They did not realize that Alice, taking advantage of the distractions of Florrie's late arrival, had eased out the book, pushing it hard with her feet, feeling the weight of her father's body and the jolt of it as the bed fell on to the bricks. It was only later that Florrie, picking up the scattered bottle of holy water as a keepsake, caught sight of Alice sitting by the dark window, with her hand stuffed hard between her legs, her skirt peeled back and Arthur's legacy firm on her knee, only partly concealing the rub of her fingers.

2. Florrie

ALICE CLIMBED THROUGH the streets towards the candy-striped lighthouse. It was a fine hot August Sunday, with the breeze from the sea hardly stirring the flags along the Hoe and the horizon hanging flat. Crowds flopped in the sun, sprawled across the grass, and on the long quay at the harbour there was the smell of tar and hot engines, the rope laid out for the tug-of-war. Even before she got to their meeting place at Smeaton's Tower, Alice wished she hadn't come. The heat was making her breathing tight, and her new shoes bit her heels. When she spotted her sister pushing through the crowds in a pretty floral dress, a dark pink hat tight to her sleek hair and slightly tipped, she was already irritated.

'It's very busy, Florrie,' she said.

'Isn't it lovely?' Florrie flung out her arms, wanting to take everything in, feeling the sun and the noise and thick summer air and wanting to laugh at it all.

'But there's so many people, Flor.'

'There's more, down the other paths and out to the pier. I could see from my room. I could see them all coming. We'll hardly get a place to stand, Ally, if we don't hurry. We'll miss the racing.'

'You still want to see it then?'

Alice was knocked by a man with a boy up high on his

shoulders. He turned to smile an apology at her, but she looked away.

'Of course. Don't you?' said Florrie, almost bouncing.

'I suppose.'

'Oh, come on, Ally, it'll be handsome.'

And Florrie led the way through the crowds, which thickened as they dropped down from the lighthouse, clotted into the narrow paths and sprawled wide on the grass banks. Boats were already working their way up and down in the shallows, the oarsmen trying out their strokes and shouting back at friends on the bank. Florrie took Alice's hand, but resisted the impulse to pull her.

'This'll do, won't it, here?' said Alice.

'But can you see, Ally, over all the heads? Can you see the water, and the boats, even in close?' She didn't wait for her sister to answer. 'It's no good. We can't – we can't see. We'll have to go down on the rocks.'

'Florrie, no. I'm not going down there.'

But Florrie had already pressed on ahead, snaking through the crowd towards the boys perched on the rocks, above the white tideline, their jackets and caps thrown into piles. Some dipped in the deep water below, hauling themselves up by their elbows. Alice caught her sister hard by the sleeve.

'Florrie, are you mad? We can't go down there. By ourselves. We can't. Everyone'll look at us.'

'Let them,' said Florrie.

And although she was ashamed of her sister, Alice couldn't help following. She did not want to be left alone.

Florrie tore a gash in her stockings climbing over the wall to the rocks. She laughed it off, jubilant, even though later, when things had calmed down, she spent a frustrating hour crouched by the low bed in her room trying to darn the tear with tiny stitches. The swimmers for the first race were getting into the water and no one paid much attention to the two girls. Alice, nonetheless, moved slowly, careful to keep her skirt tucked tight between her knees as she slid off the wall and crabbed sideways along the rocks, her cheeks burning.

'There's hardly anywhere to sit. It's all taken,' said Florrie, but not discouraged. The rocks sloped sharply down to the sea and only at the back of them, near the walls, were there any flat places to sit. Alice bent down to ease the pain from her heels. She saw she had scuffed one of her shoes.

'Here! Here, Ally. These men have said we can sit here. Isn't that kind?'

Looking up, Alice saw that Florrie had moved away and was beckoning her with quick arms. She thought she could not bear the way her sister shouted, her brazen wave. She thought nothing could have been worse. But by the time she caught up, Florrie was chattering to the men, shrieking with laughter. She appeared to have no shame.

'Ally, Ally, look! They're off. They're swimming. Oh, isn't this just the best thing? Isn't it marvellous sitting here, so close? Look at them all, how fast they go, even in the waves.'

And they watched the races, one after the other, as the lines of sleek heads ploughed out to the breakwater, almost out of sight, before turning and swimming slowly back, making splashy, uneven clusters as they reached the shore. Florrie called out sometimes to the swimmers, took a sip of something from a small flask offered to her by the men standing now precariously behind them, put her hat on the rock beside her to get a better view and felt the sun full on her head. She smiled so widely at the way the day was turning out that she looked pretty in the light playing off the sea. Alice dabbed her bleeding heels with her handkerchief and wondered what it was that had made her sister so coarse.

The men behind them, who turned out to work in the kitchens at the Continental Hotel, introduced them to Eddie. It was after the third race.

'That one there, he works with us,' one of them said, proud, even though Eddie was still pulling himself from the water while the winner was running up and down at the edge of the tide, splashing great arcs of spray with his feet and waving his arms to the crowd. The girls watched as Eddie made his way through the shallows at the edge of the bay, grinning and flicking the water out of his hair, his long-lashed eyes blinking up to where they were sitting. He could see his friends, perched alongside two sharp-faced girls, pink in the sun, and he clambered up to them, still dripping. He lay back on the hot rock, seeping dark around him, and he closed his eyes against the glare. He was sinewy, stick thin, his hair lank around his ears even as it dried.

'Slip us me baccy,' he pleaded, holding out his hand, his eyes still closed.

Instead Florrie tapped out a cigarette from her own packet and passed it to him.

He was surprised by the sleek feel of it on his palm and opened his eyes. He twitched his mouth. 'Thanks,' he said, turning from her to get a light.

It was a long afternoon. There was a series of rowing races after the swimming, and long pauses where nothing seemed to happen. The day got hotter. The tide turned and started to churn noisily against the foot of the rocks. 'I'm going back,' said Eddie, to no one in particular. 'It's late. I've got to get smartened up before service.'

'You should see him, girls, in his shiny buttons,' said his friends, laughing.

Florrie was feeling light-headed. She had not eaten and was not used to the sun.

'Do you think we should, Ally?' she said.

Alice had no idea what her sister was asking. 'Should what?' she asked warily.

'Go home,' said Florrie.

It was a relief. 'Yes, Flor, I think we should. We've been here ages,' adding, as if it mattered, 'and the tide's coming in.'

Florrie nodded. 'I'm tired,' she said. 'All of a sudden.' She reached for her hat.

'Here, let me help, my love,' said Eddie, seeing her fumbling with her hatpin, and Alice overbalancing trying to get her shoes back on. It was just instinctive kindness on his part, nothing more. But for the sisters, both of them, it was the minute they became sharply aware of him. When he gave Alice his arm to lean against, she felt the charge of his touch so that it almost unbalanced her again, and when he reached over Florrie's head to steady the hat while she took the pin from her teeth and slid it through the band, feeling the scratch of it against her scalp, her cheeks blushed red, her heart thumped, and she felt the flash of the future full inside her.

Eddie walked with the girls back up the hill to Smeaton's Tower without touching either of them again. He walked briskly and none of them spoke, though Alice's breath came noisily, like quiet song. At the lighthouse Florrie needed to take her own path across to the white Victorian villas where she worked. Eddie and Alice would be walking another way, towards town. They would, she realized, have time alone.

'Do you want to come for tea, Ally?' She did not have anything else that might divert her sister.

But Alice wanted to walk with Eddie. 'I might catch the bus,' she said. 'In these shoes, I can't hardly walk.'

'But you could come first, for tea, if you like. I've got the rest of the day.'

Alice shrugged. 'I'm fine.'

Florrie smiled at her sister. There was no way for Eddie to know they were arguing. 'Right then,' she said. 'Right you are.' And the two girls kissed lightly.

Eddie was anxious to get on. He wished he had got away once they had climbed over the rocks. They had slowed him down.

'I must get back,' he said. 'It was nice to meet you both.' He held out his hand.

'It was lovely,' said Florrie, taking his fingers lightly and hiding her face with her hat. Then she turned and walked away across the grass. She did not look back at them but, much later, sitting by the high window of her attic room, she tried to work out where they had been standing. She tried to picture Eddie as she had left him, though the details, even now, were vague. She held her arms about herself, as though it might be cold, brushing the swell of her breasts so lightly with her fingers that the shock of it surprised her, watching the slim blue of the horizon as she stroked the soft pad of her thumb against her skin, feeling the rise and fall of her breathing in her warm hand. Florrie cried slow, thick tears then and was sick, opening the window just in time to spit the dregs of the day's excitement on to the roof tiles.

Alice watched her sister go, trying to think of a way to keep Eddie.

'Right then,' he said, but Alice did not take his offered hand.

'I could give you the address where my sister works. If you like. You could see her again. You could send a note.'

Eddie saw for the first time that he might have made an impression. 'Did she say something? Did she talk about me?' He didn't know when this could have happened.

Alice smiled wide at him, encouraging, not quite ready to lie.

'I never know with you girls,' said Eddie, pleased with himself. 'I never quite know.'

But although Alice was careful in telling him the address and how the note should be marked so it would get to Florrie through the housekeeper, she still took those moments with him to heart, as her last. She could not imagine that after jogging back to the Continental in the late sun, sprinting up the stairs to his room to change, and spending long hours waiting on tables in the hot dining room, Eddie would have any idea of what she had told him. It just did not seem possible.

When the note came, it was written tidily on paper printed with the hotel name and address, flourishing in blue and gold, making it seem more momentous than it was. The housekeeper passed it to Florrie with a smile, and Florrie trembled. Since the weather was still fine, and the days long, Eddie proposed a walk on the Hoe, first of all, and a swim in the flat round pool that dipped down to the sea. But it was several weeks before their time off coincided, and they finally met one early September evening at low tide, when the weather had changed. It was cloudy and cool, and there was a dampness in the air that was not quite rain but that made Eddie's hair slick, even under its layer of Brylcreem.

Eddie sat on the steps near the Drake memorial while he waited for Florrie, lifting the hems of his trousers out of the greasy damp. Other girls went by, one wheeling a bicycle, and one with her blonde hair hardly stuffed under her headscarf. He was not sure if he would recognize Florrie. All he could clearly remember was her awkward height, and the way she had flinched when he had helped her fix her hat. But when she came, a few minutes early and her cheeks flushed pink, he knew it was her and felt an unexpected jolt of pleasure.

'You've brought your things, for the pool?' he asked. 'It's not too cold?'

Florrie had had to borrow a bathing costume. 'We'll see,' she said.

But by the time they were changed and standing together, awkward, by the tiled steps into the water, she was shivering.

Eddie ran along the sweeping edge of the pool and jumped high, tumbling into the water with a splash. He said something to Florrie as he ran, but it was lost in the excitement of things. Florrie felt the pull of the unfamiliar costume around her legs, the brisk air from the sea and a sudden fear of the rippling water below her. She pulled her cap tight down over her ears.

'Come on,' said Eddie, swimming back to her. He stood in the shallows, holding out a hand. 'It's not cold. Not once you're in.'

And to please him, because she had to, Florrie eased herself down the steps, holding hard to the rail. She reached out for Eddie's hand, stepping carefully, although the water hardly came up to her knees. Eddie laughed at her.

'Come on,' he said again.

And he swam out then to the fountain, kicking white water high behind him, still laughing.

When he looked back, Florrie was where he had left her, beacon tall among the children bobbing around her. He hauled himself on to the platform and beckoned her. And then he stepped back into the plume of the fountain and could see nothing but the blue spray and the splinters of sky and the dance of the rainbow light around him. He felt himself disappear for a moment. And then he looked for Florrie, wanting to pull her up beside him and into the stream of the shower, but he was surprised to see her still standing by the edge of the pool. She was hardly up to her waist in water. He could not understand. And because Florrie could not tell him that she couldn't swim; because, when he came back to her, he could see the blue tinge of cold around her lips and because there was no fun to be had walking through the shallow water, they agreed it was not the weather for it, and hurried back to their towels.

'Nice though, for a change,' said Florrie, when they met up again outside. She offered him a stick of chewing gum, but he shook his head at it even though she had already peeled it from its wrapper. She put it in her pocket, and found it there the following Sunday, bent over on itself and brittle.

They walked for a while, heading towards Smeaton's Tower, a landmark. Eddie offered Florrie his arm. She was shivering still, which, for no good reason, annoyed him. The sea was quiet and grey and the patches of sand dark with damp.

'Do you swim a lot?' asked Florrie, desperate to make the trip to the pool less of a failure. But Eddie, looking out towards the breakwater, was nudged into thinking about the regatta races and the warm rock on the back of his legs, and Alice.

'What does your sister do?' he asked.

'I've got two sisters,' said Florrie. 'Mary, the youngest, is still at school. She's only a maid, she's only nine. And the other one, the one you met before, that's Alice. She's seventeen. She works at Cranshaws, in town. They make things for the navy, for ships. But she's in the office, typing.'

Eddie blew through his teeth at the impressiveness of this. 'Nice,' he said. 'Nice work.'

'She was good at things, at school,' said Florrie.

They walked about until it got dusky and the streetlights came on and out at sea the lights on the ships started to reflect dimly off the water. The air was thick and still, and as the day faded it seemed suddenly quiet. They did not talk a great deal and did not drop into town, but stayed up high on the Hoe. Eddie was stiff in his lower back from their slow pace. But although he felt that he should have been disappointed with things; although he felt it would be hard, when he got back to the hotel, to explain just what had been worth the trouble, something about the calm of the evening, the soft warmth of Florrie's voice, the undemanding, undemonstrative ease of it, edged itself into him. He found himself holding her by the gate in the back wall of the house where she worked, and kissing her. He had to reach up and felt the bones in his neck click.

'When's your next night off?' he asked her.

'I'll write you a note,' she said.

Which she did, as soon as she was in her attic room, before she had even taken off her coat. She sat on the bed, resting a scrap of notepaper on her knee and pressing hard with the pencil. She tried to tell Eddie how much she had enjoyed the evening. She admitted then what she hadn't been able to say, that the pool had frightened her, that she had never learned to swim. And she gave him notice of her next day off. It was the first proper letter she had ever written. It ran to almost three sides of paper and, because she did not write well, it took her a long time. Several words had to be crossed out and attempted again. Her spelling was erratic and, despite her best efforts, the soft lead had a tendency to smear. When she looked back over it, it did not seem quite right, it was not elegant, and she did not post it. She kept it folded in the pocket of her uniform, alongside the note he had first sent.

In the quiet of the nights, reading awkwardly by the light from the street creeping through the high window, Florrie laid out her note side by side with Eddie's. As the thought of him became smudged and indistinct, reading him brought him nearer. But her own note nagged her with its ugliness; more than anything she wished she could form her letters more gracefully. She felt she was letting herself down somehow; she felt he would not want her. She suspected she might be clumsy and stupid, coarse. It was a feeling she kept with her.

Alice did not know that Eddie had taken Florrie out until a long time later. She thought she had lost him. She tried not to think about it. She concentrated very hard on her work. She typed quickly, kept her desk immaculate and was so quick to answer the manager's bell that he sometimes thought she must crouch outside his door, waiting. She practised shorthand in a notebook on her knee as she sat on the bus, and, at home in the evenings, away from Queenie May and Mary, she read. She renewed her books diligently at the lending library, and in the few weeks after meeting Eddie at the regatta she finished a number of murder mysteries; several selections of poems; a book of knitting patterns; three weighty Victorian novels about love, and a political history of the American Civil War. She read every single word of every book, no matter how dull, including any acknowledgements and references. She read steadily and carefully, finishing each evening's reading at the end of a chapter, which she marked with a folded strip of headed paper she had found at work. But she did not remember what she had read, and something about every volume disappointed her.

She did not touch Arthur's book. And the more time went by, the more frightening the prospect became. She could not bring herself even to brush her open hand against the soft cover. But she so wanted to sit with it again, on her knee; she so wanted to feel the dense paper in her hands and the animal warmth of the leather, that sometimes she could not sleep at night for thinking about it. And she was looking at where it lay on the table under her bedroom window, trying not to, trying instead to concentrate on the library edition of the *Young Secretary's Guide*, when Queenie May called through to tell her about Florrie and Eddie.

'Ooh Ally, you'll never guess. Florrie's been walking out with a young man. From the Continental. Eddie he's called,' said Queenie May, sounding almost as breathless as Alice and standing in the corridor outside the bedroom unbuttoning her coat.

Alice put down her book and watched her mother through the open door. She could not, for the moment, speak.

'They've been twice up on the Hoe and once out to Jennycliffe. He sent a note up to the house. Out of the blue, she said it was.'

'Eddie wrote to her?'

'You know him?' asked Queenie May.

'We met him at the regatta, both of us,' said Alice.

'You didn't tell me this.'

Alice took a deep breath. 'It didn't seem anything,' she said. 'He walked with us up at the Hoe, that was all. He was in one of the races.'

'What a hot day that was,' said Queenie May, folding her coat over her arm. It was all she could remember about it, the hottest day of the year. Then she thought again about Florrie. 'Oh, that girl,' she squealed and as Alice came out to her she was almost lifted off the ground by the force of her mother's embrace.

They went through to the kitchen. Alice began the preparations for their supper, turning her back on Queenie May's storytelling.

'He's at the Continental Hotel, you know. That used to be the Albion,' said Queenie May again.

'I know,' said Alice, cutting bread, each slice identical to the last.

'And he's got a good position there. He earns a good wage. He's smart, Florrie says, being a waiter and all.' Queenie May pressed her back hard against the kitchen chair, stretching out the pain in it, and wiggled her feet loose from her shoes. She was still wearing her outdoor headscarf. She waited for Alice to say something. 'Ally?'

'What?'

'Aren't you pleased, for your sister? Having a young man?'

Alice did not look around. 'It's just three times, Ma. It might not come to anything.'

'Still,' said Queenie May, confident.

The water for their eggs came to the boil. Alice took her time dunking them in, letting each one sit in the bowl of the ladle until it had filled with water before she rolled it finally into the pan. She put one aside for Mary and flicked over the timer. They both watched the sand.

'He sounds such a nice young man,' said Queenie May as Alice brought their eggs to the table. She took off her scarf then, and put it on the floor under her chair, fluffing up the hair on the crown of her head with open fingers.

'And Florrie? What does Florrie say?' asked Alice.

'I can't get much out of her,' said Queenie May with a shrug. 'It's like she doesn't want to... Alice!'

Tapping off the top of her egg with her spoon, Alice had swung into it with such force that the shell had splintered, the egg cup had fallen, and a paste of bright yolk was splattered across the table and high on to Alice's cream blouse. There was a moment's sharp silence, and then Alice left the room, slipping her arms from the spoilt blouse as she walked.

The bus engine churned, clouding the pavements with smoke. Alice dabbed at her nose with her handkerchief; the tip of it was raw and split where she had rubbed it over and over, anxious. She sucked in the fumes. Waiting for the day to start she called to mind everything Arthur had taught her about love. It was all she knew.

Florrie got on first, carrying the picnic carefully and choosing a seat halfway down the aisle by the window. Eddie allowed Alice on ahead of him, too, and, because it was polite, another woman with a baby. Florrie looked up at Alice as she came down the aisle and did not smile. Alice said nothing and went to take the seat in front of her sister, but by then Eddie had caught up and was close behind her.

'Sit with Florrie, if you like. I'm fine by myself. I can stretch out, have a smoke. It's a long ride,' he said. 'Best have the girls together.'

Alice, who was already halfway into the seat she had first chosen, hung on tight to the cold metal edge along its top to keep herself half standing. She was very still. She felt heavy and sleepy now the day had come; her thoughts were splayed.

'Aw, won't you sit with me, Eddie?' sidled Florrie, holding out a hand above the mound of the picnic basket.

'Later, my love,' said Eddie, and he took the seat on the other side of the aisle, sliding in sideways with his back to the window and his legs half bent over the seat beside him. He was puffed with the prestige of being seen with the sisters and he took his tin of cigarettes from his jacket with an unaccustomed flourish. Florrie's hand was still there, inviting, but he ignored it.

Alice slid down in her seat, very quietly, and watched out of the window while an old lady with a stick was helped up the front steps of the bus. And they travelled all the way, the three of them, apart, even though the bus filled up quickly and a young mother with red hair sat down heavily next to Florrie, her daughter in front, alongside Alice, sucking a vivid pink lollipop on a stick. And though it was lost in the chatter, in the faint chorused songs that oozed from the back seat, each of them, for some reason, was angry and Florrie flicked away tears as she watched the thick hedgerows roll by.

When they got off the bus a breeze nudged at them from the reservoir. They stood by the low stone wall looking out across the ridged water. One or two of the trees high up on the rocky slopes towards the Tor were tinged tawny with the start of autumn, but the woods closer to were still green. The cluster of people who had travelled with them on the bus gradually broke away, the children running on ahead, making noise.

'Let's walk,' said Eddie. 'There's a path takes you right round, all the way.'

'But what about the basket?' asked Florrie. 'We can't walk with the basket.'

Eddie took it off her to feel its weight. He huffed. 'Blimey, Flor, what's in it? You brought the kitchen sink?'

She giggled. 'Just lunch.'

'What did you bring all that for, when you knew we would be walking?'

Florrie thought about her best shoes, delicate in the heel, and the heavy wool of her Sunday coat. 'I thought it was an outing,' she said. 'For a picnic.'

'Well we'll have to leave it here, behind the wall and come back for it later.'

'We can't do that. Someone'll take it.'

'What? Sandwiches. Who's going to take blimin sandwiches?'

'The basket then, as well. And I bought ham.' This, Florrie felt, explained everything.

Eddie kicked a stone at one of the crows scratching near the wheel of the parked bus. 'What're we going to do then all morning if we don't go for a walk? We can't just stand here.' He looked at Alice now as he spoke, but Alice continued to look out over the water. Eddie followed her gaze.

'Look at it there. Waiting,' he said, gesturing vaguely across the reservoir to the Tor, his voice pitched high like a child's.

Florrie sighed. She did as she was told, and looked across the dark water, but all she saw was a lump of rock, stony and squat. Something strange had happened to the softness of the land-scape, making it half wild and unfamiliar.

'I'll carry it,' she said, picking up the basket.

'What, all the way?'

'We'll see.'

They had walked twenty minutes from the dam, and had turned off the wide even path on to one that twisted through a wood, and still Florrie was carrying the basket. She tried switch-ing hands, again, but the weight of it brought an ache to her neck and shoulders, separate from the sharp pain in her palms, and at last she put it down. They were a few feet from the edge of the reservoir where a small sandy beach pushed out from the stones at the limit of the woods.

'I'll wait here,' said Florrie. 'With the basket. You can go on a bit, if you like, and then when you come back, we can picnic here. Down on the sand. It's nice.'

She did not, of course, expect them to go. But Eddie took the basket only long enough to carry it down to the sand and wedge it in behind a rock in the shade, and Alice just said, 'Will you be all right, Flor, by yourself?' without waiting for an answer. And although they had neither of them planned it that way, Eddie and Alice were alone. They felt they had been let off something and turned back up into the dappled shadow of the woods. Florrie was hidden from view.

'Stupid ruddy picnic,' hissed Eddie.

Eddie set off briskly, his heart set on walking a complete circuit of the reservoir. He hurried up the path, bounding over rocks and tree roots, frolicking almost when they emerged from the trees and he could see the Tor again. Alice struggled to keep up with him. She fixed her eyes determinedly on the curve of his back, and stopped seeing things around her, just the pull and snatch of his shirt over his shoulders, and a sense of green air stretching away on all sides.

'You're very quiet, my love,' Eddie said at last, slowing for a moment when they rejoined the main path.

Alice was trying to control the rush of her breathing and nodded.

'That's good. There're not many girls like that. They chatter,' he said, matter-of-factly, and set off again hard, throwing back a smile at her. And with the clamped pain in Alice's chest and the strain of her breathing, and Eddie's giddy delight at the high-blowing clouds and the moss shadowing the rocks and the fast-running water, silver in the rocky streams, they did not say another thing until they had passed under the Tor and were well down the path along the far side of the reservoir.

'Is that you? Wheezing?' asked Eddie then, noticing for the first time as Alice caught up with him.

'It's like that, sometimes.'

Eddie saw how strange her cheeks were, blotted red. 'I'm going too fast,' he said. 'I'm sorry. I didn't think.'

Alice, waiting to speak, looked across the reservoir, trying to pick out the sandy inlet where they had left Florrie. She saw for the first time how far they had come and how long it would take them either to turn back or to continue around the circuit.

'We've come a long way,' she said, still breathy.

Eddie thought she was regretting it. He sat down on a hump of granite, full in the sun, looked up at her and winked.

'We'll have a rest,' he said. 'We'll be fine then.'

Alice did not sit down.

'Do you think she'll be all right?' she said.

'She'll be fine.'

Eddie stretched back on the rock, his feet wedged into a gnarled stem of heather. He closed his eyes. A bee hummed close to him, but he did not seem to mind. He was very still.

With the burr of the breeze, with the birds and the insects and the soft irregular splash of the water, the scrape of Alice's wheezing irritated Eddie. It made him want to prod her. He sat up.

'Can't you stop that? Now we're having a rest, can't you make it stop?' he said.

Alice did not apologize. 'Not yet.'

'I don't remember it, from before.' Eddie tried to think back to the regatta. He could not remember much.

'It comes and goes,' said Alice. 'Some times of year, too.'

She was tense as well, she knew, being with Eddie, seeing her chance, but she could not tell him this.

'It'll not bother you, after a while. You'll get used to it,' she said.

'I suppose.'

There was a pause while they both looked out across the reservoir. A small grebe ducked down into the water not far from them and seemed to disappear.

'Look at that,' said Eddie. 'Look how long it's staying under. Catching fish, I warrant.'

Alice did not look at the grebe. She was thinking of the right thing to say. She was trying to find the apt phrases, something that would beguile him. She felt the grip of the words as she tried them out in her head.

'You know, Eddie,' she said. 'I know what men like. Even boys like you. I'm not like Florrie.'

She spoke flatly, and Eddie could not be sure what she meant. He blinked in the sun.

'I know what to do,' she said. 'If you want, while you're sitting there…'

She moved forward, her hand out, offering. Eddie, staring at her, did not see the grebe pop up. 'You'd like it,' she said, sure.

Eddie scuttled up the rock, bringing his feet up high as though from an encroaching wave, protecting himself. Alice stopped then.

'Blimey, Alice. You're… you want to…' Eddie did not know how to put it.

She was twisting a stem of heather in her fingers. She could think only of touching him and what she could make this mean.

'It's not like Florrie, being religious and all,' she said. She spoke steadily, though he could hear the flicker of her breathing, stuttered and fast, and in the end, she looked up at him. She wanted to smile, he could see that. She wanted to reassure him. But she was shy, and only her eyes were giveaway soft.

Eddie took a moment to look at her. She was not flirting with him, not flouncing or flicking, but, still, she was drawing him to her. He peeled into a grin.

'What are you trying to do?' he said, shifting on the rock.

'Nothing, just talking.'

'Do you think, if you talk like that, I'll…' He slid down to the ground. 'Are you always like this?'

'I'm not like anything,' said Alice, not understanding the way he was looking at her. 'I just wanted to be nice to you. I like you.'

She expected his face to clear then. She expected him to rush at her, anxious and eager, perhaps rough. But he stood apart.

'But being nice – like that – it's unusual though,' he said.

He moved to her very slowly and patted her gently on the shoulder.

'I'm sorry,' said Alice, 'if I've – I didn't mean to upset you. I just thought…'

'It's fine, by me,' he said. 'I don't mind, you see.'

He was surprised how just that could make her smile. He smiled broadly back, his dark eyes shining. It was a long moment. Alice's breathing was quiet.

'Backwards or onwards?' said Eddie.

'It looks about the same.'

'It is.'

'Onwards then,' said Alice. 'We might as well finish. But she'll be waiting ages.'

They set off side by side, ignoring the thought of Florrie.

'You talk like you know things,' said Eddie, before they had got their rhythm back.

Alice laughed.

'You can talk to me some more, if you like,' he said, unable to resist.

'What about?'

'I don't know. Anything. What you know.'

'I'm not sure I know very much; not really,' said Alice, still laughing.

'Well, whatever you like then,' said Eddie.

Alice wanted to talk about love, but it was something unfathomable and she did not have the words. There was everything she had read, but now she needed it, this didn't seem to touch her. Which left her with only what she had learned from her father, his broken-phrased longing. And so these were the words she brought out now instead, hoping, letting them pour molten off her tongue.

It was a few hundred yards before the bus stop, as they were walking along by the fence, that Eddie finally flushed her talk out of him with a low groan. There were people around now and he turned quickly to hide the small dark stain that began to leach through his trousers.

'Here, you'll need this,' said Alice bluntly. She took her handkerchief from her pocket and stuffed it down his waistband, reaching briefly behind the fly with cool fingers. Her hands were quick and Eddie hardly felt them, but the thought of them, for the first time, embarrassed him.

'I look… swollen.' He grimaced, trying to adjust the handkerchief without attracting attention.

'You're fine. No one'll notice. Who looks down there?' said Alice.

She seemed tired out now. They finished the circuit of the reservoir in silence.

Florrie had fallen asleep long before, her head propped up against the bank and her feet in the sand. The sun had moved around and was now shining full on the picnic basket, and half across her arm, which was flung out at an angle. She did not hear Eddie and Alice approach and woke with a start when Eddie picked up the basket.

'I'm starving,' he said.

Florrie blinked at him. She was sorry to have slept; she felt the day had slipped away from her. 'Have you been all the way round?'

'All the way.'

'And you too, Ally. All that way?'

Alice nodded.

'So what time is it? Have you… ?' began Florrie, but she was distracted by Eddie rummaging through the lunch and taking a long swig from a bottle of lemonade. 'You'll spill it. It'll spoil. Be careful,' she said, and she snatched the basket from him, peeling back the lid and laying things carefully in the sand around her. 'Look, you've already got some of it on your trousers.'

Eddie, despite everything, was surprised and looked down.

'It'll wash,' said Alice.

Eddie lay back in the sand as soon as he had finished eating, and closed his eyes, though he did not sleep. As he stretched out, the wedge of Alice's handkerchief was obvious. Florrie packed things away, chattering.

'They say that you can hear the bells from the village under the water. Like ghost bells,' she said.

'What village?'

'They drowned a village, to make the reservoir. Everything. People's houses and shops and the school and the church, all under there still, just like it was.'

'Only wetter,' said Eddie, without moving.

Florrie ignored him. 'And if you listen carefully, you can hear the church bell tolling the hour, that's what they say. I listened when you were gone, ever so hard, all the time. But I didn't hear anything.'

Alice didn't quite know what to say to this. 'It must just be a legend, Flor. The kind of thing people make up.'

'Maybe,' said Florrie, unconvinced. 'But you would think it might happen, wouldn't you? That the bells would still ring.'

'It might be like farting in the bath,' said Eddie. 'Perhaps only bubbles come up.'

This made Florrie laugh. 'Oh don't, Eddie,' she said. 'Don't make me laugh – I have to pee.'

'Go on then. We won't look.' Eddie sat up and opened his eyes. 'Go into the trees somewhere.'

Alice could not believe her sister would consider this. 'No, Flor – don't you dare. What if someone comes?'

'They won't,' said Eddie, winking. 'And anyway, I'll look along the path. I'll whistle.'

And Florrie climbed the bank and found a spot close by a silver birch, and Eddie, as he had promised, kept his eyes fixed on the dirt path ready to whistle a warning. And Alice, even though she wanted to look away, could not help seeing everything, the way Florrie squatted, toppling backwards once and having to stretch out a hand against the tree to steady herself, the way she hitched up her skirt high around her thighs, the dull sheen of the nylon in the late light and then, worst of all, the slight wisp of steam rising from between her legs.

'I've never done that before,' said Florrie, when she had come back. 'I've never peed outside like that.' She glowed with achievement.

'That's my girl,' said Eddie, ebullient. He reached for her hand and kissed it extravagantly, making a show of it.

'It'll not do at home, nipping out into the yard.'

'But out here it's different,' said Eddie. 'It's fine, Flor, to let yourself go, out here. No one'll blame you for it.' He nuzzled then in the crook of her neck, pushing his nose against her ear.

Alice was curled up inside. 'You're disgusting, Flor,' she spat, and she said nothing more for the rest of the afternoon.

Eddie and Florrie sat together on the bus on the way home, close, the lengths of their legs touching. Alice had the empty picnic basket. By the time the bus pulled into the city station it was dusk and a flock of starlings pulsed around the high chimneys. As Eddie came down the steps by the driver, Alice noticed that the slight bulge of her handkerchief had disappeared.

'I'll walk you both home,' said Eddie, even though the Continental Hotel was closest by far.

'Not me,' said Alice. 'I'm fine. I'll get another bus.'

'Right you are,' he said, relieved. 'I'll take the basket then.'

He stood back as the sisters kissed goodbye, but as soon as Florrie was free he took her hand. And because of the way things had been, it seemed a great comfort to be walking up the grey streets with her, both of them quiet, feeling weary.

'That was nice, Eddie,' Florrie said, when they got to the gate. She stood still waiting to be kissed in the soft amber light from the streetlamp. He reached up to do it.

'It's a good place out there,' he said. 'We'll go again perhaps, my love, one day.'

Which Florrie took for a commitment on his part, a promise. She could not have known that, try as he might to rein it back, his mind kept sliding away to the path around the reservoir, the ridges and the pebbles and the root-rucked steps perfectly remembered and every word of Alice's dirty monologue hard and bright in his mind, like another world.

Barely a week after the outing Alice and Eddie passed each other in the street in a rainstorm. The wind was pushing hard against Alice's back and with her umbrella clamped tight behind her she saw Eddie coming. He had his cap low and his head down, and was walking fast. She stopped him by putting a hand on his arm.

He had thought so much about her that he could not, for the moment, be sure she was real. It was something about the rain, perhaps, dripping fast off the brim of his cap that blurred the edges of her, making her shimmer. He blinked. And then there was nothing at all dreamlike about her, smudge-eyed, sodden around the shoulders and with her fringe flat under her scarf.

'Just my luck to have to go out for baccy in this,' he said.

They moved in close to the entrance of the building alongside them, but the rain still hit them hard, pummelling off Alice's umbrella like stones. They didn't know what to say.

'Have you seen Florrie again then?' It was Alice who thought of something first.

'No... I was waiting,' he said, scuffing a gathering puddle with his shoe. 'Have you?'

'No.'

There was a long quiet. Alice thought it might be a prelude to something, and did not dare interrupt. Eddie was confused by the girl who looked so ordinary.

'Well, then,' he said at last. 'Well.'

'Do you want to come under?' Alice tilted the umbrella slightly and a thick trickle of water poured from one edge. Eddie shook his head.

'It's not like this, with Florrie,' he said, and Alice thought, for a moment, that he meant the weather. 'She'd have been chattering away nineteen to the dozen by now. The rain, the wet clothes, where she's been, what's for supper... you name it.' He shrugged. 'You're a quiet one, I'll give you that. When you want to be.'

Alice brushed her wet fringe to one side. 'Sounds like you've fallen for her,' she said.

'Well, sometimes… maybe… I don't know.' If Eddie was blushing, the tip of his cap concealed it.

Alice heard the rain on her umbrella and felt a damp cold around her shoulders. She shrugged up her coat and waited for him to speak again. This, she knew, was when he should declare his love for her, putting Florrie aside.

'I should get on,' was all he said.

Alice took a step back. 'She's not like me, you know,' she said quietly.

'Oh, I know that. She's a good girl.'

It was a throwaway compliment, but Alice snatched at it and held it between them.

'Is that what you want?'

Eddie looked across at her, her hair hanging limp, her nose red and her eyes narrowed at him.

'Look, I'm sorry, Alice, if you were thinking… you'd be too much for me, you see. It's not that you're not… you're a nice girl, really you are – proper nice. But…'

'But if I loved you, Eddie…'

He flinched, as though he'd been stung. She'd said the words quietly, little above a whisper, but there was nothing soft in them. They were sharp and stiff, a threat.

'Blimey.' He blew through his teeth. 'Look – Alice… I'd better get my baccy.'

'I mean it, Eddie. I mean it. Is there something I can say? I don't know very much about what to say,' said Alice. 'But I do mean it always.'

'I know,' said Eddie. He pulled up his collar.

'Really, Eddie. Florrie. Think about it. Is that what you want?

Is that it? Is it going to be Florrie?'

Eddie looked away to where the traffic was backing up at the junction ahead of them.

'It's a bit of fun, with your sister, that's what it is, Alice. I like her. Like I say, she's a good girl.' He shrugged. 'Anyway…'

Alice stepped out on to the glossy pavement and dropped the umbrella low so that it hung behind her head, cutting out the world beyond. All Eddie could see was her pale face, haloed, and the rain falling fast.

'You'll have to choose, Eddie,' she said firmly. 'You'll have to think if that's enough. You know that, don't you?'

But Eddie slipped out of the doorway without answering, turning his face into the wind. He did not look back. He splashed through the greasy streets, and across the road, keeping up such a trot as he escaped that his shins ached. When he got to the tobacconist's he was panting hard. He leaned against the wall in the shelter of the awning, pressing flat and trying to swallow down the surge of panic. He waited until his breath had eased. Then he took off his cap, shook the wet from it, and went into the shop, nodding at the shopkeeper.

He stood for a moment by the counter reading the newspaper headlines, not taking them in, teased by what Alice had said. She had spiked things with urgency. The thought of Florrie seemed to have soaked him suddenly through, hot and heavy like the press of his sodden clothes, surprising. The idea that he might choose Florrie, for ever, in the way that Alice had demanded, dripped noisily into everything and he handed over his tobacco money with unsure hands.

Alice was late for work and so wet that her skirt dripped

water on to the floor beneath her desk. By lunchtime there was a deep grey puddle, stained with wool dye and trickling down a ridge in the tiles towards the open corridor, and by the time she got home that evening, having got wet again in the still falling rain, her damp tights rubbing in her shoes, she felt utterly deflated. She could think only of Eddie, but not with any joy. With her hair still damp, and a chillness within her that wouldn't shift, she opened Arthur's book again.

It was exactly how she remembered it. There was nothing to shock or surprise her. And actually, with the gloom of her mood and the evening half-light, the plates seemed awkward, crude in places, their colours flat. But Alice hardly looked at them. It was the words she was after. Although she could have recited them without the pages to help her, she had never tried this. Since the death of her father, the poems had been lost to her. And now, starting with the first, slowly at the beginning, slightly afraid, she read each one, word by word, gathering pace as she read until she was galloping through the stanzas, leaping from poem to poem, her head full of the shapes and rhythms, her heart racing with the thrill of archaisms, odd spellings, beating sing-song rhymes and arcane poesy. She thought of Eddie still, it was true, but only the sense of him, vaguely, caught up in the words, as her father inevitably was. She did not think of the pain of him. Reading the poems, her misery left her, slipping away, and the anxiety of finding herself melted, because somewhere between the lines of them, she knew from experience, she had always known, there was love.

Queenie May had to call the doctor. She found Alice lying on her bed, slumped back against her pillow, her face pale, her eyes closed, and her struggle for breath so violent that her whole body heaved with the straining of her lungs. Arthur's book was lying open beside her but was turned over, the pages hidden.

'Mary! Mary, get a doctor. Run for a doctor,' Queenie May shouted through to the kitchen where Mary was aimlessly cutting patterns in blank paper with a pair of nail scissors.

Mary shouted back, protesting. 'In the rain? Ma!'

'Oh, for pity's sake, my girl. Go and get him. For Ally. She's bad.'

This made Mary curious. She could not have hoped for a genuine emergency. She came down the corridor and saw Queenie May with Alice propped against her, rubbing her chest.

'Can't she breathe?' Mary would have liked to be ill too, if it meant she could be part of it.

Queenie May didn't turn. 'Mary, will you run. Go now and run. I don't know what to do.'

Mary heard the urgency but still hung at the door, watching. 'Mary!'

When Mary had gone, Queenie May peeled away from Alice and reached for the book. She turned it open on the bed, and looked for a moment at what was there, then she stacked it with the other books on the shelves. She did not look at Alice but she came back to her and held her. And it seemed no time at all until the doctor was there, easing Alice from her tight arms, trying to get her daughter to stand.

'Get her to the kitchen, if we can,' he said, and between them they shuffled her down the short corridor and sat her heavily in one of the wooden chairs. Her breathing rattled. Mary pranced behind them, bobbing, but they did not notice her. The doctor was busy all the time, not looking at the mother. He was fitting a syringe. 'Has she had attacks before?'

'She has wheezes all the time. But not like this, not an attack.' Queenie May was frightened of the word.

'Get the kettle boiling and pans, if you can, on the hob. We need steam.' He was rolling Alice's sleeve and holding the needle in the light. 'And a wet blanket even, in front of the fire. Whatever you can.' He pierced her arm and injected her.

'What's that then?' said Mary, who was hovering by the door. Queenie May had not seen her.

'Mary, get the pans boiling. Make yourself useful my girl,' she said, but the doctor answered her as if she mattered, as if her question were a good one. Mary remembered that.

'It's adrenalin. It'll help her. Give her a boost,' he said.

But it didn't. Alice continued to slump on the chair, the edges of her face tingeing blue, the room gradually filling around her with steam and the doctor sitting across from her, just watching. She heaved, wide-eyed with the effort of breathing.

'She's not getting any better,' said Queenie May at last from the stove where she was re-filling the pans with water.

'It doesn't look like it,' said the doctor, not moving.

'Isn't there anything else?'

'Just give her time,' he said, but Alice's arms were limp now by her sides and the contours of her face slipping and it was only a couple of minutes later that he opened his bag again and took out a small glass bottle. He emptied the grains from it on to the palm of his hand. 'Morphine,' he said, looking at Mary before she could ask.

And he gave the grains to Alice, with water, and sat back again and watched.

Queenie May kept the pans boiling hard. She filled a glass with water and let it trickle slowly down the grey blanket that was hung in front of the fire. She did not dare touch her daughter until the doctor gave permission and so she circled, finding things to do. She even breathed out hard herself, noisily, to charge the air with more of whatever it was that Alice needed.

'Is she the only one in your family that has asthma?' asked the doctor.

'There's just me and three girls now,' said Queenie May. 'And she's the only one.'

'You don't get wheezing that wakes you up? Or a cough?' he said, turning to Mary, and although she would have liked to say yes, she had to shake her head.

'Good. Well then. And how old is she?'

'Eighteen,' said Queenie May.

'Sometimes, you see, they grow out of it. But maybe not, in this case.'

He bent forward towards Alice, as though looking for something, and then shook his head. Queenie May felt the horror of it.

'It's a nasty business,' said the doctor, leaning back again.

Alice was spluttering, but when the coughing passed she was stiller. Her eyes were wistful and her face pale, but she seemed to be straining less to breathe.

'You see, she'll be all right, won't she, now?' Queenie May was accusatory.

'Yes. I reckon so.'

'With what you've given her, and the steam and everything. She'll be all right.'

The doctor nodded. Queenie May reached for the back of the chair to steady herself and held out an arm to draw Mary to her.

'It's like drowning, isn't it?' said Mary.

As the rasp of Alice's breathing calmed, the doctor began to pack away his things.

'Can I take them off the boil now?' asked Queenie May, looking towards the pans. The windows were dripping with condensation.

The doctor nodded. 'She'll be fine.'

'She's getting colour back, I can see. She looks better,' said Queenie May, though the difference in her daughter was faint. 'Will it happen again, like this, an attack?'

The doctor shrugged. 'It's hard to say. If this is her first, then it may just be one of those things. She may have been overdoing it, or getting in a state. It can be nerves, you know, that brings it on.'

He looked closely again at Alice. He brought his face up to hers, peering, searching for something there. Even when she looked straight back at him, he kept his gaze on her.

Alice could smell the blunt peppermint on his breath, and the close scent of tobacco behind.

At last, hardly turning, he spoke to Mary. 'I came with a coat, but it was wet. So I left it in the hall. If you could fetch it for me, my dear.'

Mary skipped away, important. The doctor kicked the door so that it swung to behind her, and spoke again, his voice low now, spitting with distaste.

'The other thing that has an effect,' he said, 'is sex. Especially for women.'

Queenie May felt her cheeks blush red but Alice was still pale.

'It's a way of the perversion escaping. It's a sign. Dirty mind, dirty hands; you know the kind of thing. It has to come out somewhere.'

He was close to Alice again now but she looked back at him, undaunted. The unspent squeak of her breathing challenged him. Then there was a rustle in the doorway and Mary, standing unnecessarily still with the doctor's coat held high. He took it from her and slid his arms in slowly. He seemed to fill the room.

'Call for me again,' he said, 'if it happens.'

Mary showed him out and the kitchen door clicked shut behind them. Alice closed her eyes for a moment and then lifted a hand towards her mother. Queenie May didn't take it. Instead she went to slide open a window. The steam curled away. Alice stood up though her legs were unsteady and her head thumped with the effects of the drugs. There was still a clamp on her lungs.

'Don't let him come again,' she sighed. She held herself stiff by the table.

Queenie May looked at her daughter's drawn face, and was surprised by what she noticed there, suddenly. 'You should be careful, Ally,' she said.

'I'll just take a few steps, go to my room. I'll be all right.'

'Ally, you know what I meant... after what he said...'

Mary came back into the kitchen, beaming. 'He says I'm to keep an eye on you, Ally.'

'There's no need,' said Alice, but Mary, full of herself, winked at her mother.

Alice could not speak again. She edged slowly back to her room. When Queenie May and Mary went to bed not very much later, they saw her there, still fully dressed and sitting propped upright against the wall. She was reading a small library book in a tatty blue cover.

'That's what does it,' whispered Mary to her mother when they had pressed their backs to each other in the cold bed. 'Too much reading. It's bound to.'

'Perhaps,' said Queenie May, unconvinced. She shivered and reached over to lay an arm across Mary's shoulders. 'You shouldn't be surprised, my love, about what happens to Ally,' she went on quietly as she felt her daughter shift beneath her.

Mary grunted, sleepy now as the bed grew warmer. Queenie May couldn't shake off the way the doctor had looked. His face loomed in the speckled dark, his eyes bulging at the thought of Alice's corruption. She would have liked to swat it away, but she had no authority to do that. So she buried herself deeper under the blanket. 'I think we might have lost her, my girl,' she said, but Mary was already asleep.

And when Queenie May closed her eyes something strange happened to the doctor's face, and to Alice's slim body, heaving with the effort of breathing, and to the way they came together, writhing and clutching and scratching, the doctor's teeth deep in the folds of Alice's skin, her taut limbs tight around him. And for a long time, even though Queenie May peered hard into the thin darkness of the room, she did not see them part. All she saw was a confusion of arms and hands, the doctor's wide mouth, the steam from the kitchen shining bright on Alice's hair, on the down above her lip and in the dip of her breasts where her blouse had been loosened. All she saw was the swell of movement, deep and full, like the surge of a pool at the edge of the tide, but resolutely silent. And when she finally went to sleep it was with the conviction that Alice's nature had finally become known to her.

Alice could not go to work, and a week after Christmas she was sent a curt, impersonal letter of dismissal, with a reference enclosed, thinly typed. After that, she stayed in the house, sitting mostly on the bed, her back propped with pillows, not seeming to feel the cold that clung to the walls and floor, and eating only when Queenie May prompted her to. She tested herself daily on the spellings of long words, scratching them out invisibly with her finger in the damp air, and when Florrie called around to flaunt the shallow-set stones of her engagement ring, she was in the kitchen practising her shorthand by taking notes from the wireless bulletins, her head bent low, her pencil blunt.

When Alice saw the glint of cat's-eye jewels on Florrie's finger she went to the bedroom and closed the door. Outside, there was celebration, a squeal of excitement from Queenie May, tears, Mary circling and Florrie skidding off to show the neighbours. It was several hours later before she knocked and called through the peeling panels to her sister.

'Is it your chest playing up, Ally?' she asked, pushing the door. It swung open. Alice was standing at an odd angle, interrupted. She was naked. Florrie could see the stain of dark blood running down the inside of her legs.

'Oh dear Lord, what have you done, Ally?' she hissed, sliding into the room and closing the door firmly behind her. She looked around for something, a knife, a blade, a shard of glass. But there was nothing.

'Ally? Are you all right? Are you hurt?'

'It's just my time of the month,' said Alice dully. The sound of her voice was a surprise to Florrie. They had not spoken in a long time.

'But don't you want to…?' Florrie reached into her sleeve for a handkerchief and held it out, crumpled, for her sister to take.

'Leave it,' said Alice.

'Right you are.' Florrie put the handkerchief on the bed. She saw then that there were stains on the cover where Alice had been sitting, dark flowering patches of blood seeping through the cotton fabric. There was nowhere else to sit so, like Alice, Florrie stood.

'Look, Ally, take this…' She bent for Alice's blouse that was crumpled on the floor, shook it out and held it towards her sister. Alice backed away and Florrie was left with the pale shirt dangling between them. She tried to lean back against the support of the door, but with her height she was awkward and she held her sister's blouse stiffly away from her with clothes-peg fingers.

'I came to say about Eddie,' she said.

Alice flinched.

'I came to say, I don't know, to talk about him.' Florrie looked away from her sister's insistent nakedness. 'I thought it'd be nice. He's joining the navy, to wait on the officers. He wants us to be married, he says, before his posting comes through.' She could not help but turn back, smiling. 'It'll be hardly no time, Ally.'

She looked around for somewhere to put the blouse but there was just the spoilt bed. So she folded it as best she could and put it on the floor near her feet.

Alice ran her hands flat down her thighs, feeling ridges of goose pimples. 'How did he do it?'

'How did he ask?'

'Yes.'

'Just quietly really. Nothing flash. He was getting worked up about something, I could tell. He was far away. And that's what it was.'

Alice frowned. 'Did he have the ring there, with him, ready?'

'We was out the back, by the gate. And there was something he wanted to say, I could see that. And I asked him, thinking there might be something I'd done, and out he came with it.' Florrie brushed her hair back from her face. 'He didn't go on one knee, though, not there, in the wet. Not in his new trousers.'

'But did he have the ring, when he asked you? Did he have it there?'

Florrie could not understand why her sister was pressing her. It irked her. ''Course not,' she said. 'We bought it afterwards, together, when we'd seen what we could afford.'

Alice nodded, her point proved. She sank on to the end of the bed, smudging the growing stream of blood between her thighs. 'Well then,' she said. 'Well, then – you don't know what it was, do you? You don't know what he was after. You don't even know that he meant it at all. You could have put it in his head for him. He could have been thinking something else, when he was in a state. He could have been thinking he'd end it with you. How do you know he's not having you on?'

'How could I put it in his head, Ally? He asked me because he wanted to. It wasn't anything I said, I swear it – it was what he wanted.'

There was a pause. Florrie concentrated on the glint of her ring, rubbing it gently with the fingers of her right hand.

'Don't try and spoil it, Ally,' she said.

Alice leaned back on the bed, slight and bony, her elongated nakedness defiant. 'I just know he doesn't love you, that's all,' she said.

They both watched as Florrie raised her hand, but the light was dull in Alice's room and the ring was flat on her skin, unremarkable. Alice sat up and crossed her arms. They both waited. And then Florrie began.

'I don't think you do know, Ally,' she said evenly. 'Just because Da…' She shrugged, half-smiling. She was not meaning to finish.

Alice looked straight at her sister. 'Because Da what?'

'Because he wanted you.' The words dipped away.

'He always did.'

Florrie let her head drop for a moment, as though it were too much. Alice thought she caught the mumble of a prayer. And then something gathered pace in Florrie. She came close to the bed, standing tall, a long way above her sister, rubbing hard at the ring on her finger. Her voice was bold.

'Ally, listen to me – that's nothing. That's just dirt, filth and dirt and grubby fingers. It's just – Ally, feeling up little maids like that, it's…' She shook away the picture of it. Her voice steadied. 'He should never have done it, Ally. It made you… you always thought it made you special, all that. You always thought it made you smart, like you was different, better. But it's nothing.' She screwed her toes into the floorboards, the leather of her best shoes scuffing. 'I can see that now.'

Alice felt tears coming and was surprised. 'Have you told him about that?' she asked.

'Who?'

'Eddie.'

Florrie sucked in the cold air. 'Blimey! 'Course not. Why would I tell him that?'

'He doesn't ask about me?' kept on Alice. 'You don't talk about me?'

'Just about how weird you're getting,' said Florrie. She saw the tears now slipping out of Alice's eyes. They braced her.

'That's you, Florrie, saying that. He doesn't say that,' said Alice, as though she knew. But there was doubt in it.

'You don't know what he says, you,' hissed Florrie, defending Eddie, bearing down on the naked girl below her. 'It's the same all over, you thinking you know everything. But Eddie's marrying me, Ally, whether you like it or not. And you – you're just weird. You're filthy and embarrassing.'

Alice realized for the first time that Eddie must have given her away. 'He's told you,' she said. She felt the bitterness like fire behind her eyes, drying the tears.

But Florrie was not paying attention. She had more to say. 'Ally, this is not like it was before, with Da. This is not like that. This is Eddie. This is the way he looks at me and holds me and...'

'It was just like that,' Alice said. 'With Da.'

'No, no, Ally this is different. This is Eddie. Me and Eddie. And whatever I do and wherever I go, even if we're miles and miles apart, I can feel him beside me and—'

Alice laughed out at this. 'Just the same,' she said, her voice hard.

It brought them to a standstill. Florrie stooped again. Alice wiped the blood from her leg with her hand and stood up, turning away from her sister. She crossed to pick up the blouse from the floor and hung it loosely over her shoulders, leaving smudges of bloody fingerprints on the pale fabric. They both felt their anger sag.

'You think I don't deserve him,' said Florrie. 'You think I'm not good enough for him.'

Alice sighed. 'It'll never happen, Flor, the wedding, you mark my words,' she said.

'Oh yes, it will. I'm going to marry him. And then you'll see, Ally, what it's like when someone loves you, like they should. You'll realize,' said Florrie. There was a final spat of rage in her. She picked up the handkerchief and threw it at her sister, but it floated in the air between them, settling without venom on the floor.

'It'll never happen,' said Alice.

When Florrie had gone, Alice was brisk. She did not realize that she was crying again. She was concentrating on cleaning herself, on setting her hair straight and on wrenching out from deep inside her the broken pan handle that was making her bleed. She crouched, her legs wide, pulling herself free and did not see Mary standing at the half-open door.

'I'll help you, Ally, shall I?'

Alice sprang upright and the bloodied handle fell to the floor.

She was fierce. 'Mary! Can't you leave us alone? I was talking to your sister.'

'No you weren't. Florrie's in the kitchen.'

'I was – before. We were talking.'

Mary pushed the door further and squinted at the odd debris in the room. She shrugged. 'If you don't get dressed soon you'll miss her,' she said calmly, and Alice heard her scatter away.

When Alice came out of her room, Florrie was leaving. Queenie May was fussing over the ring, then bringing Florrie tight, then holding her away to look at her. Mary was swinging on her oldest sister's free hand, getting tangled in the embraces. Their parting took a long time. Alice hung by the end of the corridor and watched them, without a word. Only when Florrie had stepped out into the street, and Mary had run up to the corner to wave her off, did she move up behind her mother at the open door. For a moment, unexpectedly, she wanted to call after Florrie. There were so many things she wanted to say now. But Florrie was walking quickly and instead Alice watched her as she turned at the bottom of the street and then, when she had passed out of sight, she watched a crane at the dockyard swinging a load of timber high over grey tin roofs.

'You'll get your chest bad, standing there in the cold,' said Queenie May.

Alice closed the door.

'What do you think he sees in her, Ma?' she asked.

'Florrie? She's a lovely maid,' said Queenie May. 'She'll do him proud.'

Alice turned away, back to her room. Queenie May noticed the slump of her walk and later, when she thought about it, she wished she'd gone after her.

It was a windy day at the end of April when they were married. The high spring tide flung damp air into the streets and the confetti blew back in their faces along with the drizzle, as they stood by the door to the chapel. They had to move aside as a navy car passed, but it slowed and beeped its horn. Florrie waved, a great arching wave, and pale yellow petals from her bouquet floated down with the confetti. One caught in the cuff of her jacket, and she brushed it away, enjoying the feel of the sober tweed of her new wedding suit. The small crowd threw up three cheers, relieved to be free of the strange cadences of the mass, and Eddie reached up trying to kiss her. Florrie was not paying attention and did not bend to him.

'Go on, Flor, let me kiss you.'

She noticed him then, and for the first time that day felt too tall. 'Perhaps you'll get taller, now you're in the navy,' she said, bending.

As they kissed someone called out to them from behind: 'You know what they say about Catholic maids on their wedding night.' And Eddie batted the thought away with a sharp arm, not quite laughing.

After the ceremony they went back to the house in a noisy huddle. Queenie May's neighbours had helped while they were out, and there were flowers on the kitchen table and a cloth so crisp and white that it might not have been fabric at all. There were plates stacked on the pristine draining board and bottles of beer lined neatly along the window ledge. A fire had been lit, even though it was not cold. All these things Florrie and Queenie

May noted with something like wonder, and they would have been satisfied with all this, and talked about it for many months to come. But Eddie had wanted to surprise his bride, and he did it with the cake.

'Just watch your backs. I've got some friends coming in,' he said, when they had all squeezed into the kitchen and he had taken off his uniform jacket and laid it carefully on Alice's bed. 'Thought we could do with a treat.' He winked at Florrie. And the cake was paraded into the small kitchen by two of Eddie's old friends from the Continental, on a magnificent hotel silver platter, its sharp white icing as smooth and firm as the table-cloth, its flowers crystal pink and so seductive that many of the guests pressing around thought they caught the heady scent of freesias.

They rested it gently on the table. Eddie grinned. Florrie's hands were pressed to her mouth but Queenie May squealed and bounced as though the floor had caught fire beneath her. Someone started a round of applause that rippled for a long time. Someone else slapped Mary's hand away as she went to touch the icing with the faintest, most reverent of touches. Eddie, still grinning, manoeuvred his way around the table until he stood by his wife, and then he took her hand. 'I love you,' he said, to Florrie of course, but looking at the cake.

Florrie did not turn to him. She was pressed hard on either side by their friends, which made it difficult to move, and she did not want to lose sight of the perfect neat features of the white-gowned, long-veiled bride on top of the cake, in case something happened to her.

'It's a present,' he said, 'for coming away – for starting

something new, with me. I thought you deserved something, I don't know – pretty.'

'Thank you,' said Florrie. And the cake seemed sad to her for a moment, nothing but the emblem of another parting, but she reached across to touch it, stroking the flowers with timid fingers, and she trembled then with the joy in it too. For the first time that day she thought of her father, wishing she could show him such a beautiful thing.

There were three tiers, far too many to feed the guests, even if they all took second helpings.

'You'll keep the top one for the christening, though,' said Queenie May, as she rummaged through the drawer for a long knife. It broke the charm. Someone nudged Florrie.

'What if it's twins? You'll need extra cake.' They laughed.

Florrie squawked. 'I'm not having ruddy twins. Can't squeeze them both out,' she said, which got them all laughing again.

Alice slipped away. Florrie was spoiling everything with her coarseness and she could not bear to watch her cut the cake.

Florrie and Eddie stood side by side, close, with the knife between them, having to press down so hard on the icing that Queenie May was afraid the blade might break. There were cheers all round, a broken verse of song, the light pouring through the kitchen window and making the colours on the cake glow. Florrie shook her hair from its clips and grinned. Eddie let his hand stay tight on hers and nudged against her. He stole another kiss, dipping against her neck close to her ear, and they both felt the prickling desire in it. There was noise all around, happy, rolling chatter, and someone pushed the chairs back so they could dance to the songs on the wireless. When they went to eat the cake, everyone taking a clumsily cut square, there was a murmur of delighted approval like a high-flung spring tide. Eddie took a bow for them, proud, and there was the clatter of applause.

When Alice emerged again later there was just the tablecloth stained with squashed currants and the icing on the kitchen floor giving a graininess like sand. The room was quiet enough for them to hear the rattle of a loose gutter blowing against the walls of the house in the high wind. The guests had gone home, Eddie had eaten too much cake and drunk too much beer, needing the prop of the doorframe to steady himself, and Florrie was sitting alone at the table, pushing the crumbs into messy lines and humming hymn tunes softly while Queenie May swept up around her.

Alice held out a package towards her sister.

'It's your wedding present,' she said unnecessarily.

Mary, at least, was excited by the prospect of this and pushed up against Alice's arm to see better. She could not imagine what it might be. Queenie May had given the bride and groom an envelope of money as well as cloths and a duster, twisted into a doll, with the white of the dishcloth made up to look like a bride. They had been given mixing bowls and a glass casserole, teatime crockery and a solid metal pail, a hog-bristle broom, two teapots and, from the boys at the naval base, a hot-water bottle with a soft cover approximating a naked woman. As far as Mary could see, they had everything they needed.

Alice held out her arm steadily; her sister still had not taken the parcel. 'I wanted to give you something,' said Alice, prompting her.

It was wrapped in gossamer paper, tied tight with a silver ribbon. Florrie thought it might be a bread board, and was rather taken aback by the extravagance of the wrapping. She unpeeled one end of it carefully. And suddenly, before she had taken the paper right away, she knew what was inside. Alice had given them Arthur's book.

Florrie felt the hard edge of the covers on the tips of her fingers, their long-remembered velvet, and anger and betrayal exploded from her, pushing Eddie and Mary and Queenie May hard against the margins of the room until there was just her and Alice there, alone, ungrown. Alice had planned what she would say. She had rehearsed the words, making them right. But she did not get a chance to speak. Because Florrie sprang up and slapped Alice hard, pummelling her with questions, slamming the wrapped book over and over against the table, sending currants and crumbs flicking high into the air and a noise like storm waves into the houses on either side.

'What sort of a present is this? What sort of thing is it, to give someone on their wedding day? What are you doing? What are you thinking? Why can't you bear to see me happy, Ally?'

Alice was afraid of her sister's fury. 'I wanted you to have it,' she said simply, and the others felt sorry for her.

'What is it, Flor? What's in the parcel, my love?' asked Eddie gently, thinking he could calm things. He moved forward at the same time as Queenie May, both of them wanting to touch Florrie. They could not understand why she was so unlike herself. But Florrie was aware only of Alice. And no one watching understood why she screamed hoarse-high at her sister, and threw the parcel across the room so that it thudded hard against the door of the cooker, and why she then took Eddie roughly by the arm and led him out of the house, leaving the front door swinging open on the cold night of the street.

3. Queenie May

MARY PICKED UP the book from the floor, brushing the soot and crumbs from Alice's wrapping. She had drunk a bottle of beer and her eyelids stung. She could hear her mother somewhere, sobbing, and she took her time sliding the book from its paper cover. She picked at the small pile of currants and icing heaped in the middle of the table and she turned up the music on the wireless until it was everywhere.

The first thing she read was Alice's letter to Florrie. It was closely written into the first sheet of the book in dark ink, the words fraying around the edges of the page. It was a lovely letter, an eloquent apology, even-toned and modest. It spelled out the mistakes of the past and promised a new future. Mary read it over again, understanding that Alice was giving something up, but not sure what. She read the names there, Alice's and Florrie's and Eddie's, clasped together in the swirl of writing, and she knew she was left out of something.

She turned the page, snatching at the paper. Inside was nothing, a litter of poems and pictures. She began to read the first lines of one of the verses but they were misshapen and stiff. She turned back to the letter.

Queenie May caught her. 'Mary!'

Mary instinctively flipped the cover of the book closed.

'What are you doing, girl? That's not yours. You've spoilt it.'

Mary pouted. 'I haven't, Ma, honest. I just took the paper off, to clean it. To wipe it down.' She held up the sheet of Alice's wrapping to show where it was stained. 'It got dirty, on the floor. I haven't touched the rest.'

Queenie May leaned hard on the back of a chair. 'Let me see,' she said, and Mary slid the book across the table towards her.

'I thought it might be that.' Queenie May hardly looked at it. The tears came again from her red eyes.

Mary did not understand. She was shrill in trying to defend herself. 'I didn't do anything, really, Ma. I just took the paper off.'

Queenie May looked surprised to see her there. 'Not you, I wasn't talking about you,' she said.

Mary stored up the rejection.

Queenie May re-wrapped the book as best she could, without looking at it, and put it away in a drawer. But she could not forget it. The thought of it hung heavy. It bewildered her. It was the thought of Arthur, as he had been, young and hopeful and edging towards her; the buckling of time between them, the nostalgia for love; the distortions of the bodies she had once seen there on the pages, a secret somewhere she could not grasp, a longing, a silence, the clatter of confusion, and again, always, Arthur, as though she could reach him. She wanted to untie the parcel and flick through the pages. She thought this might make things clearer. But each time she pulled the book out from the back of the drawer, she lost heart. Still, she kept it. She waited for Florrie to claim it, or for Alice to see that it had not been given. But it was never mentioned, and in the meantime, though she did not quite like to, she treasured it.

Eddie was sent to strange seas. Diligently he posted letters home and diligently Florrie tried to read them, puzzling over the baffling turns of phrase. She underlined in pencil the words she could not read or did not understand, pushing down hard on the paper and often snapping the leads. Sometimes whole phrases were underlined. She would read them out loud, falteringly, to her mother. *'It seems to be the tropical currents which are responsible, according to the meteorological reports, for the unexpectedly turbulent passage and the inordinate number of crew who find themselves indisposed for service.'* It was all Florrie had of him. When she prayed for Eddie, as she always did, she found it was the letters she saw in her prayers, neatly stamped and enveloped, while his face would not come to her.

A few months after the wedding, at the low tide of late summer, Florrie called by with one of these letters. Alice answered the door.

'Oh Ally,' said Florrie, the sheets flapping in her hand. 'I didn't mean…'

Alice glanced at the paper. 'Another one?' She knew Florrie and her mother read Eddie's letters together. She had heard scraps of them drifting along the corridor to her room.

Florrie nodded. 'It's a long one. And—'

'Ma's out,' said Alice, but she was not abrupt. It was as though she were waiting for something.

Florrie was quiet.

'We could read it,' Alice offered, 'if you like. I could help.'

Mary had seen her sister coming up the street and now bounced in the doorway behind Alice.

'Can I, Flor? Can I read?'

'Not now, Mary. It's not for you,' Alice said sharply. 'You're too young.'

Florrie watched Mary's pleasure collapse. 'Perhaps another time,' she said. 'Get us some tea – that would be better.'

Mary scraped her knuckles against the wall. She kicked at something, a mark on the skirting board or an unswept pebble, glaring at her sisters, wanting to matter. But Florrie and Alice didn't see her. Florrie was steadying the first page of Eddie's letter against the doorframe and they were both bent over it, beginning to read. Mary spat at the floor and ground the bubbles of phlegm into the boards with her bare heel. For a long time she stood in the shadow of the corridor, watching her sisters.

They did not move inside. They stayed on the step where the light was good and where there was a view of things beyond, the bright-doored houses and the flat water and the wheeling gulls. The letter was long and dull and they began slowly at first, too aware of each other to concentrate. But they had been close before, many times over many years, and soon it felt ordinary. They read more fluently. Alice helped unpick the difficult words. And with the sun warm on their faces, and the bracing smell of rhubarb drifting from next door's kitchen, they found their hair touching as it fell across their shoulders, their hands brushing aside the pages together. They laughed at Eddie's pompous empty phrases, full and loudly and long, until their stomachs cramped with the effort, and, breathless, Alice had to lean on her sister for support.

'He's a bit puffed with himself, Flor,' breathed Alice. 'It's nonsense, this stuff that he writes.'

Florrie nodded and took her sister's arm conspiratorially. 'Yeah, but Ally, he's good in bed, you know.'

And they looked at each other for a moment, unsure, and then Florrie winked, and then they laughed again, together, raucous.

After the letter, they went for a walk, taking the hill steadily arm in arm. Mary, who was finally setting out the tea things for them inside, heard the sudden quiet and went to the door to look for them. She sat on the empty doorstep, her feet tucked hard under her, and watched, but all she saw was Queenie May, struggling from the other direction with a heavy bag of shopping.

'Give us a hand then, my girl,' called her mother, when she was still near the end of the street. But Mary slunk away so that Queenie May was short with her later, slapping her around the legs for bringing mud into the house on her shoes, and refusing her a slice of bread. Waiting for Alice and Florrie, they could not settle. Queenie May could not bear the chatter of the wireless, and turned it off. She dropped a cup as she was washing up. Its handle sheared off cleanly leaving two short stumps and Mary dried it without comment, stacking it with the others on the shelf.

When Florrie and Alice finally got back, they were hot and weary. Queenie May heard them, their voices high and clear in the twilight. She began unstringing her apron to greet Florrie but it was Alice, alone, who came into the house, puffing only slightly, red-faced, her eyes glossy, and wanting to talk about the book.

'She says she doesn't have it,' she said, peaceably enough.

'Florrie says she never got it. She didn't take it. She hasn't read it, what I wrote. But she won't want it. Not now. I should have it back.'

Mary was at the kitchen door, still holding the tea towel. Nobody noticed her. She could see her mother shaking.

'You can't take it back. It was a present,' Queenie May pointed out.

'But still.'

'But still nothing, my girl.' Queenie May's voice rose. 'It was a present, Ally, a wedding present. For Florrie and Eddie. And that's that. You can't just say you'll have it back.'

'But you haven't even given it to them, Ma,' said Alice. 'Florrie told me; she didn't take it. She thought I meant something else, so she didn't take it. But we've talked now and—'

Queenie May couldn't let her finish. 'I haven't given it to them – yet – because of the fuss. But I will give it them, when Eddie comes back. They should have it.'

She spoke fiercely. Alice backed away, wondering, and made herself speak quietly, dispassionately, to show her mother how right her case was.

'I wrote something in it, though, Ma, and Florrie doesn't need to see that now. It would muddle things again. Give it me back and I'll make it right. It's mine after all, not yours. Da left it to me.'

Perhaps, without bringing Arthur into it, Alice could have had the book back. But Queenie May shrank from the triumph she thought she heard ringing in her daughter's voice, the confirmation of Alice's continuing victory, and with a hiccuped yelp she turned away into the back of the house. Alice listened to the tap dripping in the kitchen, and saw Mary then, watching from the door.

'What do you want?' Alice spat, suddenly sharp.

Mary twisted the tea towel and shrugged. 'I've seen the book,' she said. 'I've seen what you wrote.'

'It's nothing to do with you,' said Alice.

''Tis so.'

Alice was not interested. 'Yes, and how's that then?'

'Because,' said Mary, defiant. Then she thought of it. 'Because you can't have secrets like that in families.'

'It's not a secret,' said Alice. 'It's just between me and Florrie, that's all. And it's nothing to do with you. You were too young.' She took the tea towel from Mary and held it up to the light to show where holes had been torn in the linen. 'It's falling abroad. You should mend it,' she said.

Mary sank back into the kitchen. When she was out of sight, she put her fingers and then her hand into one of the holes, tearing it wider. The tea towel hung limp. She threw it on to the back of a chair.

Left alone, Alice went to the window to look across in the direction of Florrie's house. It was a beautiful evening, a slip of moon rising low and the flush of the day still strong. She noticed these things with a shock, as though they were new. There was a reflection in the window, of a girl, bright-eyed and hopeful. It was not her. The reflected girl wore her hair differently, closer cut and pale; she had long lashes and a nose that ran slightly crooked. There was something familiar about her, but that was all. Alice pressed her forehead to the cool glass and the reflection disappeared. Then, without saying a word to her mother or

Mary, she took a light headscarf from the table and let herself out into the soft air and the low-voiced rattle of the evening streets, walking away towards the sea.

When Alice had been gone almost a week, Queenie May stopped expecting her back. She stood by the open drawer of the flimsy bedroom chest, linen scattered around her, looped over handles and strewn on the floor, and the shimmer of dusk making the room uncertain. She had unwrapped Arthur's book and was holding it in her hands. She felt quite calm. No real thoughts would come to her, just a thick swirl of sounds like the muffled voices of the wireless, scraps of words, unsteady tones, and the everlasting hum that was Arthur.

Standing quite still, she opened the book. The lie of the pages seemed to direct her towards the back, but she bent it more forcefully towards the middle instead, hearing the growl of the binding as she pulled the covers apart, a small animal moan. Perhaps it was this, or something about the flesh of the leather or the resistance of the stitching as she pushed the pages open, but whatever it was, Queenie May did not fulfil her intention of sitting quietly to try to trace something from the unfathomable words and dark pictures. She did not even sit down. Instead, with the whimper of a sigh, she took the thick paper in her hands and tore it. And when one page was shredded, she took the next and then the next, not looking at what she was doing but gazing out at a point somewhere on the grubby bedroom wall, listening only to the remarkably quiet sound of the book being destroyed.

Nothing of Arthur came to Queenie May as she ripped the

pages, not the slightest scent of him, and very soon there was exhaustion in the way she stood there. The book clung to itself, the paper heavy and unyielding, the binding still tight. So when Mary found her mother in a sea of paper scraps and trampled linen, the weight of the volume in Queenie May's still shaking hands was not greatly diminished, and only the sag of Queenie May's shoulders proved how great the loss had been.

Mary looked at the back of her mother for some time before deciding to intervene. When she did step forward she was wary.

'Ma, what are you doing? What are you doing to Ally's book?'

Queenie May shook her head sharply, as if to dismiss the shrill voice. She did not turn around.

'Ma!'

Eventually Mary had to touch her, feeling the sting of nylon from her mother's housecoat. Queenie May spoke quietly then. 'I just thought it was better this way. We don't need it.'

Mary picked up some of the scraps at her feet, ragged jig-saws of bright colours, spoilt words suspended. She turned the pieces over in her hands. 'You've made a proper mess, Ma.'

Queenie May handed her what was left of the book. 'You take it, Mary. It's best. Clear up for me, my love.'

Mary held the book lightly. She did not reply. Queenie May felt angry for the first time. 'Mary. Do as you're told. Take it away, out of my sight. Get a broom, girl.'

She stepped out of the debris, brushing herself down, scraps of paper floating from her. The colour grew in Mary's cheeks.

'Before Alice comes and there's a row,' said Queenie May, more quietly.

Mary held tighter to the book. 'Ally'll not come, not now,'

she said. 'She's gone off somewhere, I warrant. Gone off with a man.'

'Mary, how can you say that? That's wicked my girl. You don't know anything.'

This stung Mary even more. 'I do, I do, I know everything,' she lied. 'She'll have taken him away, so they can do things. She'll never come back. And you'll not want her back. Not now.'

'Taken who away? Mary, what are you talking about?'

'The man. The man she's with.'

Queenie May lunged at her daughter, her arms out, wanting to shake her. But she spoke slowly. 'What man? Mary Craythorne, if you know anything, my girl, anything at all…'

The sudden solemnity frightened Mary. She wished she hadn't started it and stepped away, out of reach, her eyes fixed on the cover of the book.

'I just thought…'

'Have you heard anything, Mary? Has anyone said anything? Anything at all?'

Mary, still not looking at her mother, shook her head. But Queenie May felt there was something there and pressed her.

'It doesn't matter, my love, if it's not nice. If it's rude. It doesn't matter. You just need to tell me what they say.'

Mary wished she had left her mother to rip the book. She shook her head again, and a tear dropped on to the leather binding, splaying. 'There'll just be the two of us, won't there, now,' she said. 'Just together, me and you, Ma.' She looked up. 'And we'll have the house to ourselves and the money from your wages, and then…'

'You must tell me, Mary. This man? Who is this man?'

'I don't know.'

'But there *is* a man, my girl? That's what they're saying?'

'Ma, I don't know. I don't know.'

'Mary, please. Did she go away with a man?'

Mary heard the baffling plea, and felt she could not disappoint her mother even if it meant making up her sister's shame.

'I think she did,' she said, at last.

Queenie May sighed and nodded a long succession of tiny nods. 'Take the book,' she said flatly. 'We'll tidy round.'

'I'll ditch it,' said Mary, bright now. 'I'll put it in the big bins behind the shops.'

But her mother surprised her again, squealing, trying to snatch the book back with unexpected energy. 'No, don't, Mary. Mary, you can't. Give it to me. Give me the book.'

Mary spun around, eluding her grasp. They stood for a moment unresolved, sculptural. Queenie May had her hands outstretched towards her daughter and Mary, sideways to her, was lifting the book high, out of reach, her hands trembling with the weight of it and the anger of not understanding. There was a silence.

'It's not worth keeping, Ma, is it?' tested Mary. 'You should ditch it.'

'I can't do that,' said Queenie May.

'Why though? Why bother so much? It's an old thing.'

There was no reply. Mary let her sore arms drop, but kept a grip on the book.

'Ma?'

'It's special, that's all, Mary. You wouldn't understand. Your father… You were very young.'

'Is it a secret?'

'No, Mary, it's not a secret. It's just, I don't know, my girl, sometimes some things are special, that's all. And Ally likes it, the book. It's hers.'

Mary flipped the front cover of the book and held it out towards Queenie May, open at the page on which Alice had written the dedication tight into the paper. 'You've seen this? You've seen what she's written?'

Queenie May pulled her daughter to her with stiff hands, and Mary yelped in protest. 'Ally?' said Queenie May. 'To who? Who's she writing to?'

Mary took time before replying. Her mother's grasp was tight on her arms and she wriggled. The book, between them, jabbed its sharp edges against her chest. She could not think of anything to say; her invention failed her. But then the answer came to her naturally, as though right.

'To Eddie,' she said. 'She's written to Eddie.' She thought of something else. 'A love letter, Ma.'

'Let me see. Show me.'

Queenie May took the book in her hands again, and looked hard at what was written there, but could make out nothing, not even the names. She nodded though, all the same.

'Read it to me, Mary. Read it out,' she said, but then, instantly, knowing she could not hear it and seeing Mary's reluctance she said, 'no, it's all right, my girl. I don't want to hear.'

There was a moment's quiet.

'She's written to Eddie,' said Queenie May, certain.

Mary knew there was no going back. Her mother's face tightened around the eyes, the colour draining from her. She nodded.

'We shouldn't let them know we've read it though, Ma.'

Queenie May glanced at the scraps around her.

Mary spoke quickly, firm. 'We'll clear up everything, all the pieces, and then we'll ditch it. I'll get the dustpan.'

While she was gone, Queenie May looked again at what Alice had written. 'Oh, Ally. Oh, Ally,' she said, out loud, because it was a relief. 'Oh, Arthur.'

And she turned the pages that were left, carefully, seeing mothers reaching out to hold their children, babies held high on strong shoulders, rows of heads bent in prayer and words entwined like blessings with the infinite blue of summer skies.

They worked hard to sweep up every piece of paper, even those that had floated under the furniture. For good measure, Queenie May ironed and folded all the linen that had been disturbed in the drawer. It took her several hours and it was dark by the time she finished. Mary had gone to bed. She was alone in the kitchen and the book was on the table beside her. Even though the house was quiet she looked around her before opening it again. She went straight to the page on which Alice had written and she looked at it by the pale light. She sat for many hours wondering about the words Alice might have used. When Mary woke, she immediately missed the weight of her mother beside her and padded into the kitchen, feeling the cold on her bare feet. Queenie May was sitting at the table, yawning, flickering golden in the low dawn sunlight. The book was beside her, re-wrapped in its wedding paper.

Queenie May spoke without looking around. Her voice was steady. 'I didn't know there was a letter,' she said. 'When I broke the book, I didn't know there was a letter. I didn't know anything like that. I thought it was still like it was when your father gave it to her.'

Mary yawned. 'But you're going to ditch it, Ma? You're going to let me get rid of it?'

'Not just yet,' said Queenie May.

When Eddie got his first period of leave it was nearly two years later, summer again, and Alice had still not come home. Her things had been cleared away and neatly packaged. Queenie May had returned the library loans, sheepishly, paying the fine on them. Mary had moved into Alice's bed.

They arranged an excursion to a beach further along the coast where the coves were sheltered and a great grass-topped rock emerged from the sand in the middle of the bay, a relic of land. The morning clouds hung low, and away from the shore the waves were tipped with white and bucking in the wind. Florrie wore a cardigan buttoned up tight, and refused to take a swimming costume. When they found an empty inlet she sat up close to the rock, facing the path up through the cliffs, her back to the sea, and she pulled the sand around her in ridges, corrugating her body shape into the beach. Queenie May peeled her skirt up towards her thighs and sat with her legs and feet in the occasional slip of sun. Only Eddie and Mary wanted to swim.

It was children, mostly, at the water's edge, splashing in and out of the low waves or collecting wet sand in buckets. One or two men, with their trousers rolled up neatly to their knees, waded in the shallows. Beyond there were the cadenced arms of a few swimmers, crisscrossing in the darker sea. Mary, eager, was already waist-deep in water, her shoulders stiff with the sudden cold. She kept her eyes fixed on the stretched horizon. Eddie was still on the sand. He looked back to where his wife was sitting. Queenie May waved at him, and he waved back. He watched Mary as she edged steadily forward. The clouds out at sea, ahead of her, seemed unfamiliarly grey.

He took a deep breath and ran through the shallows. His feet stung. He passed Mary, and thought he heard her laugh. He pushed on until the water was high up his legs, above his waist then, a bitter tideline on the curled hairs of his chest, and he dipped into a wave, a bulge of black water that swelled towards him. As he always did, he slipped his head into the sea, but when he came up he was panting, straining for breath, his limbs numb. He had never felt such cold. And flicking his dripping hair from his eyes he turned immediately for the shore, flailing, running as soon as his feet touched the bottom, desperate for the feel of the dry sand. Dodging the children scattered at the edge, he scampered up the beach, throwing himself next to Queenie May, shivering.

'Blimey, that's the last time I'm going in an English sea,' he said. 'It's not what I'm used to at all, that.' He shook his hair again. 'Blimey, Flor. Ruddy freezing, that water is.'

Florrie smiled at him, disappointed. 'P'raps it's got colder since you've been away,' she said.

'Wretched weather,' he spat, taking the towel from her and rubbing himself hard.

When they looked again out to sea, Mary was swimming. She was keeping her head high above the water and they could see her bobbing about, not far from the shore.

'There you are, Eddie, my love,' said Queenie May. 'That's the way to do it,' and just then the sun came out, too, making the water suddenly blue and slowing everything.

'Not if you paid me,' said Eddie, striking a pair of matches with desperate fingers and cupping them from the wind.

Florrie was folding Mary's clothes and balancing them on her shoes so that they would stay proud of the sand. She waited for Eddie to lie back again, with his cigarette secure, and then she nudged Queenie May.

'Here, Ma,' she said. 'Look.'

She held out Mary's pink-flowered panties, but down low between them so they were hidden. In the gusset was a small dark spot of blood.

'It's her time of the month, Ma, look.' It was little more than a whisper.

'Mary? Not yet. She doesn't... not yet,' said Queenie May, but she took the knickers anyway and, a moment later, let them fall in the sand. 'I'd better fetch her back.'

'She won't have seen, Ma. She won't have thought of it,' said Florrie, loudly enough now for Eddie to catch the rush of words. He propped himself on his elbow, sand blowing into his face as Queenie May heaved herself upright and pulled down her skirt. He spat it away.

'All right, my love? Are you all right Flor?'

Florrie shoved the stained knickers under Mary's other clothes. 'It's Mary, she's been in too long,' she said. 'That's all.'

Mary saw her mother beckoning from the tideline and splashed towards her, smiling. But Queenie May's face was set hard. She pulled her daughter by the arm as soon as she could reach her, dragging her across the sand until they were standing away from the families around them. Mary's wet swimsuit left a long stain of damp down Queenie May's side.

'Mary, you have to come,' said Queenie May.

'Can't I go back in, Ma? I'm not cold.'

Mary's lips were lilac and her face pale.

'You'll come back with me, my girl, and get dressed, that's what you'll do,' said Queenie May, looking away over the grooved sand. 'Swimming around like a ... when there's ...' She puffed hard. 'I won't have it, Mary.'

'But Ma, everybody's swimming. Look.' Mary swept her arm across the sea, but still her mother would not look up from the sand. 'I'll just be a minute, Ma, that's all,' and she went to pull away, but Queenie May slapped her then, in front of everyone, her broad hand smacking against Mary's wet cheek with the sound of winter waves. Mary took a step back. She felt the side of her face with cold fingers. The wind was making it sting.

'You've had enough, my girl. I said.'

Queenie May turned and began to walk back to their clothes. Mary, bemused, dragged up the beach behind her mother. Florrie had been watching them, and as they got near she peeled herself away from the rock and bent over Eddie.

'Come with me, Eddie, for a bit of a walk,' she said. He did not move. 'It'll warm you up.' She touched his arm very lightly and he looked up at her, still against the moving sky. 'Come on, Eddie, put your trousers on, and your shirt. You'll feel better.' She moved her hand up his arm, feeling the prickle of the sand and the chill of his skin beneath, and ever so gently, because it was new to her again, she touched the rise of his chest.

Eddie sat up. 'Oh, come on then, Florrie,' he said content-edly, and he winked at her as he pulled his still damp skin into his clothes.

When Queenie May and Mary got back to the cove they were alone. Queenie May kicked at Mary's dress and shoes piled on the sand. Then she bent down to find the panties, turned her back on the expanse of public beach behind her, and exposed the smudge of blood. It meant nothing to Mary.

'Haven't I told you, my girl, to be careful? Haven't I told you it would come? You should look out for yourself now, now you're growing up.'

Mary, shivering, wanted to get dressed. She was still aggrieved that they had stopped her swimming.

'You just can't be like this,' said Queenie May. 'You can't be so loose, my girl,' and she threw the knickers to the floor, kick-ing two or three big showers of sand over them until there was just a scrap of white cotton poking through, unidentifiable. Then she brushed down her skirt and stalked quickly out of the cove leaving her daughter alone, surprised, bleeding very slightly as she recovered from the cold.

Queenie May walked first to the water's edge, but she did not like the way things flattened there, exposing her, so she turned along the sea and walked to the cliffs instead, still moving fast. She strode along the broken line of coves and inlets, cutting across their tops so that she did not disturb the families clustered inside them, dodging around the weed-pooled rocks that jutted out and ducking once through a stone arch with puddles trapped around its base and closed anemones bulging orange from its sides. She covered the edges of the beach quickly, her feet slipping sideways in the dry sand and she hurried on, but still it was as though something were chasing her. She could not understand it. And seeing that she was nearly back at their own patch of sand, where Mary was sitting now, dressed, her legs up tight against her chest, Queenie May pulled across the bay towards the rock, striding out as though with a purpose, seeing nothing of the games skimming around her.

On the other side of the rock, the sand was narrow and the cliffs taller, leaning over the bay. It was more secluded, dark almost in the dull light. Young couples slunk away and groups of boys clambered on the sharp promontories in the search for something extraordinary. The dampness from high tide lingered. Queenie May sensed the sand colder on her bare feet, and slowed. She could hear the blood thumping in her ears but the panic in her head seemed flat now and far away. She felt suddenly awkward. She went to turn, thinking that the others might be waiting. She thought Arthur should be there, to laugh with her, and she looked up at the rock at her side, craning her neck to where patches of pink thrift clung to the short turf, overhanging. For a moment she closed her eyes and then she started back.

The couple she saw then, tight up against the base of the rock, entangled, did not notice her. It was only a moment, anyway, and she was past. Even for Queenie May it was an impression, as much as anything, a sense of things. She could not see the faces, not fully, the girl having her head tucked into her lover's neck, the boy's hair hanging low. But there was something about them, about the girl especially and the way her skin shone in the shadowy light, and Queenie May was out beyond the rock, on her way across the open sand, when it struck her that it was Alice there, so close. She stopped again. A shriek of something, children or gulls, slid off the cliffs above her, and it felt for an instant as though the whole world were cheering. She felt a smile come and her legs buckle. She bit hard on her lip. She filled herself with breath, ready, lifted her hands towards them and went to hold her daughter. For a moment, blinding, it seemed that things would come right again and she reached out to draw her family back together, whole, untarnished.

But then when she stepped further she could see the grip of the boy's hand under a cotton skirt, and the way he was nuzzling, squirming close, here, in public, on the beach; she saw the way their legs were twined indecently, the sand blown all over them, and the rude flick of the girl's fingers as they tunnelled in the damp below the rock. Another couple, walking like Queenie May, respectable, muttered something sternly. The clouds closed across. Queenie May felt the catch of nausea hot in her throat, and she stole away, turning her back on them. She faced out to the sea, the breeze on her face, and in the smell of it, of the damp-sand salt air, memories of other places pressed in on her, dusky rooms and quiet shadows and the never quite knowing her husband. Everything seemed spoilt. She kicked hard at the sand.

Further up the bay she saw Eddie and Florrie, hand in hand, and she waved, waiting then until they came up to her. They walked on together. Back at the cove Mary was curled up, asleep, her wet costume hanging limp from a tooth of rock, but they woke her to share the sandwiches. The clouds brushed apart and the sun came through again. Florrie and Eddie sat close, and after lunch they took Mary along the ripples of small pools.

Queenie May was alone then. She stared back towards the rock, to where she knew her daughter was, hidden, and she thought of the doctor and everything he had said to her. She closed her eyes against the glare.

On the way home she was quiet. The others put it down to the weariness of the day and let her doze, curled uncomfortably against her youngest daughter. Eddie and Florrie held hands again, and watched the city grow back around them. Mary felt the weight of her mother's head tipped against her chest, bumping slightly with the uneven road. It was sore. But there was something about it too that made her newly aware of her taut skin and a soft pleasure swelling beneath it, and a warmth there under the ache, and she did not complain.

Alice was not at the beach. She was in London, in the heavy quiet of the library, pushing her trolley of books through the narrow lanes of the stacks. The dusty silence comforted her. Of the jobs she had tried since leaving home – behind the counter at a haberdasher's, typing again and, briefly, because she had to, cooking at a department store canteen – she found this was the one that reconciled her to the clamour of the capital. After almost a year among the high banks of shelves, away from things, trying to memorize the erratic configuration of the Dewey Decimal classification and accustom herself to the half-light, she felt settled. She knew the clicks of the heating pipes and the varied tones of slammed doors, far away. The other staff were used to the idea that she preferred the most tedious of jobs, deep among the disciplined lines of off-prints and periodicals, and they rarely spoke to her. She thought of her mother now only in passing.

Alice's hair had grown long, splitting at the ends where she tried to tie it back with an elastic band. Her shoes were scuffed and worn at the heel. In the netherworld of the library basement she had little physical sense of herself; she never bothered now with lipstick. When she found a card in her locker from her manager, Malcolm Whitcroft, to mark her twenty-first birthday, she found she had forgotten the date.

'I looked it up in the staff files,' he admitted, waiting for her that evening at the back door, his keys twirling in his hand. 'Happy birthday.'

She smiled wanly.

'If you wanted to, you know, celebrate, we could go somewhere. If you liked,' he went on, but Alice only blinked at him and shook her head.

She caught him watching her sometimes, waiting to take the morning register, his arms folded, his hair slightly damp, close cut. Once or twice he came down into her basement territory and loitered, fingering the medical periodicals. But he did not speak to her again, except on routine matters, and when, almost a year later, he proposed marriage, it came as a surprise.

He leaned forwards across the table in the milk bar, the unromantic glint of chrome hardening his solemnity, his hands fixed together in a tight arch, and she thought he was going to reprimand her for some irregularity. She felt the sting of disgrace before he spoke. So that when instead he asked her to marry him, there was the relief of escaping something and she took her time before replying, picking up a glossy grain of sugar with her nail and rolling it with her fingertip along the bevelled edge of the table before letting it fall into the metal ashtray where Malcolm's cigarette smouldered.

'I'm sorry,' Alice said at last, pushing her glass aside, 'I can't.'

His expression did not change. 'Is there someone else, Alice? I thought not. I thought you were available, but I've never asked, so if there is someone else… well, then I would understand.'

She did not know how to answer this. 'I am, as you say, available,' she said, after a while. 'But it makes no difference, to me. I couldn't marry you, really. I'm sorry, Mr Whitcroft.'

'But you *do* like me, Alice?' he pushed.

She had not thought much about it. 'Oh yes,' she said. 'Of course. Of course I like you. It's just… it's very unexpected. I never thought… I never imagined marrying you.' She thought of the way he sat at his desk, unbending, stacked like one of his books into a niche by the entrance. 'And anyway, I wouldn't know what to call you,' she added, clinching it. 'Mr Whitcroft wouldn't do, would it?'

He considered this, sucking the remains of his drink through his straw, swirling it then through the froth that clung to the sides of the empty glass.

'Well, never mind, we'll see what happens,' he said.

By the time Alice got home, walking the long way around from the bus stop, matching her strained breathing to the rhythm of her steps, she had more or less forgotten Malcolm and what he had said. It did not seem important. When she tried to remember, it slipped away from her. All she could picture was the girl behind the counter who was polishing something, over and over, with a green cloth, and the desperate stillness of

Malcolm's hands. Before many more weeks had passed she had changed jobs.

'It's just one of those things, an opportunity,' she said, when he asked her. 'It's a law firm, advertising for a clerk. It's just down the road from me – much nearer.'

She was embarrassed by the pucker of his mouth. But she kept the gift he gave her, an Everyman edition of *The Pilgrim's Progress*, and she arranged it on her bookshelves alongside her growing collection.

Her new office was crowded and noisy. The traffic burred outside and the telephones were shrill. The other girls tried to claim her and were offended when she kept apart. Alice sat at her desk, marking ledgers in her tidy longhand, juggling hard-edged legal papers, waiting for something. She bit her nails, making her fingers bleed.

One Sunday morning she woke early to find the street covered with snow. She walked for a long time, along the packed roads where she lived and towards the river, the trees conspicuous, the aspiring lines from wheel ruts and tram tracks marking the city into close grids, the statues veiled. Clumps of grass hung heavy in the patches of wasteland, and the street signs were mysterious. Coming out into a wide square boundaried with white-porched houses, she walked around every side of it, keeping to the railings and watching the birds in the central gardens rummaging in the brown corners below the bushes. She was upset by a scruffy boy, coming in the other direction, who flicked off the perfectly balanced hoods of snow from each pike of the fence. The calm of the city troubled her.

Later, after war had been declared, she found herself back in the genteel square, stripped now of the snow, its railings pulled up. A doorman at one of the buildings approached her.

'Do you want anything, miss?'

'No, thank you,' said Alice, composed. She did not realize how long she had been standing on the pavement. 'I was just wondering how things were going, you know, out of London, in other places.'

He sucked through tight lips. 'Badly,' he said.

Alice nodded. 'I suppose so.' Then suddenly. 'Do you remember the snow? I came here last winter, in the snow.'

'It was my day off, miss. I was in bed,' he said.

'I'd never seen snow before, in the city.'

'Well, I s'pose you're not from round here, from the sound of you.'

'Oh, I am now,' said Alice.

But when she got home there was something on the news about the Devonport dockyard and she picked up the wireless before the article was finished and threw it against the door. It crackled and the back board lay in pieces. She did not get it fixed. So the rest of the war arrived first-hand, encroaching from the air and blasting change into the landscape. She spent the nights in the cupboard under the stairs, the door propped open, reading by the light of a torch. She could not sleep. She had the gnawing feeling of something forgotten or hidden somewhere, or lost. And in the dim yellow glow, all she could think of was the snow that day, and the way the boy had flicked it from the railings, not seeing that it was beautiful.

★

Maggie was born early and small, after a hurried labour. Florrie had miscarried twice already and she arranged for the baptism almost immediately, just in case. Her daughter was tiny and quiet, improbably light, and she could not help comparing her to the bodies of her brothers that she had washed and wrapped so carefully, feeling for warmth on them long after she had been told they were dead. Hour after hour she held her ear to her daughter's face, feeling for her breath, never quite convinced by it.

The service was held at the new church, which had been built in a wide avenue alongside the shops, square and clean, its gardens laid out with concrete steps. Maggie was lost in the white shawl, and Mary was embarrassed by having to hold the candle like that, out in front of the congregation.

'There's no one else,' said Florrie, pale still. 'Not with Alice gone.'

'But I don't know what to do. And it doesn't feel right,' complained Mary.

'Someone'll do it for Eddie, and you'll do it for Alice. It'll have to be like that, that's all,' said Florrie, not allowing regrets. But Mary's fixed pout bulged ugly in the candlelight and Florrie said a prayer for Alice although not being sure what God might do for her sister, the intention was hazy.

Afterwards, Florrie took the baby to Queenie May's and they sat together, looking out at the bomb craters that pocked the land around the dockyard. Mary changed out of her best clothes and wrapped a scarf tight under her coat, even though the weather was mild.

'Where's she going?' asked Florrie, hearing her sister leave but not looking up from where Maggie was sleeping beside her on the couch.

'Mary? She's doing the ambulances again.'

'I thought they'd said she was too young.'

'Not now she's turned sixteen. And she likes it, sitting up high, hoity toity. She's getting good with the bandages.'

'I couldn't do it,' said Florrie, shaking her head. 'Not at night, in the dark, during a raid.'

'It's what she wants.' Queenie May flipped a cover over Maggie. 'It's like that now.'

Even though they sat together a long time, feeling the dark creep around them from the unlit city, Florrie had left with the baby before Mary came home. There had been no bombs, and Mary had not been needed for emergencies. But it had been an unexpectedly mild evening, and she had walked with a boy in the shelter of the railway banks, feeding him tales of gory wounds. He reached inside her coat, feeling the warmth of her, and when a train scuttled along the track, screeching, they both jumped, and then laughed at their sudden fear.

'It's the raids, making us like that,' he said, drawing Mary close again. She slipped her hands into his pockets.

'But it's good too, the war. It lets us do things.'

He huffed. 'Not if you get bombed.'

The city smelt of stale smoke. Burnt-out buildings smouldered weakly; demolished houses disappeared, leaving only panels of bright paper glued stubbornly to the ends of fallen walls, intimating something. But Mary was used to all this.

'No, not that,' she conceded. 'But some of it, don't you think, some of it's exciting?'

Queenie May had waited up for her. 'It's late, my girl, when you've got school tomorrow.' She rubbed her hands with the cold.

'I've nearly finished with school now, Ma.'

Queenie May tried another accusation. 'But I see nothing of you. You're always out. And I don't know what's happening out there.'

Mary hung her coat neatly on the peg and smiled at her mother. 'I'm fine,' she said. 'They need volunteers, you know that.'

'You should be careful, though, my girl.'

Mary yawned. Her breath hung opaque. 'They say the worst of it's over. The crews said there might be no more raids,' she said, shivering. 'Ma, it's cold in here. Colder than outside.'

'Really, they've said that, the warden and everyone?'

Mary nodded.

In the end, it was several disappointing years later before victory was finally announced on the radio. Only then, when the debris was cleared away and bunting hung in flapping zigzags across the street, did Queenie May take out the metal chest from under the solid enamel of the kitchen sink, where it had been kept safe from bombs, heaving it into the middle of the floor. She eased the book out and brushed off the dust she thought she saw clinging to it. It was right to renew things. The windows were cleaned, the back yard meticulously swept, the rugs hung out to blow in the tranquil breezes, and three hyacinth bulbs planted in a pot tied to the windowsill. The days were lengthening. Queenie May imagined that Alice might come back, and it was in a new spirit of optimism that she thought about getting the book restored.

Mary had found varnish for her nails and was painting her toes, her bare foot looped crooked over the back of the kitchen chair. She was between shifts at the hospital where she had just begun work, and was weary. She watched her mother dreamily as Queenie May slid the chest across the floor.

'I can help with that, Ma, if it needs cleaning under there. Leave it till my day off.'

Queenie May, on her knees, looked up at her. 'I'm getting everything straight,' she said, holding tight to the tin box. 'That's all. Now it's safe to unpack things.'

Mary shrugged, and went back to her toenails.

'And I'm getting it fixed,' Queenie May added. 'I'm taking it to be mended.'

Mary nodded, not listening.

'The book,' said Queenie May, straightening up and holding the box out ahead of her.

The varnish was clotting, thick, and Mary could not paint it straight. She huffed and reached in her pocket for something to wipe away the smudges. Queenie May left her.

Two days later, Mary came home to find her mother sitting on the bed, the open book between her splayed legs, her head bent low over the page, her hand tipped towards the words. She was trying to read. She looked up as Mary threw her coat across a chair.

'I was trying to see it, to make something of it,' she explained apologetically. 'But Mary, I can't. It won't do it. Won't you read it to me, my love?'

She patted the counterpane beside her, inviting, and Mary sat down with the slightest of sighs. She could see Alice's scrawl.

'What is it, Ma? Is it from Ally? Has she… ?'

The question trailed beyond but Queenie May wanted it thrust away.

'It's the book,' she said.

Mary shrugged. 'The book?'

Queenie May snorted a breathy laugh. 'You're not such a scatterbrain, my girl. You remember the book.' She smoothed the already smooth paper with her flat hand and Mary began to read what was written there. Queenie May was remembering the slow blizzard of paper scraps, poetic and majestic. 'You do remember, Mary, how you read it to me – when you were young – or told me about it – the letter Ally had written? You remember me tearing the book?'

There was everything in between, the war especially, dense and deep, and for Mary the elongated years of growing up.

'I don't know Ma,' she said.

Queenie May was unexpectedly upset. 'Oh Mary, come on, my girl – the letter – the love letter from Alice to Eddie. The one she wrote before she went away. The one that explained it all.'

Mary remembered something shifting and only half real, like the games she had played as a girl. She tried reading what Alice had written, to consolidate things, feeling the press of her mother's legs against her own, but there was nothing on the page to help her; no love letter. Just something ordinary, trite words between sisters.

'Read it to me, Mary,' wheedled Queenie May.

Mary frowned. 'You want to hear it, Ma? You're sure? It's

just… it's just Ally, a long time ago,' she said. 'It's not much, probably. Best left.'

'It's all right, Mary. I think it's time. After everything.'

Mary thought of a way out. 'But Florrie. What if Florrie hears… now Eddie's due home and everything?'

Queenie May was definite. 'After all these years? She won't hear.'

Mary edged away from her mother. She spoke without looking at her. 'It's best left, Ma,' she said again. 'I'm not sure it's quite, you know, how you remember. After all this time.'

She closed the front cover of the book and there was quiet. Then the stutter of her mother's tears.

'But I can't do it, I can't do it on my own, I can't read it, Mary. And I just wanted to know why she went, that's all. I just wanted to know what took Ally away.'

Mary did not understand. 'But I don't see… if I read?'

'I wanted to be sure,' said Queenie May, 'about Eddie.' And she sobbed, once, as though her lungs were cracking, and then the misery broke out of her with such force that she curled up hard, thrusting the book to one side as she clenched the bed cover tightly in her hands, her face and soon her chin and chest wet with tears. Mary held her and cried too, because she could not resist. It took them a long time to be quiet. Then Queenie May held Mary's hand as she explained, her slow sobs still snatching the words.

'I thought – I didn't know – oh, poor Ally – she's been gone so long. And I wanted to see – I thought if it was Eddie – if she was in love with Eddie – then she would have left because of that. I thought that was it.'

Mary nodded, not understanding. She squeezed her mother's hand but there was no response.

'Because if not,' Queenie May went on. 'If not – then I thought it was something else – me – or Arthur – I thought she left because of something else. And I couldn't bear... it had to be Eddie.'

Mary wrapped both her hands around her mother's, dipping her head over them, burdened by Queenie May's distress and the way it excluded her. They sat for a long time together on the bed, tired, huddled, not even moving with the dark. Every now and again a heavy sob would surge out of Queenie May's past and Mary would touch her briefly on the shoulder, reassuring. She didn't read to her mother.

'It'll be all right, Ma,' she said at last. 'I promise.'

So Mary wrote the love letter to Eddie, as Alice might have done, making it true. It was not easy. She sat for a long time, trying out lines on scraps of paper, and practising the twist of her letters. She tried to imagine how Alice might write, but all she could think of were the tight-packed pages of shorthand she had sometimes watched her sister concocting, a mystery to her. She thought about love and tried to describe it. But when she read back the words they were stilted and strange, quaint. She did not like the sound of them.

She continued to practise. She tried out phrases in her head; whispered them to herself to get them honed. And the words, in time, began to sink deep in her, playing their sounds out as she slept. Sitting by the window on the bus, watching the city; sweeping out the ward; standing on the corner by the cinema arches looking out across the dockyard, and, in the twilight, waiting for boys, the thought of the letter seemed to lift her from things, making the world around her swollen and tremulous, and only herself sharp-edged, knowing. Day by day, and word by word, she began to understand. And in the end, when she tore Alice's writing from the front of the book and wrote her own letter there instead, she pushed the words breathlessly to the limit of the paper, scrawling quickly, the pen tingling in her fingers, her thoughts scattered, and only the tincture of love hot on the page and within her, writhing. At the end of it, Mary sat back, blotting the sheet with an old rag. She did not read again what she had written. She set the book open on the floor by her feet until she could be sure the dark ink was absolutely dry and she stretched out, content.

Mary's work was finished just in time. Less than a week later Queenie May packed up the book and took it into the city, to a bookseller's not far from the town hall. The shop's original premises had been bombed, and it was cramped now into two small rooms piled high with muddled shelves and boxes of books, stone dust falling from the ceiling on to the paper covers. The shop girl, gawky and thick-lipped, reassured Queenie May with her open clumsiness and lack of pretension.

'It's lovely,' she said, when Queenie May showed her what remained of the book. 'What a shame it's so spoilt. Was it a raid? We get lots of books from raids.'

Queenie May nodded. The girl turned the pages gingerly.

'I don't know what you can do, but if you can fix it somehow, some of it. It belonged to my daughter,' said Queenie May. It sounded so much like the making of a memorial that she was embarrassed.

The girl looked carefully at the binding and the stitching. She glanced at Mary's letter, but did not, just then, read it. She bent the cover back and forth. She pressed the pages between her thumb and finger, as though testing their ripeness. After that, she did not know what to do, and was no clearer as to how the book might be repaired. She looked again at its configuration. Queenie May waited, trusting her.

'You see, it's in two parts,' said the girl at last. 'From here, where it says *Songs of Experience*, that's a whole new section. And the damage is all before it, here. It must have been the way it was lying. But there's just these first few pages, which are still all right, and then scraps and tears, and then…' She flicked through to make her point, her confidence growing. 'Perhaps we could start again, with this bit, the end, and make a new book.'

She did not know if this was possible, but it sounded reasonable and she smiled up at Queenie May, waiting for an answer.

'Half of it then,' said Queenie May.

'More or less. The good half. We'd save whatever we could – the cover, of course, trimmed back, and the page she's written on. It would be in a good state.'

Queenie May thought about it, unsatisfied. 'It's better than nothing I suppose.'

'It'll still look nice – and old,' said the girl, hoping this would clinch it.

The thought of it looking something like the same was very tempting.

'How long will it take?' asked Queenie May.

The girl breathed heavily in the direction of the piled boxes. 'We're very busy. Just at the moment. I think it may take a while. It's a specialist job. But if you leave your address we can write to you when it's ready.'

Queenie May gave the name of her street. 'And then,' she asked, 'I would need to know how much it might cost.'

The girl puffed again. 'Hard to say,' she said. 'Just now.'

Queenie May, frightened of making a scene in such a seat of learning, left without an estimate.

The letter arrived several months later, informing Queenie May, in the most polite way, that the job had been satisfactorily completed. It said nothing about cost, nor did it tell Queenie May that the book had been re-stitched with intimate care by an experienced binder, a Polish refugee, who savoured the feel of the paper, like bird's wings in his hands, and who kept the discarded pages for himself. Florrie read it out loud to her mother when she called by with Maggie. Eddie was coming home after the war and there was such a rush to make things right for him, that everything else brushed lightly by her, but still the letter made her start.

'What's this, Ma? What book?'

Queenie May bent to wipe Maggie's runny nose. 'Alice's book,' she said, seeing no way out of it.

Florrie pulled Maggie to her so that her mother had to look up. 'What book, Ma? The book? The one from the wedding? That one?'

Maggie whimpered at the tightness of her mother's grip on her bare arm, and Florrie slapped her. They listened for a while to her tight sobs.

'It got damaged,' said Queenie May at last. 'I thought I should have it put right.'

'We don't want it, you know, Eddie and me. We don't want it, not even as a present, not after…'

'No, best not,' said Queenie May flatly. 'But still, it wasn't right to let it spoil. It might be worth something one day.'

Florrie huffed. 'You should have ditched it, while you had the chance,' she said. 'It's not worth anything; it's not worth any trouble.'

'Well, it's done now,' said Queenie May.

'We don't want it,' said Florrie again.

'No, I suppose not. I'll keep it,' said Queenie May.

Florrie waited on the Hoe for Eddie's ship to dock. Maggie pulled hard on her hand, wanting to be put up high on her shoulders, wanting to see, but Florrie resisted, her eyes fixed to the battle-grey vessel that was emerging so slowly from the far edge of things. She recited the rosary in her head, trying to be calm, but the routine prayers leapt and soared, refusing to be still, and the crowd pushed around her. A thick drizzle smudged the distance and then she saw the ship, sleek and terrible, and, eventually, the bright battlemented rows on the deck that only became figures at the very last moment. She looked out for Eddie, but she did not see him, not until the sailors had landed and everyone was at the dock, shouting and whistling and reaching out. And when she did see him, she was suddenly, unexpectedly shy. He looked brawny and tanned. So although she had planned to run to him, to throw her arms around him, to kiss him, of course, she found she could not do that. She held back. And then she picked up Maggie and held her out like a gift. And the other things she had brought with her in her basket – the bottle of beer and the cigarettes, the packet of lemon sweets – she kept hidden and on the way home, even though it was still raining, she took off the new red headscarf she had been wearing and slipped it into her pocket, sorry that Eddie had not noticed it.

With everything going on, Florrie forgot about her mother's arrangements for the book, and so no one knew when it was, exactly, that Queenie May went into town to collect it. The girl showed her what had been done.

'Can you read me something then?' asked Queenie May.

The girl blinked. 'They're just the same, the poems. We haven't done anything to the pages, just taken out the damaged ones and rebound it,' she said.

'But if you wouldn't mind… just a line or two. To make sure.'

'I don't read very well,' said the girl, sheepish. 'Not out loud.'

'That won't matter. You'll be better than me. It was my husband, you see, that used to do the reading.'

There seemed to be no escape. The girl cleared her throat. Queenie May held tight to the counter, waiting. The lines came slowly but right. Queenie May heard them as though it were Arthur. After a verse, the girl stopped and closed the book.

'It seems all right,' said Queenie May. 'It seems like it was before.'

The girl, relieved, packed the book in a large box. Queenie May paid, although the sum alarmed her. When she left the shop she was afraid to take the bus in case she would have to leave the box in the luggage rack, away from her, so she walked home with the weight of it pulling her arms. She took the book out, once, when she was safely in the kitchen, feeling the coolness of the cleaned skin of the binding, but she did not dare open it. She put it away in its box and burnt the paper that Alice had used to wrap it for the wedding.

When Alice finally came home, letting herself in quietly through the open front door, she found a woman who might once have been her mother swathed in an indeterminate, multicoloured cloth bag, kneeling with her ear to the skirting board, the grubby soles of her feet pointing skywards and one hand poised on the stained wooden handle of an old spade. On the floor beside her was a small slab of furred meat, torn apart, leaking dark blood, twitching slightly. Alice did not know quite what to say.

'Ma? Is that you, Ma?' she tried.

Queenie May jumped. It was a voice she only half recognized.

'I've come to see you,' said Alice.

Queenie May turned on her knees, but did not yet get up. 'Can you see the head, my love?' she said. 'I think it might be by the door.'

And Alice looked, despite herself. The head was there, apparently undamaged. She nodded.

'Good,' said Queenie May. 'I thought so.'

She got up then, slowly. Her movements were stiff. She had been crouched a long time, waiting, her back tipped against the wall and her hands propped on the hard floor, everything about her still. She liked to let the mice come. She watched their soft fur flick with the movement of quick deft steps; she liked the shape of their ears and the sinuous pitch of their tails. She allowed them to taste a raisin, their whiskers twitching, and then she pounded the shovel into them.

'Aren't your feet cold, Ma?' asked Alice because what she was really amazed at were the dripping folds of Queenie May's extra weight.

'I can feel the mice better that way, my love.' Queenie May was matter-of-fact. 'You get a sense of them. They scratch, you know, nibble at things, and it's everywhere in the house, in the floorboards.'

Alice reached forward now and took both of her mother's hands, helping her straighten up. They hung for a moment, balanced. And at that moment, as Queenie May looked at Alice, there was nothing to disturb her pleasure. The past had been scrubbed clean, shrinking between them so they could reach across it.

'Oh Ally,' she said. 'I thought you were dead. I was so sorry.'

Alice let go of her mother's hands and looked at Queenie May's face. She noticed the pallor of it, the wrinkles wedged deep by the salt air.

'Do you want to sit down, Ma?' she said.

Queenie May shook herself. 'I want that ruddy mouse's head.' She reached behind the cupboard for the dustpan and brush. Alice thought afterwards that she should have helped, but at the time she just watched as her mother knelt again and swept the head into the pan, turned it over once or twice with the tip of the brush, sniffed it with her nose close, and then threw it briskly into the open bin by the kitchen door.

'There,' said Queenie May when she had finished. 'That's better.'

Alice did not know much about mice. 'I like your dress, Ma,' she said instead, and she reached out to touch the edge of the patched material.

Queenie May swung her hips to make the fabric flutter. The dress was unfitted, with a frilled drawstring neck and no belts or ties or darts to nip. They both watched as it continued to move without her. Then, seeing Alice there, realizing, Queenie May felt a burst of joy, and all at once she dropped the dustpan with a clatter, gripped Alice hard by the arms and pulled her close. It was the feel of Alice she wanted, and she did not let her go for a very long time.

While she was still holding her daughter, Queenie May talked about the book. She knew afterwards that she should have waited, but it was lively in her mind and the words welled up, unstoppable.

'I've been wanting to tell you, my love; I've been waiting all this time. There was… I don't know… an accident. Something happened. It got torn.'

Alice, deep in the folds of her mother's arms, felt the words drift by her.

'But you see, Ally,' went on Queenie May, 'I couldn't give it to Florrie, not with what you'd written, and I didn't know where you were.'

Alice hardly moved. She felt sleepy. 'You should have given it to her. It was hers.'

'Mary read out for me what you'd written,' said Queenie May. 'And so I couldn't, could I? Not then, with Eddie away, and

Maggie… and anyway it's fixed up now, my love, if you want it. I've kept it for you.'

Alice heard the murmur of the sounds rumbling through Queenie May's heavy arms, but it meant nothing.

Eventually they drew apart. Queenie May boiled the kettle for tea and Alice flung her coat and scarf down, but by then all kinds of things had swept back between them like the returning tide. They only spoke once more about the book.

'Well, it's best off out of harm's way – and that's where I've kept it all this time. And you can take it now along with you and have it back,' said Queenie May, when they were sitting together. She did not yet dare tell her daughter about the repair; she thought this would come naturally when Alice had the book again.

But Alice surprised her. 'I don't know. Perhaps it's best thrown away,' she said.

'Oh, but Ally, no – you couldn't do that – it'd be so sad.' Some kind of anger was pitching inside Queenie May.

'I don't know,' said Alice.

In the long silence that followed, Queenie May sat with her feet splayed wide, flat on the floorboards, feeling for mice. Alice wrote her name, in bold italics, in the dust on her mother's windowsill. The accumulating flotsam was sinking them both. After ten minutes, Alice made an excuse to leave and Queenie May let her go. On her way home, Alice stopped at a van and bought an ice cream in a thick cornet. She felt like she was celebrating something. Several days afterwards, she found the bruises from her mother's grip turning yellow on her skin, even though she could not remember any pain.

★

Mary walked carefully and quietly through the house, her movements deliberate, as if they mattered, making hardly a sound. Her breath did not come. This is what she enjoyed and she walked slower, paraded, opening the chest of drawers and sliding the book out from under the linen, careful to cover the slightest trace of her intrusion. She knew the exact configuration of her mother's clothes, the way the edges folded against each other, their measured patterns.

Despite its slimness, it felt heavy in her hands. She rested it partly on the top of the chest of drawers as she opened it. Her mother had gone with neighbours on a picnic, pushing a pram full of sandwiches. Now, the patches of blue sky lengthening with the tide, Mary swung the open book wide across the room, offering up the bright pictures to the empty house. She circled for a while, gathering pace, but it was when she slowed, the colours coming close, that her head spun, disorientating her. She felt the spit of excitement. The letter, she knew, would remind her of love.

There was a knock at the door. Mary jumped with the surprise of it, and the book fell to the floor. Then the knock came again, louder. It left her no choice. She trudged through the corridor and, letting in the rustling air of the street, saw a man holding four dahlias, like splinters of stained glass. He had clearly shined his shoes. He seemed nervous, and when she saw it was Charlie, Mary sighed.

'I thought we could have a walk,' he said. 'If you like.'

She was thinking about the ridge in her hair, and the splashes of grease on her old skirt. She knew she was not wearing lipstick.

'Come in,' she said. 'I'm doing something. I'll be with you in a minute.'

She left him there in the hall and went back to the book. She thought of putting it away and going to tidy herself up. But Charlie, after a minute, followed her, and, because the door was open, stood and watched her in the bedroom. She caught the ripple of his gaze. And for no good reason she held the book out to him.

'Here – look at this.'

He took it in one hand, awkward with the dahlias.

'Give me the flowers – here – and open it at the beginning.'

Charlie did as he was told. He read the book's title, and then the words that Mary had written. He scowled.

'Is it yours?'

'Not really. It's a family thing. Ma has it now. But that...' and she could not help herself. 'I wrote that.'

Charlie said nothing.

'It was a while ago,' added Mary.

He was standing very stiff. 'Who's Eddie?'

Mary laughed and moved towards him. 'Eddie's Florrie's husband – you know that. It's nothing to do with him. I made it up.' She nudged into his arm and leaned across. 'It's a love letter,' she said, feeling it needed more explanation. 'From Alice, my other sister, to Eddie. But it's not true. I made it up. For a lark.' She nudged again.

'It was all just in your head?' said Charlie, admiring. 'Like a kind of story? With words like that?'

'I suppose so.' Mary nodded.

They came close. And in a whisper Mary read it, her voice hoarse.

It all happened in rather a rush, on the floor, which was littered with the crushed petals of Charlie's dahlias, like bruised butterflies. They hardly spoke, though Charlie buried his face in the crook of Mary's shoulder to hide the sound of his unexpected grunts. They had a walk afterwards, once the room was set straight and the book put back in its drawer, and the world around them glowed in the light breaking off the sea. Queenie May was sitting in the kitchen half asleep when they got back, and so Charlie didn't stay.

'He's asked me to marry him,' said Mary, nonchalant. It wasn't true. But she saw that it could be, and she wanted to prick her mother from her stupor.

Queenie May, however, had her mind on mice and was considering ways in which she could sharpen the edge of her spade, by filing it perhaps. 'Right you are, my love,' she said, testing the imaginary blade between her thumb and forefinger, closing her eyes on the pain of it.

'Did you hear me, Ma? Charlie – he wants to marry me.'

Queenie May looked then at her daughter. She was surprised. 'I thought it was the other one you liked, him from the quarry.'

'I said he was asking, that's all. I didn't say I was going to marry him. I didn't say I was marrying anyone. I'm only just twenty, Ma.' She was annoyed at her mother's indifference. 'But it's nice to be asked.'

By the time Charlie said the question out loud, the bump of their baby was swollen hard and he stumbled over the words. Mary found she was tense with him, unyielding, and she kept the bulge of her stomach resolutely between them. After the wedding she stood apart and when they went back to the house to cut the cake, she refused to come through from the bedroom.

'It's the baby, making me sick,' she said to Florrie, sending her sister in her place.

And so Charlie made the first cut alone, and Florrie afterwards carved neat squares that she passed around. They saved one for Mary. Queenie May, when she could not be seen, also wrapped a piece in a paper napkin and put it aside for her second daughter.

'Do you think I should have come, Ma? I could have come,' said Alice, as she ate it a few days later at her mother's house.

'I don't know, my love.'

'It's just, after so long…'

Alice ran her finger through the crumbs. Queenie May nodded, reaching across to take the napkin, refolding it carefully, letting nothing fall.

'I thought by now… I thought you might have told them about me,' Alice said. 'You haven't, have you?'

'No. No, Ally – I thought it best.'

Alice finally flapped the cake debris from her skirt and stood up, moving away from her mother, towards the window. There were mouse traps lined up along the skirting board there, primed with almonds.

'I should have just gone to Florrie, in the beginning, like I wanted,' Alice said. 'I should have just gone. I shouldn't have let you keep it secret. She would have been all right. She would have—'

'It's best not to upset things,' said Queenie May, flatly.

'But a wedding, Ma – Mary's wedding.'

Queenie May crouched and began to sweep the few fallen cake crumbs across the carpet with her open hands. Alice watched her.

'The mice'll be after them,' Queenie May pointed out.

She manoeuvred the crumbs into a ridge and then flipped them into her palm. She looked up at her daughter.

'You can't go about, Ally, just upsetting things. I'm not having it. I don't want them to know – not yet.'

'I know that, Ma. That's what you always say – the same. But it's not that, is it? How can I upset things? You're just keeping me to yourself.'

Queenie May sat back on her haunches. 'Why on earth would I do that, Ally?'

There was no answer and Alice shook her head. 'It's just I can't do it on my own,' she said quietly. 'I can't just go back to them after all this time, out of the blue, not if you don't help me. You can explain to them that it's not like they think; it's not like they've heard. I'm not…'

Queenie May stood up, straightening stiffly, the hand full of cake crumbs flat and steady in front of her.

'Alice, they know, my girl. It's no good pretending. Mary's told me all the things you did; she's told me about all the – men.' The word came out too hushed between them. 'I can't just say… she has all kinds of stories about you, Alice. They know what you're like.'

'But Ma, it isn't true! When you told me what they said, what they thought I was like… But I don't know where it's come from. It's not fair, what they say – it's not right, Ma. You have to listen to me.'

Queenie May swallowed a series of sharp tuts under her breath, blinking away the ancient, wearying maelstrom of warped faces, of her husband bending close, and Alice straining for breath, of the long-dead doctor, peering; shaking away the ache of sharp-imagined men, sneering at her from Mary's tales, entwined on beaches, clasping. The exhaustion of it overwhelmed her.

'Well then, what about Eddie? What about that, my girl?' Her voice was weary with unasked questions.

Alice didn't understand. 'What's wrong with Eddie?'

She looked at her mother, puzzled, and Queenie May saw such a young girl there, such wide, clear eyes washed bright with unfallen tears, that she couldn't, just then, accuse her with the letter.

'Nothing, my love,' she said. 'Nothing. But you know very well what men can be, once you set them going.'

She shuffled away, her hand outstretched with the crumbs, her bare feet silent on the carpet. Alice picked what might have been cake from under her nails until her mother returned. Then she spoke quickly.

'Are you not ever going to tell them, Ma? Are you not ever going to have them here when I come? Florrie and Mary, Eddie?'

Queenie May pursed her lips and her flesh folded around them. 'Shall we see, Ally, how it goes?'

'Because if I see them once – if I explain… it'll be all right then, when they hear. I don't like it like this, Ma – like a fugitive.'

'You made your own bed, my girl,' said Queenie May firmly.

Alice looked away, defeated.

★

Winding her way through familiar streets on the bus from the city, the view from the window fixed itself oddly in Alice's mind, sharp and clear, strange again after her absence. When the bus set her down, she slipped along the line of shops to buy something for her mother. The buildings were shabby. One or two were boarded up and there was litter jammed in their doorways. A squat brown dog was tied with thick string to the metal bicycle rails, over which two small girls were looping. Alice felt conspicuous. But she took her time, passing from shop to shop, and in the end she chose a small-flowered yellow rose, the colour of custard, its heads drooping low over its pot. She did not have much money, and it was expensive, but the moment she saw it, she knew it was the thing, and she carried it up the hill with great care.

Queenie May opened the door promptly, her baggy dress floating about her. It was a different cloth, with small coloured circles imprinted, but if anything it was looser than ever, and the low bulge of her breasts pushed it out in odd places. The house behind her was dark and quiet, and Alice felt the lurch of disappointment.

'You haven't said anything to Florrie then, Ma? You didn't tell her I was coming?'

Queenie May took the rose without any ceremony, bending over it to kiss Alice on the forehead.

'I thought it best not,' she said. 'She's busy just now, my love. Eddie's away again in a week or two. South Africa, you know. And Maggie's grown now, too. She's turned six – a pretty little maid.'

Alice heard the complaint. 'I know, Ma. I'm sorry I've not been for a while.'

Queenie May shrugged. She had counted the months: it was almost two years.

'It's been summer,' she said, as if that was enough and she turned to lead Alice into the lounge. There was a stiffness now in the way she moved, shuffling her feet close to the floor and keeping her back bent slightly forward. Alice watched the labour of her mother's waddle from behind.

Queenie May invited her to stay for lunch even though it was still nearly an hour until midday. Alice sat by the window on to the street while her mother worked in the kitchen. They said very little to each other, the distance between the two rooms and the noises from the stove making chatter awkward.

'Can I help, Ma?' called Alice, once.

Queenie May shuffled through then.

'Let me do this, Ally,' she said. 'Let me cook for you,' and Alice left her alone.

Queenie May brought the plates of sausages through on wooden trays that Alice had not seen before. On each of them there was an identical pair of small blue plastic salt and pepper pots, and a paper napkin, folded. Queenie May brought each of the trays from the kitchen slowly in turn, afraid of falling, and she went again at the end for a saucer of mustard, the powder still lying dry at the edges. By the time they ate, the meal was cold. But Alice enjoyed it, nonetheless, and saved the thought of it.

'That was lovely, Ma,' she said.

'It'll keep you going,' said her mother, as though there were a long journey to be got through. Then she took the plates away, repeating her slow procession to the kitchen. Alice heard the clatter of dishes on the draining board, and the sound of something falling. Then she heard the radio, suddenly loud, songs slipping confidently into the quiet. It seemed a long time until Queenie May came back. When she did come, she was brisk.

'Are you all right, Ally?' she said.

Alice had to say she was.

'You're managing all right, for money? You're eating well? Your chest's not playing up too much?'

The way the questions came together made each of them avoidable.

'I'm fine, Ma, really.'

'Right you are,' said Queenie May, not believing.

There was only the slightest of pauses.

'Can't you find someone?' asked Queenie May then.

Alice sniffed a laugh. 'I don't want anyone, Ma. I don't like, you know, that sort of thing.'

Queenie May did not laugh back. 'But Ally, what is it? What is it that you're after? With all the men you've... with all the...'

'Don't start that.' Alice was sharp.

'Right you are.' But Queenie May had to go on. 'At your age, though, Ally – you're thirty, my girl – you're on the shelf. You should settle down with someone, with someone you love. You'd see then...'

'I don't think I would,' said Alice.

'You're too like your father, Ally, that's the trouble. You want too much. You'll just get yourself in a state, like he did.'

Alice remembered the wide ridged palms of her father's hands, but his face was faint. Queenie May sat back in her chair, wincing at the shifting configuration of her pain.

'He spoilt you, Ally,' she said.

'He did,' said Alice. 'He spoilt me. But that's a long time ago, Ma.'

'Not to me,' said Queenie May.

Queenie May tipped her head back against her seat and closed her eyes. Her face was loose. Alice spread out long on the sofa. They breathed quietly together, remembering things. They were both weary. The house was still. And even though it was the middle of the day, they slept for a long time. Alice opened her eyes once or twice, dreamily, and, seeing the consoling bulk of her mother in the large armchair, sank back to sleep. When they finally stirred, the light in the room was grey and the radio pips were bleating the lateness of the hour. Alice was in a hurry to go for her bus and Queenie May was matter-of-fact again.

'You'll call by, Ally, when you get the chance?' she said, at the door.

Two days later, Queenie May woke in the night with unfamiliar pains twisting in her chest and a grip of such loneliness about her heart that she could not breathe. When she tried to get up from the bed, she fell, catching her foot in the trailing end of the sheet and wedging herself at an odd angle between the wardrobe and the floor, half on her knees. The draught from under the door stirred the edges of her nightdress, but otherwise she was still. From her peculiar vantage point, she noticed an abandoned handkerchief lodged under the bed, pale in the half-light, and she closed her eyes. But the faces that came to her then, leering and smirking, whipping close around her, clinging like cobwebs to her skin, had no solace in them. They were not quite recognizable, distorted and antique, the unready features of her flimsy sons, blank-faced ghouls, strangers, peering and pinching at her, mocking, menacing her with bony hands. She died calling out in the dark for Arthur, knowing he would not come.

Florrie did not find Queenie May until two days later, already rotting, her stench deep in the boards of the house and mice shredding her clothes for their nests. It meant that even in the end, Florrie did not hold her mother, retching instead across the thick folds of the corpse. She left the windows of the house wide open to clear the smell. Once or twice children in the street held competitions to see if they could throw stones through into the rooms. A cat climbed in. The slice of new moon shone cold on to the furniture. Florrie sat at home, waiting for things to clear. And when finally she went back to the house, the landlord pressuring her to empty the rooms, she found that small things had been neglected: dishes left unwashed in the kitchen, a pile of mending tucked behind a chair and a pot-plant rose, wilted and brown, unwatered. She was angry with her mother for surrendering in that way. She also found the book, wrapped and pristine, settled comfortably among Queenie May's stockings and yellowing vests. She recognized it immediately. She thought of it as Alice's; she did not remember that it was hers. And she left it on the floor while she tidied. It was at the end of the day, addled then by the creeping sadness of touching her mother's things, that she put it on top of the box that she was taking home. She did not think to mention it to Mary.

★

At Queenie May's funeral they looked, of course, for Alice. They stood on the open ground of the new cemetery extension huddled around the close-packed button of yellow flowers at the foot of the open grave, and each of them, in turn, swept a gaze across the mounds and headstones, right up to the boundary fence, across to the new estate of houses packed against it, and away then to the low grey film of sea. But Alice was not there.

'She must be dead then, too,' concluded Florrie, and Mary, taking her sister's arm tightly in her own, nodded in confirmation.

But Florrie could not shake the sadness of this. Her prayers fractured into little more than just the brooding repetition of her sister's name, and when she thought of her mother's funeral, as she did often over the coming years, she sometimes suspected she saw Alice there; sometimes obscured by a tree, or the parked bulk of the hearse; sometimes at the edge of the small crowd, tucked far back, but unmistakeable. The look in her sister's eyes transfixed her.

'Did you hear, Mum, what I said?' persisted Maggie.

They were cooking together, making trays of angel cakes for the church bazaar. Maggie was mixing the butter icing, pressing the fondant hard with the back of a wooden spoon. Her mother was supposed to be cutting the cakes, but she was still, her knife suspended above the board.

'What, Mags? Sorry.' Florrie shook her head and the picture of Alice dissolved, quivering. It was almost ten years since Queenie May's death, but still the ridged sweep of the cemetery was fresh-coloured in her mind and Florrie felt as though she were grieving for something.

'I've got some things for the bring and buy,' Maggie repeated, unspectacularly. 'I looked them out, a couple of prayer books from when I was little.'

Florrie was still distracted. 'Prayer books, Maggie?'

'The ones for children. There're two of them. I don't know where they came from.'

Florrie began again cutting wings from the sliced lids of her buns, her knife strokes steady. 'I got them at church, at my first communion,' she said. 'A long time ago.'

Maggie sensed she might have made a mistake. 'I'm sorry, I didn't know. I just thought… If they're special, I can keep them, of course. They don't take up room.'

'You don't use them though,' said Florrie.

'No.'

'Well, then.'

Florrie spooned out the butter icing on to the cakes and stuck the wings in at angles on their tops. Maggie set a cherry carefully in each. They were quiet, concentrating, but over her shoulder Florrie could feel Arthur, bending over her as he had done on her communion day, his breath peppery. She could feel the swirl of the borrowed veil on her shoulders and the smoky breeze from the dockyard unsettling her hair. She could feel her father's hand light on her shoulder, the warmth of it through her thin blouse, and the sanctity of the prayer books clutched in her hand. She finished the buns and turned away to the sink. Maggie brought the slender books down from her bedroom. They looked fragile and outdated, the colours on them sugary.

'Here, Mum, what do you think? Shall I keep them?'

Florrie shook her head. 'Put them with the tins,' she said.

'We'll give them to Mrs Morimer for the bring-and-buy, like you said.'

Maggie hesitated.

'Everyone got one,' said Florrie plainly, wiping her hands. 'In those days, everyone got one when you made your communion. They're nothing special. The nuns dished them out at the back of the church, I remember.' Then, for the moment, there was a question. 'But there's nothing written in them, is there, Mags?'

Maggie flicked open the books. 'No. Nothing,' she said and she put the books with the pile of things to be taken to the bazaar.

Later, packing the box to take to church, Florrie held the prayer books in her hand. They seemed very small. She read a rhyme from one of them, but it was childish, so instead she took her rosary from her pocket and recited a brisk decade, flicking the beads quickly through her fingers. Still, though, the prayer would not hold the past away. It was swelling back now, inexorable, and there were still traces of butter icing around her nails and flakes of hard flour in the creases of her wrists when she took the lid off the box that held, unsorted, her dead mother's things. There was not much of any interest. In less than half an hour she had sorted through the heirlooms and set most aside, unsentimentally, for the forthcoming bazaar. A small green glass vase she put away for Maggie and she took Alice's book downstairs and put it on the dining-room table. She noticed how light it felt, and as she unwrapped it she saw how dull it was, how ordinary. It was just Alice's odd wedding present, neglected.

The new binding was tight. The pages clung together, and so Florrie had to ease back the front cover. The letter surprised her.

She knew Mary's handwriting immediately. It was slightly twisted by the format of the page, slightly askew, as though she were using a broken-nibbed pen, but Florrie recognized it nonetheless. So although she saw Alice's name there, she was not fooled. And when Florrie first read the letter, she was so busy puzzling over when Mary could have done it and how Queenie May could have let her, that she hardly took in the words. So she read the whole thing again, slowly and clumsily, the peculiar passion her sister was speaking to Eddie only gradually becoming real to her.

At first she thought about it quite clearly. She saw what Mary had done as a child's thing; a dare. But the clearness did not last long, because there was Alice's name, and Eddie's, there was the throb of lust, and there were the words combusting the past. And Florrie could not help thinking then about Eddie and what he might have done and how he might have betrayed her; about the way her sisters had plotted against her, uniting in their rancid desire for her husband; about the million possibilities that might shame and defeat her. And within a few moments all she had was her anger, vast and unlandmarked. Dressed as she was in her apron, her hair straggled and unpinned, Florrie stuffed the book high into the back of the airing cupboard where no one could chance upon it. Maggie heard the click of the front door as her mother left the house.

Florrie cantered down the hill as a light rain began to fall, but she saw nothing of the puddles gathering around her, and never stepped aside to avoid the spray of passing cars. She did not see how people looked at her. All she could see was Eddie, the beautiful man she had married, and, clicking through her vision like stuttering frames of film, the moments he might have spent with Mary or Alice, the looks he might have flashed at them, the evidence of betrayal. She saw when it might have started, at the wedding or before, Alice's dramatic treachery bold in the scenes, and always the rest of them circling away from her, leaving her, because she could not keep up with them. She ran faster.

It seemed to Florrie that Eddie had let her down. She was disappointed. It was Alice, perhaps, or Mary, who had deceived her. It was perhaps the two of them. But it was always Eddie. As though she had been waiting for it from the first, she accepted it, but it stung her nonetheless. It did not seem right that she should be discarded. It did not seem just. Her anger welled up from the past, where she was gauche and ignorant and clumsy, where Arthur was turning from her. They had written a letter that stunted everything.

When Florrie trotted out into the road that led down to the dockyard, and was hit hard by a delivery van coming from the city, she was trying to decide what she could do. Her pace had slowed; she was no longer running. This is what, in the end, killed her. Had she been running still, the van would have slid past her, honking. But things were becoming clear to her. She was feeling the dribble of rain for the first time on her neck and reaching behind to pull her collar tight. With the cool of it on her skin it was as though, suddenly, she could see what the future might be. The radiance of it made her stop, and it was then that she was hit. Spinning up into the air, light for a moment, warm, she saw her reflection in the wide windscreen, askew slightly but sharp, her face firm with the expectation of freedom, and she was surprised.

4. Eddie

When Eddie first found the book, going through the things at the back of the cupboard almost two years after Florrie died, he could not think what it was. It was wrapped in torn white paper that was blotched and stained along one side, browning with age, and when he felt the weight of it he could only think it might be some kind of album, photos perhaps that his wife had kept of Maggie when she was growing up, or an unfinished collection of something. Even when he unwrapped it, it still meant nothing. He did not recognize the soft brown cover and, although it seemed old, he could not remember it.

And he got distracted for a while by a scarf that caught his eye, dark sprigs of thorns on a deep red ground; the same scarf Florrie had worn, he was sure, when she had stood up high on the Hoe in the squalling rain, waiting for a glimpse of his ship returning after the war. He had seen the colour of it vivid in the crowd, he could remember that, and he could remember the thump in his heart at the first sight of her, just the scarf and a wisp of hair and the half-familiar way she held her head, high over the other women but dipped down, askance. He remembered trying to be sure of who she was, in those moments before they touched, but it never came to him, and there was just the scarf, tickly on his skin, and the smell of land, the warm, damp nylon, the scent of hairspray and cigarettes and the musk of the city, the strangeness of Florrie, a smell that sickened him. Kneeling on the narrow landing, he held the scarf to his face now. It smelt only of the cheap wood of the cupboard. He put it to one side, for a jumble sale. He had no use for it.

Eddie was disappointed to find the book did not bulge with photographs, or cigarette cards, or stamps, or even scraps from family outings, stuck down with sticky corners. He could imagine that Florrie might have found pleasure in collecting odds and ends, to mark her place in time, and he would have liked to see the things she chose to save. But it was just a book, with nothing personal about it. And Eddie put it to one side while he continued to tidy the cupboard. He found other things: the thick plait of Maggie's hair cut off when she left primary school and laid in a shoe box; Christmas cards; an old dog licence; a neatly rolled newspaper celebrating the Queen's coronation six years earlier; a small brown velvet purse, faded and much worn, empty, and the letters he had written home from his tours, bound with a dry elastic band that crumbled away the moment he went to unwind it. He read one or two paragraphs but somehow they rolled by him, without burrs to catch his attention. There seemed to be nothing there. And Eddie cried, for the first time since he had received the call at the dockyard offices telling him that his wife had been killed.

By the time he looked at the book properly it was late and he was tired. Maggie had come in from work and was upstairs in her room, playing records. He could hear the faint noise of her moving around, perhaps dancing. He unwrapped a mint sweet and twisted the empty wrapper deftly into a bow. He had come home from one of his long navy tours with almost two thousand of these bows, which he had fashioned into a rug, pulling the papers through a square of sacking with a crochet hook. This one he balanced on the edge of his metal ashtray; he would later throw it away. He opened the book and sat back in his chair with it spread wide on his lap. He had to force the binding, which was tight. He pushed it open at a page towards the back and sat with it for a long time. He finished his sweet and then rolled a cigarette with the tobacco from his tin and lit it, knocking the mint wrapper to the floor and sprinkling a few dark fibres of tobacco on to the pale pages. He did not know what to make of what he saw, odd distended paintings splashed around, almost over, poems that were more like hymns; the resonant blues of tropical waters, swirling orange where they lapped the sands; sun-deep greens sweeping into gold. He read one or two lines of verse, and he ran his fingers over the pages. They felt thick and warm, like dark flesh dripping from the sea.

Eddie stubbed out the wet paper end of his roll-up and tried to concentrate. He turned back to find the information given at the beginning, to get some idea of what he was looking at, at what it was that Florrie had hoarded. It was then that he saw a different page at the front, densely covered in blue-inked writing, a looped stretched hand that he didn't recognize. There was something alluring about it, about the boldness of it, the letters tangled and intense and when Eddie picked out his name there, clearly, he felt it for a moment like a spell.

He sat back. Maggie had stopped her dance and was silent. A blackbird sang in the hedge by the window. He could hear the stutter of his own breathing. And then, with his fingers drumming a hornpipe on the worn arms of his chair, he read for the first time the love letter that was inked into the blank paper of the book. When he had finished, he read it again, sitting in the dimming light by the bay window of the sitting room and, later, when he had eaten his toast and drunk his tea, he read it sitting on the stool by the draining board and then again, before bed, although he did not take it into the bedroom with him.

Florrie never had the words for such a thing, he knew that, even before he saw her sister's name signed at the bottom. Alice. It was written with a flourish, bold, the ends of the letters peeling away like promises. Eddie ran his finger over the shape of it and tried to find a face to match, but he could not picture her. He had last seen her over twenty years ago, picking at the curls of wedding-cake icing, her eyes down, quiet, her face turned away. Now all he could summon was a sense of her, something like a taste, and the words she had once tempted him with on their walk around the reservoir. These were still bright.

That Alice had written to him in this way was somehow not a surprise. But the anger and regret of not having known about it until now kept Eddie awake, gloating in his half-dreams and tossing him towards morning in the tangled sheets. The thought that he might have lived the years differently tormented him. He whimpered in the dawn hours at the unkindness of fate and found many ways to blame Florrie.

'Did you ever hear, Mags, what became of your Auntie Alice?' he asked his daughter fiercely the next day, not entirely sure that Maggie, too, was not guilty somehow.

Maggie was sitting on the kitchen stool, peeling an apple and swinging her legs. She was more surprised by his tone than by the question. She tugged at the rising hem of her skirt, presuming that might be something to do with it. 'She wasn't at the funeral,' she said, 'nor at Nanny's.'

'She wasn't,' said Eddie. 'But maybe she's not well. Or maybe she's dead herself. I've not heard anything of her all these years. I just didn't know whether your mother—'

Maggie interrupted. 'She's not dead, Dad. She's just peculiar. That's what Nanny said. With all the... you know.'

Her shoulders and eyebrows flicked, but Eddie did not understand the code. It had been like this since the moment he had stepped on shore for the final time, Florrie waiting for him at the dock with Maggie alongside, always somehow daring him to catch up. He had to ask.

'All the what? What do you mean?'

'She's had a lot of men,' muttered Maggie, blushing, and slicing into the apple.

Eddie looked away. 'Oh, I see.'

'They used to talk about them.'

'Who?'

'Mum and Nanny and Auntie Mary. They said there were all sorts – some of them were, you know, darkies, foreign, sailors.' Maggie saw no incongruity in this. 'It's disgusting, that's what Auntie Mary says. Auntie Alice threw herself away, that's what she says, getting mixed up with people like that.'

'But you never saw any of them?'

'The men? Dad! How would I see the men? I've never even seen Auntie Alice. It's just things I heard, at Nanny's funeral – before Mum died. And anyway, you wouldn't want to, would you?'

Again, Eddie did not understand. 'Wouldn't want what?'

'To see them. Or her. Not after that. Not a woman like that.' Maggie was sure of this. She slid off the stool. 'Why do you want to know for?'

'I just wondered,' said Eddie, cowed by her certainty.

He could have just torn Alice's letter from the book, but he wanted to make a neat job of it. So later that morning, when Maggie had gone off to the post office where she had started work, he took it out to the pebble-dashed shed in the shadowed, green-walled corner of the yard, and he cleared a space for it on the workbench. In the bright strip lighting of the shed, it took him some time to uncut the binding and ease back the cover. He worked slowly, with careful precision, using a magnifying glass to bring close the weft of the stitches. More than once he changed the blade on his knife to be sure of slicing cleanly. He was surprised at the quality of the workmanship. It pleased him. He enjoyed the dissection.

The pages fell loosely on to the workbench, releasing the accumulated dust of quiet years. He separated the one at the front on which the letter was written and cut carefully between the small pin-prick holes where the stitches had been, joining them with sharp-pointed scissors like dot-to-dot and finally cutting the sheet into perfect halves. He put the letter on to the window ledge, making room between a packet of cabbage seeds and a jar half-full of turpentine. Then he spent a long time scrupulously collecting together the rest of the loose pages and putting them in order. When they were done he stacked them at the end of the workbench and covered them with a cloth. He had enjoyed being so close to the book and had touched it with tenderness. It was a beautiful thing, even in pieces.

He took the separated letter inside. He put the kettle on the stove to boil, switched on the radio for the lunchtime news, rolled himself a cigarette, and then read it again. The voice he heard speaking the lines was breathy and light. He did not know if it was Alice's, but it made the words pulse and sparkle, and he read them over and over, their meaning dissolving even as they became written into him, the kettle singing on the hob, his head throbbing and his hand pumping hard inside the flies of his trousers until he was completely free of Florrie.

Eddie climbed the hill from the dockyard, the wind from the sea on his back. He had the evening paper rolled in his hand and a new tin of tobacco in his pocket. He nodded at the neighbours and stopped on the front path to pick up a scrap of litter that had wedged itself into a gap in the paving. It was only when he felt the scratch of the key against the lock that he got a tingle of nerves.

'I'm going to find your Auntie Alice,' he said to Maggie, as soon as they were quiet together. They were watching television, though Eddie had the newspaper open too on the arm of his chair and Maggie, her legs bent underneath her, was picking at something on her bare knee. 'In case she doesn't know. She needs to know, my love. She's Florrie's sister, after all. Family. It's only right she knows that your mother's dead.'

It made Maggie look up, but she didn't say anything. Eddie saw the shadow of Florrie around her eyes.

'It'll be a shock to her; it'll be strange – I know that,' he went on. 'And there's Queenie May, too. She may not even know her mother's dead. But anyway, I think it's only right, you see.'

Maggie went back to her worn knee. Eddie's hands trembled.

'Well then? What do you think, Mags?'

She looked across at him. There was the intimation, suddenly, of all the things she might want to say, but she did not have the courage to begin and her eyes flopped from his face.

'You'll never find her. She's not been heard of for years. What can you do, go to the police?'

'I'll look her up in the phone book,' said Eddie.

But Alice lived away from the sea now, in a small estate of prefabs on the edge of the moors, so she was not in the Plymouth city phone book that Eddie consulted at the library. There were no other Craythornes listed.

'Are there other ways of tracing people? Family,' Eddie asked the high-haired librarian behind the counter.

She looked at him for a moment before deciding there was nothing unpleasant about the question.

'There're war records,' she said, 'if it was someone who fought or died in the war. And there's the electoral roll, but you'd have to have an idea whereabouts they might be. If you know the parish, for example. And it's only any good for people registered to vote, so…'

'I don't suppose she's done that. From what I've heard,' said Eddie.

The librarian nodded. 'If someone doesn't want to be found…' she said.

Eddie nodded back, without actually agreeing. 'I could hire a private detective,' he joked.

The librarian laughed, bubbling spit through her teeth. She

picked up the directory and turned to take it through to the back room. 'Good luck,' she said, over her shoulder.

Eddie did not, of course, hire a private detective. He would not have known how to do such a thing. But over the months that followed, he consulted the electoral roll; the war records (just in case); Queenie May's old friends and neighbours; the former teacher at the girls' school (who was too sick to remember anything); and the registers for all the parishes he could think of within a reasonable radius. When nothing came of these he had to ask Mary.

'Oh my good Lord, Eddie. What are you bothering with that for now?' was the first thing Mary said, taking his coat from him and shaking it, though it was a clear dry day. She steered him through to the lounge.

'Charlie and the boys are out, cycling,' she said then, as if the thing about Alice was decided and there was nothing more to say. 'You can stay though, if you like, and wait for them. They won't be long.' She smiled hard at him, her eyes fixed diligently above his head.

'It's all right. I just called by, quickly, to ask about Alice, that's all. I won't wait.'

Eddie reached out a hand as if to lean on the fireplace, but immediately felt it odd, like standing at a public bar, and pulled back his arm uncertainly in mid-air. The clock ticked loudly from its niche in the stone-clad wall that twisted up from the electric fire. It insisted on drawing Eddie in.

'Is that new, Mary, the fireplace?'

Mary blushed. 'A friend of Charlie's did it for us,' she said and just for a moment settled a flicking gaze on her brother-in-law.

'It's nice,' Eddie said.

Mary touched one of the grey-green bricks lightly with her hand. 'It's granite,' she said. 'Real stone, polished up.'

'Is it? It's nice.'

'There's a lot you can do, these days.'

Eddie nodded. He wanted to leave. He could not tell her about the book or the letter in case she judged him by it. 'Well, then, if there's nothing… about Alice. If you can't help…'

Mary smiled again. 'There's nothing to say, Eddie. You know it all. Alice left home not long after you and Florrie were married, and that was it. She never bothered with me, or with Charlie and the boys; never came round or wrote or anything. At first Ma worried herself sick. She thought she'd had an asthma attack somewhere in some backstreet, but then we heard things – we heard she'd been seen with a man, doing something, behind a rock at Jennycliffe… Well, what can you do then?'

Eddie did not know if he was expected to answer. 'Something must have set her off,' he said, hoping it was enough.

'I think you can tell these things,' said Mary. 'I think you know when someone's like that. Especially family. I think it shows.'

'I meant something must have made her leave,' said Eddie. He touched the edge of the fireplace. The stone was unexpectedly warm.

Watching him, Mary reached out a hand as though to hold him back.

'Is it local?' Eddie asked, seeing the hand. 'It looks local. From up on Dartmoor.'

Mary retreated. 'No one made her. She left. Just like that,' she said. 'She just went away.'

'And you and Florrie, you never...' He didn't want to sound critical. 'You didn't try to find her? You never heard anything from her?'

Mary shook her head. 'She was a dirty slut, you know,' she said firmly.

Again, Eddie nodded. What Mary said did not surprise him. From what he could remember of Alice, he thought it might be true. It made no difference.

There was a clatter of bicycles on the front step. Mary jerked back her head, stiff-necked, as though a chain had been tightened.

'It's the boys back. Are you sure you won't stay, Eddie?' Her tone was softer.

'I'll walk out over the bridge, I think, and get some fresh air,' he said. 'It's a lovely day.'

'It is,' said Mary.

Eddie got tangled with his nephews in the hallway as he tried to get his coat from the banister. They were rowdy, pushing each other and getting in the way. Charlie, stepping over them, shook Eddie's hand.

'It's lovely out there.'

'I'm off for a bit of a walk,' replied Eddie.

'Right you are then,' said Charlie.

Mary fussed with her sons' dirty shoes and did not say goodbye to Eddie, though she waved to him, afterwards, as he went down the path. Charlie, feeling the sudden warmth of the house, lit his pipe by the open kitchen window. He watched the smoke squeeze out and unfurl over the yard. He saw Eddie, briefly, as he passed the gap in the broken fence. He was walking quickly, his head bowed. Something about the sight of him made Charlie purse his lips tightly around his pipe stem.

Alice was untraceable. There was no clue as to where she might have gone and all Eddie had was the page from the book with the scalding words, drawing out the distance and taking her away from him. There was nothing more he could do. But in the way of these things, that just made it worse. He couldn't stop thinking about her. Being alone seemed sharp now and sore, and so he found a face for her, somewhere from his past, from a conglomeration of likely faces, and he found her a wide-legged way of walking and dressed her in the pre-war fashions he remembered. He caught the scent of her, some kind of flower, skin-fresh, and he pulled her hair close to her head so that he could see the shape of it, broad and round, reminding him of Florrie. And every evening he read the letter after he had unplugged the television to prepare for bed, and he had her voice, unimagined, ringing in his ears through the night. It was as if he had always been in love with her.

Alice's letter lay in the drawer alongside Eddie's bed for several years. After the first few months, he did not read it. He gave up on the idea of searching for her and did not mention it to the family again. He let other ordinary things happen to him. As he walked to and from work, the pull of the tide was never exactly the same; this marked off the days. From the small oblong window at the top of the stairs, he looked along the coast, watching the light on the sea bring in the change of season. This seemed like enough.

Closed into the late November streets, Eddie walked quickly, arriving first at the Continental Hotel. The city was grey and Victorian, the hotel quiet and shabby and old-fashioned. Eddie had not been there for well over twenty years, but the familiarity of it was exhilarating. He dropped down two stone steps from the street and along a narrow corridor. There was no one in the bar, and apparently no one serving. The door thudded shut behind him, and still no one came. He stood near the beer pumps, fingering the box of darts in his pocket. He waited. And then, as he expected, it all happened at once, two men from the home team arriving with a new board packed in a box, the barmaid coming up the steps from the cellar with a red crate of bottles, the dockyard team calling for beer, the stools and tables being pushed back and the oche unrolled, the quiet calm of the Sunday morning displaced. Someone chalked up the scoreboard and, while Eddie took a sip through the froth on the top of his pint, the team captains tossed the coin and shook hands. The blunt rhythmic thud-thud of the darts began.

Eddie missed three darts at double sixteen and when the dockyard team lost, by one leg, he had to wonder if he had let them down. The defeated men left together, laughing and downhearted. They stood for a moment outside on the pavement, lifting their collars against the brisk cold wind, loosening their ties and looking up and down the quiet streets. Someone, kindly, invited Eddie to go along for more beer, but he did not want to be with them and used Maggie as an excuse.

'She's cooking. I'd better not,' he said.

They joked with him for a moment about this mysterious Maggie.

'Maggie's my daughter,' said Eddie flatly, aware that he was disappointing them again. 'Grown up now. Nearly.'

They shuffled on the pavement and a taxi went by, spraying up dirty mist.

'She's a good girl,' Eddie added. 'I'd better be off.'

But as he turned the corner to the front of the hotel the brisk pace of the competition drained suddenly from him, and his feet felt stiff. Maggie, he knew, would not be at home. She was having Sunday lunch with a friend, someone Eddie didn't know, a girl from work. The ashen drizzle of the day, just about bearable in the city, would be denser if he headed back towards the house, the river flat and black, the bridge hidden, the streets oily. He would feel more alone. He looked up at the sky and could see nothing. A greasy damp slid across his skin and he wiped his face with the back of his hand. There was the chance, he knew, that he might disappear. Eddie turned across the front of the hotel and went into the faded womb-red entrance hall by the revolving door from the main street. If it had been a finer day, with the sun making the sea glisten and the breeze swinging in with the scent of spring, then he might have thrown off the disappointment of the morning for a stroll on the Hoe. It might have been different. But it was November, and cold, and deeply grey, and Eddie allowed the waitress in the tight black skirt to show him to a table in the half-empty dining room that smelt of Sunday greens.

Eddie was given a thin, bright tomato soup with a single slice of buttered white bread, and shortly afterwards three wedges of muddy beef. He ate it all without looking up. He did not even think to order a beer until he had almost finished his main course. He turned then to try to catch the waitress's eye but she had her back to him, serving a quiet family sitting in the window and he felt awkward looking at the bulge of her buttocks through her skirt, so he finished his meat and waited.

Eddie pushed his plate back, rucking the dark cloth beneath it into folds. He looked around him for the first time at the brown and red dining room, the half-lit chandeliers yellow and heavy, a highly patterned carpet on the floor that he did not remember. He watched the other diners for a moment, discreetly. The family in the window was eating dessert, an elderly couple in woollen suits, a man of Eddie's age who shared their sharp nose and chin and a woman who seemed apart from it. There were two other women on the table next to them, waiting like Eddie, looking around. He turned his eyes from them.

Then there was Alice.

It was not that he recognized her straight away. She was not what he had conjured since finding the letter. There was a limpness about her face, and slack folds about her eyes, that he had not envisaged. Her hair was cut short, and bulged into a strange loop at the back where she had struggled to reach with her hairbrush. Her dark blue dress drained the colour from her and gave her body sharp, unfamiliar angles. Nonetheless, it was Alice, and Eddie knew this the moment he heard her speak. Hearing the voice, there could be no mistake.

She called to the waitress for her bill.

'I was wondering if I could pay by cheque. Would that be all right?'

That is what Eddie heard, at first, almost without noticing, but then something flashed inside him, and he leaned forward, waiting for her to speak again. The tablecloth crumpled hot in his hand.

'That's fine, madam,' said the waitress.

'If I could borrow a pen... I'm sorry.'

It was such an ordinary thing, but the gravel in her voice scraped something clear and bright in Eddie's memory and he felt himself stand.

Alice had her hand in her bag. The waitress was bending to take her side plate. They both looked across at the slight, thin-mouthed man in the tweed jacket who had knocked his chair backwards against the wall with a clatter. The other diners looked too. It felt to them like something should happen. For a moment, everyone was still, waiting, but then the waitress started briskly for the kitchen. Eddie tasted the meat as something far away and faint, and clutched the edge of the table to steady himself.

'I'll bring you dessert, sir, if you like,' said the waitress as she passed. 'Ice cream or fruit salad?'

Eddie felt the end of the toppled chair leg sharp against his calf. He stared across at the woman he knew was Alice, but she was brushing crumbs from the cloth.

'No, no dessert,' he said, more loudly than he meant.

The waitress shrugged. She would eat his ice-cream portion later, out by the back stairs, shivering in the cold.

Eddie could not think what to do. He could not move. He was absolutely sure the woman at the table was Alice. She was not what he had expected, but she was Alice. And he was so afraid of her now, of what she might say to reject the past written in the letter, that he was held back.

He watched as the waitress brought the pen and Alice wrote out the cheque. Then she took her coat from the seat next to her where it had been folded, and stood to button it. She turned her back to Eddie as she did this, looking out across the heads of the other diners to the view from the window. Eddie followed her gaze. An advertising logo, painted on the side of a passing lorry, floated across the glass like a flag. Then there was just a view of the bank building opposite, its milky windows half-mast.

Alice was in the lobby when he caught up with her. She was looking at herself in the heavy gilt-framed mirror, adjusting the buttons of her coat, and it was the reflection of him she saw first, his dark eyes wide and anxious. She remembered his eyes.

'Oh,' she said, looking hard into the depths of the mirror. His reflection caught up with her.

'Alice?'

'I was having lunch,' she said, turning to him.

'Yes – I had lunch. The beef.'

'It was rather dry.'

Looking at the back of her reflected in the mirror, Eddie could see her scalp through the bend of misplaced hair.

'Alice,' he said again, softly.

'It was my birthday,' she said. 'I'm forty-eight,' she added sheepishly.

And of course they did not know what to do, after all this time, with the strangeness of gathering age between them. They did not know how to start.

Eddie saw the reflection of the waitress coming through the door from the dining room. She held out a small plate to him.

'Your bill, sir? For lunch.'

Eddie did not stop looking at Alice. 'Will you wait, one moment? Just while I… I've got something to tell you.'

'I'll wait,' said Alice. Even all these years later, the way she said it, it seemed like an invitation.

Eddie paid his bill in cash, leaving a tip. The waitress took his notes away again on the plate and disappeared back into the restaurant.

'Come in here,' said Eddie. He reached out to take Alice's hand, but realized at the last moment what he was doing and put his hand into his pocket instead, where he felt his darts. He opened the door to the right of the lobby, a magnificent high door with carved panels and a thick brush seal. It opened, he knew, into the ballroom.

Inside it was gloomy. There were no windows, only a row of skylights high in the domed roof. The room was more or less empty. The curtains had been taken down so that the stage was bare at the far end, and only a few trestle tables remained, folded and stacked against the back wall and haphazardly covered with sheets. The banks of mirrors and the glass chandeliers, the smooth pale ash floor, the gilt decorations and brass railings were all dull and lifeless. There was no hint of sparkle or glamour. Eddie was surprised. It was not what he had expected.

'They've closed it up,' he said, hardly moving from the door.

Alice took a step or two inside, her heels clicking on the floor.

'They dance at the Pavilions now, the youngsters, I think,' she said. She looked around carefully. 'It's beautiful. I would have loved to come here. I would have loved to dance, with the band.'

Eddie had danced, here, with Florrie. He remembered that. He remembered everything about it, suddenly drawing it from the dark, the small cream and blue flowers of Florrie's dress, the double layer of polish he had laid on his shoes, the way they had waltzed, gingerly at first, self-conscious, and the way the crowds about them, always changing, looked always the same, looked light and poised and merry. And Florrie, sheltering him beneath her tallness, had spun with such grace that neither of them had found anything to say about it.

'I used to dance in the navy. It was tap dancing,' he said, because it was his memory alone. 'We had a place on the ship where the floor made a good sound. I can't remember; I think we had something for our shoes. I got quite good. I liked it.'

Alice was surprised. 'I'd forgotten,' she said. 'About you being at sea.'

'Forgotten?' Eddie couldn't believe this. He felt she should know him better. 'It's what I did – for years. And even after, now, at the dockyard – I'm in the offices, working shifts. You can't have forgotten about the navy, my love.'

'I didn't know, I suppose,' she said.

'But you did, you did know. When we were married, me and Florrie, I was in the navy then. Some of them made the guard of honour at the church – you remember that?'

Eddie was unexpectedly angry at so much of himself vanishing so suddenly.

Alice breathed a half-smile, nearly apologizing. 'But it wasn't like that when I met you, not at first, was it? And I've always thought of you, I suppose, as I first saw you. It doesn't matter.'

This wasn't what Eddie had supposed it would be like. They were prickly together, out of joint. Alice's indifference hurt him and what he said next came out fiercely.

'I found what you wrote, in the book. I found it when Florrie died.'

His head was full of the neat close lines of text. He felt the glow of it. There was a flush to her cheeks, too, he could see, as she came towards him, as she, too, felt the crush of what she had written all those years ago.

But it was not that.

'Florrie's dead?' Alice said quietly, her eyes sliding from his face.

Only then did Eddie remember that Alice had not known. 'She was killed,' he said. 'She was knocked down. A while ago, now – I'm sorry, my love. We looked for you at the time, you see, to tell you, but... I'm sorry.'

Before he had moved, she turned from him and walked away across the expanse of dance floor. He listened to the click of her heels and watched the pale patch of her scalp. He could not tell if she was crying. There was no sound from her. He waited while she walked, watching, until eventually she took a turn around the sweep of the ballroom and came back to him. She was breathing heavily with short stiff breaths. He thought he'd better tell her everything.

'And Queenie May? You knew about Queenie May, that she was dead?'

Alice nodded. 'Yes, I knew about Ma. I used to go and see her, at the end. I saw her just a day or two before she died. I knew about that. It was just Florrie.'

Eddie took his tin of cigarettes from his pocket and clicked the lid open softly with both thumbs.

'But they said you'd lost touch. I thought no one knew where you were. Even Queenie May…'

'She never told anyone,' said Alice. 'Even Florrie. She was ashamed of me.' She breathed a soft laugh.

Eddie took out a cigarette and slipped the tin back into his pocket.

'I'm sorry you didn't know,' he said. 'You should have been told. You should have been there at the funeral.'

'I wouldn't have gone anyway.' Her quick anger was surprising. Eddie thought she might flounce away, abandoning him, but she took his arm, pressing her fingers into the fabric of his coat. 'So you're on your own, Eddie. After all this time.'

Afterwards, Eddie thought he should have mentioned Maggie. He should have told Alice that Maggie was taking care of things, filling in, but she smiled at him with such sudden vehemence that he was flustered.

'I found what you'd written, all those years ago, in the book,' he said instead, feeling Alice's arm rested on his.

Alice showed no surprise. 'But Florrie? She never found it? Never read it?'

'Good Lord, no,' said Eddie. 'I don't think so. It was in a pile of old stuff.'

Alice was quiet. In the echo of the disused ballroom the years peeled away from her; the confusion of Florrie resounded everywhere like the shatter of breaking glass, kindling a desire that she had presumed was dead. She looked at Eddie, dazed, and smiled again.

Eddie pushed the door with his shoulder and the brush seal swooshed open. There was an elderly man with a walking stick making his slow way through the lobby. He did not seem to notice Eddie and Alice as they left the hotel, dowdy and unremarkable and with something inside each of them like fireflies.

They spoke on the telephone that evening, when Maggie was in the bathroom washing her hair. They agreed to meet again the following weekend. Neither of them could drive.

'We could catch the bus into Cornwall, to Looe,' Alice suggested.

'In November?'

'We could play the slotties,' she said. Eddie had no better suggestion.

Since it rained hard all day, they played the machines in the arcade many times over, changing their notes for halfpennies at the booth and watching them trickle away. Alice won once on the one-armed bandit, a meagre win that rattled into the tray faintly, but Eddie soon ran out of coins. He went out of the shimmering darkness to look at the sea. It was grey and choppy, the horizon shrunk. He felt Alice behind him.

'Would you like tea?' he asked, because they had to do something, and they went to a lace-windowed café tucked up behind the harbour. Alice ordered a scone with clotted cream. Eddie was suddenly uncomfortable, watching her eat, and Alice, looking across at him, took her time with the thick cream, fingering the crumbs, tempting him. He could not tell if she knew what she was doing.

After tea they wandered for a while in the rain, Alice keeping him at bay with the twirl of her umbrella, the spray dripping from the peak of Eddie's cap. They looked at the fishing boats in the harbour, moored up for low tide and they watched a child throw an apple core to the screeching gulls. They did not talk much. It was as if they could not risk it. Going home on the bus, crossing the new bridge back into Devon, when Eddie wanted to say something about what might have happened to them, he just watched instead as the great steel hawsers marked time outside the window. And when he got home that evening, he found he hadn't enjoyed himself in the way he'd expected. He felt as if he'd lost something.

They did not arrange to meet again. And even though Eddie had Alice's address now, and a phone number, he did not contact her. He found he could put her out of his mind. He did not read the letter.

But then Maggie found the loose pages of the book.

She had gone out to the shed to look for a screwdriver to tighten the handle on a saucepan. A large spider, thin-legged and quick, had scuttled across the bench in front of her making her stumble backwards, panicky, a scream tucked in her throat. She had knocked things, a spade and a bottle, and in the confusion of grabbing hands she had pulled the cloth from the pile of unbound sheets stacked in the corner of a low shelf. She was surprised at what she found. She brought one of the pages back into the kitchen, holding it gently by one edge, the screwdriver in her skirt pocket.

'What's this, Dad?' she called through.

She yanked back the edge of the corrugated plastic partition that pulled across between the kitchen and the lounge, a mucky bone colour. It squeaked on its runners.

'Look. This. From the shed.'

Eddie knew what she had found. He was surprised to feel his heart racing. 'It was Florrie's,' he said, not looking. 'A book. I found it when I was clearing the things.'

He turned to her then and held out his hand for the page. Maggie slipped it to him before disappearing behind the partition to deal with the crackles and spits from the stove. The paper was crisp and heavy, but not damp. Eddie held it up to the light from the wide bay window, looking for mushroom-brown spots or the stain of watermarks. It looked no different than the day he had dissected the volume. Nothing had affected it.

Maggie came into the lounge having turned down the heat. She took the page from her father and looked at it again. The forms and colours were strange. Creeping fronds of something, a tree or a vine, slid dark into the head of a snake. The page held her, but she did not like it. There was something brutal about it.

'It's beautiful,' she said nonetheless. 'Was it really Mum's? I've never seen it before. She never showed me.'

She handed the page back to Eddie, not wanting to think about Florrie with it. For a while they were both quiet.

'I never knew,' Maggie said at last, shuffling. It was the first time the memory of her mother had let her down.

Eddie felt sorry for her. 'Nor did I, my love, nor did I. It wasn't just you. It was hidden away in a cupboard, you see, at the back. She'd probably forgotten all about it.'

'But where did she get it, something like this?'

Maggie couldn't help touching it again and she fingered the page. Eddie watched her.

'I don't know.' He hesitated. 'It was a wedding present, I think. I remember it, vaguely. Someone gave it to us. It's a bit strange, a book, but there you are. I suppose they thought it'd be a change from mops and dusters and what have you…'

There was a sudden spat in the kitchen and Maggie hurried through. She was gone for some time, and their meal was ready and sitting on the plates on the high counter when she asked her father more about what she had found.

'It's not a book, though, is it, really? It's just pages. Separate pages. Why would someone give you that?'

'It was a book, before, when I found it,' said Eddie, bending to take the plastic bottle of sauce from the flip-doored cupboard beneath the counter. 'Just like a normal book.'

They carried their plates into the small dining room alongside the kitchen, little more than a large windowless cupboard. Eddie laid the page between them on the table.

'Why did you take it apart then?' Maggie slid in between the wall and her chair, knocking her knee, as she always did.

Eddie looked hard at the bacon chop on his plate. He cut a slice and chewed it, and while he was chewing he looked around. He had to think of something other than the letter, but Alice was there suddenly in the leaping shadows of the page in front of him, pert and provoking, and he could not look at Maggie or think of any answer for her.

'Dad? Why? Why take it to pieces?'

There were two side-by-side prints pinned to the wall above Maggie's head, their frames split at the corners and their colours faded, even in the dusk of the dining room. Eddie, surprised to see them, and not quite sure whether they had always been there, held on to their anonymity.

'I thought of making them into pictures, making some frames for them, perhaps,' he said, not quite looking at his daughter and aware of heat rising from the page on the table. 'They're handsome, I thought. It seemed a shame to keep them hidden away. Your mother would have liked it, you see; something of hers to have around.'

Maggie wiped her hand on her skirt and picked up the loose page again. She was wary.

'They're odd, though, don't you think? Are they all like this, the other pages?'

'More or less,' said Eddie, realizing he could hardly remember anything of them. 'But if you don't like them… it was only an idea, my love. I haven't done anything yet.'

Maggie thought she would not like them. Something about the pictures disturbed her. They warped the way she thought of Florrie. But she could not disappoint her father.

'No, it's a good idea. It'd be lovely. We could have them in the lounge, above the fire, if they're pretty ones. I could have one in my bedroom. How many are there? How many are you making?'

'Half a dozen I suppose, while I'm at it,' said Eddie. 'I could get the wood from Harper's – just a bit of half-inch, nothing fancy.'

'I could stain it though, or paint it.'

'If you like.'

Later that evening, taking a torch, Maggie brought in the pile of pages from the shed and sat on the floor in the lounge with them spread around her, their colours repeated in the brazen swirls of the carpet. They were very fine things, in their way. She tried hard to admire them, and she chose the ones that did not offend her, swapping pages in and out as she made up her mind. She resisted thinking of her mother.

Eddie tried not to watch. But Maggie in the half-light, her bare legs crossed and her hair falling long against her face as she deliberated over the pictures, was beautiful, and he could not help looking. And as he cut and sanded the wood for the frames in his shed over the next days, measured up carefully for the mitre joints, glued and pinned and sanded again, he knew what he was doing was an act of love. He did not want the work to stop, and when he had finished the six, and the pages were straight and flat inside their frames, he made two more from the remaining wood, beginning the meticulous process all over again with relief.

Tamed by their home-made frames the pages looked flat and orderly. Eddie wrapped the ones for Alice in brown paper and when he called around he held the parcel in front of him against his chest, feeling the slight warmth of it where it blocked the wind. The grey corrugated-metal walls of Alice's prefab, the iron-red door and the small windows could not be made to look cheerful even with the bunch of holly she had tied with scarlet ribbon to the knocker. The garden looked bare under a light covering of hard snow and the house next door was empty, the land around it tall with dead weeds. The granite outcrops of the moors loomed too close, as though they might tumble on to the fragile buildings below and crush them. But Alice was smiling as she answered the door, and inside the little lounge was bright and warm, with paper chains strung crisscross all ways, tinsel over the ornaments and bookcases, and a threadbare Santa propped up on the mantelpiece. There was the smell too of something, rum or sherry, warm and slightly musty, and Eddie felt the encircling, metallic consolation of his naval berth.

He did not sit down, but held out the parcel with stiff arms, forcing Alice to take it.

'I brought you something,' he said. 'For Christmas, I suppose. Happy Christmas.'

Alice sat down and put it next to her for a moment on the sofa, unopened. She rubbed her knees with her hands. Eddie watched the way her fingers clamped into the cloth of her skirt.

'You can sit, Eddie, if you like,' she said, but she did not press it because his unease was obvious.

They faced each other, their glances sliding away. Then Alice opened the paper and pulled out the first of the pictures. She held it far in front of her and for a long time it was there, suspended between them, the reflection of Christmas decorations spangling across its glass. They both watched the pulse of colours.

'Eddie,' said Alice, at last quietly. She pulled out the other pages quickly from the paper, propping them up against the back and the arm of the sofa. There were three of them. They were all, although Eddie did not know this, from towards the end of the book. Alice knew them exactly.

'You took it apart,' she said, in a tone Eddie could not catch.

He giggled. 'I had to get rid of what you'd written, my love.'

Alice ignored him and sat back from the pictures, not wanting to touch them. Her face was pale.

Eddie felt he should explain. 'I know it's a bit strange, when you gave the book to Florrie, to me and Florrie, for our wedding, and now things are, well, different. But I thought you'd like them, you see. I thought they were nice. And the book was doing nothing, in the cupboard, tucked away. No one was looking at it. And they are nice, aren't they?'

Alice could not speak, so Eddie filled the quiet.

'I could put them up for you. You can get things into the wall here, picture hooks or something, can't you? I brought some, in case.'

He held out a pile of shiny new picture hooks in the palm of his hand. He had not brought the bent and painted ones from his toolbox but had got a new packet from the hardware shop with Alice in mind.

Alice looked mechanically at what he was holding out to her.

Eddie sat down. 'Your decorations are lovely,' he said. 'Maggie used to make paper chains.'

'Where's the rest of it?' Alice's voice was uneven.

'The rest of the book? We've got some, Maggie and me, around the house. She picked them out, you see, the ones she wanted. And there're a few more pages which we've just put back in the cupboard. They're all right, though – they're not lost. It's just a bit much to have around.'

'I can't believe you took it apart,' said Alice, and she looked at Eddie for the first time. He felt like somehow he had cheated her.

Eddie flipped the picture hooks in his hand. Alice turned away from the frames on the sofa.

'Didn't you think it might be special? Didn't you *think*, Eddie?'

'Of course it's special. It's what you gave us. It's what you wrote in, my love. It's what brought us together again. It's a lovely book,' said Eddie.

Alice nodded slowly. 'I had the book a long time before I gave it to you at the wedding. It's like a part of me,' she said, her voice suddenly old, as though a lot of her life had passed since she had last spoken.

In response, Eddie was bright. 'And all the better you should have a bit of it back, to remind you.' He leaned forward, soft. 'It'll make you think of me, you see, when I'm not here.'

Alice looked at the pictures again.

'They make me think of my father,' she said, but Eddie had never known Arthur Craythorne and without an image in his mind the idea of him did not stick.

It could not go on, this staccato ballet of theirs, the emptiness of the years welling between them; it could not go on without them parting, and neither of them quite wanted that yet. So they drank tea laced with whisky, and they talked, after a while, about easier things, the snow that was forecast and heating costs. Eddie felt that the awkwardness had gone. He told a story he hardly remembered about one Christmas when his ship had been anchored off the South African coast and the crew had swum in the warm sea and lit bonfires on the sand and sung 'Silent Night' in Afrikaans.

'Christmas was never the same again,' he said. 'It was never so… well, exotic, after that.'

On and off, Alice looked at the pictures, warily, as if they might burn her.

'Shall I put them up for you?' said Eddie, after one of these glances.

Alice had hammer and nails of her own, but said yes anyway.

'Where do you want them then?' Eddie took the picture hooks from his pocket again and they twinkled in the light like more festive decorations.

'In the bedroom,' said Alice firmly.

For a moment, Eddie wondered if this was an invitation, but Alice padded past him in her slippers without catching his eye and when he followed her through with the pile of pictures to the little tin bedroom she was standing apart by the window.

'Opposite the bed, in a line,' she said. 'Where I can see them.'

And then she left him and Eddie struggled with the mechanics of fixing the pictures to the flimsy walls. As he straightened them finally in a row, he imagined turning back to see Alice spread-eagled on the bed, waiting for him, but he heard her clanking a pan in the kitchen instead and knew his visit was almost over.

'Thank you, Eddie,' she said primly when he had finished. She had her hands in a bowl of soapy water and Eddie stood by the entrance to the closeted kitchen.

'I just thought you'd like them,' he said. They were both aware of the soft shuffle of Eddie's hands against the wool of his best winter trousers. 'If you'd like, for Christmas, you could come round. You could meet Maggie.'

Alice smiled at him, leaning into the bowl, the bubbles rising up her arms. 'I don't know, Eddie… I'm not sure…'

'How about Boxing Day? Boxing Day at ours?' Eddie pressed.

'I don't think I should,' said Alice, resisting.

'Oh, but after everything – surely you don't want to let it go, Alice.' Eddie tried to think of a phrase from the letter, to entice her with, but he had only the unsteady sense of it; he could not pin it down. Instead he stepped in closer.

'After everything…' repeated Alice, lifting her hands from the bowl, letting them hang there, shiny and dripping. 'Well, yes, I suppose.' She shook off the suds and was suddenly matter-of-fact. 'I'll have to look at the buses.'

'Or I could order you a taxi.'

'Don't be silly, there's no need. It'd cost a fortune. I'll let you know,' said Alice.

When Eddie had gone, she went into the bedroom without turning on the light and though she could see nothing of the new pictures on her walls, she imagined every detail of them, the maddening curves she had traced with her finger when she sat with Arthur to read the poems, the threat of the familiar lines. And somewhere in what she saw were the faces of Eddie and her father, elongated, distorted, pulled tight as though reflected in the back of a spoon, but with the essence of them pungent. And above all this were the running words, the scrawled verses that pounded their unlost rhythms in her head and trampled her deeper and deeper into the soft mattress until she felt she could not breathe.

For the first time in many years, Alice's lungs clenched within her. Throughout the night she wheezed and puffed and rasped and in the morning she was too tired to leave her bed. She lay unmoving, hungry, watching a robin singing out by her window, and gazing a long time at the pictures on the wall, flat in the early light, unremarkable even. She thought then, at last, of Eddie's invitation.

'I'll not go,' she said, out loud resolved. 'I'll let her have him.'

She turned on her side, breathing heavily still, and closed her eyes. But the picture of Florrie and Eddie, together, was fixed there now; it would not shift. And Alice screamed out at it, broken-breathed, pushing herself up in the bed, slapping her hands hard into the pillow, screaming and pummelling, the echoes stinging from the corrugated walls. Only her exhaustion quietened her.

Alice took her time coming up to the house. She stood for a while by the open gate, without entering, apparently taking in everything there was to see, the sweep of the Tamar Bridge, the low flat school being built high up on the open fields opposite, the bungalow across the road with all its curtains drawn. She walked slowly up the path, taking each step purposefully, gingerly, as though the game she was playing would punish her for stepping on the crazed edges of the paving. And she spent a long time on the doorstep, quietly, deciding something. Maggie, who was waiting by the convector heater in the hallway, thought she must have gone.

But when she opened the door, Alice was there, looking back at her, unsurprised.

'Oh,' said Maggie, knowing already she had failed.

'I'm Alice.'

'Yes.'

'Your – aunt.'

'Yes.' Maggie had expected to feel sorry for Alice, or ashamed of her; she'd pictured someone shabby and dented. But now, with her aunt in front of her, she felt a skitter of fear.

'I've come to see your father. Well, and you too, if you're Maggie.'

Alice smiled a tense smile, fading flat. It brought Maggie to herself.

'Yes, of course, sorry. I *am* Maggie. Come in, won't you?'

Alice wiped her feet unnecessarily thoroughly on the brush mat, and stepped just far enough into the hall for Maggie to close the door behind her.

'You're one too, then,' she said, as if it were funny, and when Maggie turned she saw that Alice had taken the small plastic bottle of holy water from its niche on the windowsill by the door, had uncapped it and was sniffing it.

'It's—' began Maggie.

'Holy water. I know. It says.' Alice read, '"*Holy Water from Lourdes.*"'

'There's some in the little dish, too, if you want to, you know, bless yourself,' said Maggie.

Alice peered at the grey drips in the dish.

'It was Mum's,' Maggie said. 'She was Catholic.'

Alice turned sharply away with a snort and Maggie decided that everything she had heard about her aunt must be true.

Just then Eddie came down the stairs beaming, his best jacket brushed and buttoned, his tie tightly knotted. His eyes were shining and both women were surprised by how charming he looked.

'Good then,' said Eddie, generally. 'Good. Would you like a drink Alice?'

He pushed open the door to the lounge, ushering Alice and Maggie inside ahead of him and letting out the thick warm smells of the nearly cooked lunch.

Alice was disturbed by how much of Florrie was in the house, in the nasty mustard of the thick winter curtains, in the unabashed exuberance of the carpet, the twee pictures, the plastic, the cheap antimacassars crumpled in the corners of the sofa, the knitted doll propped drunkenly against the veneer of the electric fire, the crucifix tied from Palm Sunday reeds. It was exactly how she had always imagined her sister's home to be. It made her ashamed of Florrie, even now. She took a deep breath, tasting the beef that would come later, and Eddie handed her a glass of sherry, syrupy and dark. Maggie squeezed through the corrugated partition to the kitchen. There was quiet for a moment, just the sound of the meat spitting in the oven.

Alice did not drink from her glass but she held it tight. She looked at the cased pages hooked above the fireplace, picturing Maggie's plump hands tilting them straight. She wanted to tear down the frames and pull them to pieces, to gather up every last shred of her book and take it home and make it whole. She wanted to show Eddie what he had done, splintering her history into parts; show him how wrong it was, how absurd. She wanted to prove how differently she could do things. But she couldn't get started.

'It's just like her, like Florrie,' she said, gesturing around.

Eddie shrugged.

Maggie was dressing the table for the meal. Standing in the kitchen, pressing her back against the warmth of the oven, she realized that what had passed for festive the day before with her father – a candle he had taken from the naval stores and a paper cracker each – would not do. There was something demanding about Alice. So she knelt on the floor and reached into the back of the low cupboards, taking out boxes, moving jars and bottles, unpacking parcels tied in greaseproof, until she had found three more or less matching tissue doilies, like limp snowflakes, a packet of red paper napkins, the rest of the box of Christmas crackers and four solid cake-top figures (three snowmen and a Santa). Reaching in the cabinet above the fridge, where Florrie had kept the first aid, she also took down a whole roll of cotton wool and a small handbag mirror. While her father and aunt were talking, she was manoeuvring these into a simple vision of arctic life, and by the time the roast potatoes had browned and Eddie and Alice were called through, she had pulled out the dining table to its furthest extent, laid three neat places with the doilies and the best bone-handled cutlery, and created a small winter pond in the centre with the snowmen perched on cotton-wool hills. On the handbag-mirror pond Santa idled perilously. It felt to Maggie like a grander Christmas altogether, and she expected someone to praise her for her inventiveness. But when her father and Alice edged around the loaded worktop into the cramped dining room there was burning air eddying between them and they did not notice, or did not mention, Maggie's decorations.

Maggie was awkward with the silence of the meal and after lunch, convinced that her aunt was rude and unreachable, she went upstairs. She had a small boxroom at the front of the house, just large enough for a single bed, a hanging rail for her clothes that her father had concealed with a curtain, and several bookshelves on which there were no books. Its window took up almost all of the outside wall, and so light poured in even on a dull day. Maggie stood for a while, looking out. Two children rode by on bicycles, Christmas-new and shiny, but otherwise the street was quiet. She listened for her father and Alice downstairs, but they were quiet too. She lay back into the thick panel of sunlight spread across the bed, her feet hanging loose over her pillow and she closed her eyes, heavy from her lunch and sleepy. She lay a long time, feeling the sun on her face, floating just outside of sleep, trying not to cry.

Eddie and Alice did not miss Maggie. They were standing close together in front of the low sink; they were moving so harmoniously with the ebb and flow of the plates from one side of the draining board to the other, that it was as if they were dancing. Alice's flourish of the checked tea towel flagged their rhythm and the hot water, spitting from the small boiler above the sink, syncopated the beat.

But as Alice bent to pick up a knife from the draining board, the chrome nozzle below the boiler suddenly spewed steam and hot water sprayed across her hands and face. She leapt back from the sink and squealed (a noise that Maggie heard vaguely in her half sleep) pressing the damp tea towel close around her face. As soon as the momentary shock had passed, she knew it was not serious, but Eddie was alarmed. He dropped the pan into the water and caught Alice by the shoulders, pushing her back until she was wedged against the fridge, at the same time hush-hushing reassurance. He trembled as he went to prise away the tea towel she was still clutching to her face, perhaps because he was frightened of seeing the raw-red blotches of a serious scald, and, for the briefest of moments, he could not look directly at her, seeing instead the way her blouse tucked down around the dimple in her neck. But then, when he did look after all, there was just a sprinkling of faint red freckles across one cheek and the ridged markings from the pressure of the tea towel, and the provocation of unspoken words in the way she held her mouth.

It was not a tender moment. Eddie's kiss was not gentle; there was no caution in the way he held her. It was rushed and fumbled and anxious, teenage in its brutality, and even before he had drawn back, Eddie felt awkward and slightly ashamed. Alice felt the walls of the years collapsing. This is what she had been waiting for, to have him come at her like this, to have him choose her. It was not a surprise. But all she could taste was the lingering mustiness of wet tea towel, the tang of soap and the stale sweetness of regret.

The look of Alice, the light on her face, the tense-drawn passion around her eyes, disturbed Eddie because it was not Florrie. Florrie would have laughed him away, struck out at him perhaps with the cloth. Alice wanted him still, wanted more of him, wanted to curl the dark edges of Christmas around them both until they were forgotten. He stood back from her, dull.

'It's always like that. It's the washer or something,' he said. 'I had a look at it once, but couldn't do anything with it. I'm sorry, Alice – I should have done something before. Florrie always wanted to change it.'

She did not look away as he spoke Florrie's name.

'I'm fine. It stung, that's all,' she said.

Eddie flicked out the tea towel. 'I'd better finish up,' he said. 'You sit down. There'll be a film on if you like.'

And she passed through the partition so that he could breathe again. She sat on the edge of the sofa rubbing a spot on her calf where a drip of water had splashed against her tights.

Eddie remembered Maggie. He listened for her, and thought he heard the scratch of her record player, but could not be sure. The first thing he did, when he finished in the kitchen, was to call up the stairs but she did not hear, or at least did not respond.

'She'll be asleep, I reckon,' he said to Alice, half turned away from her, holding the door to the hall still open so that they could feel the cold air rolling over them.

'Florrie all over, that's what she is,' said Alice.

It was not a compliment.

'Still, she's a good girl,' said Eddie.

'Keep the draught out, Eddie. Come and sit down,' said Alice, flinging a gesture vaguely towards the other end of the sofa.

But Eddie went to sit apart, in his armchair.

Maggie turned up her music and they heard the faint trickle of it.

'With her mother – well, you know, she's…' Eddie looked at the ceiling. 'I want to tread carefully with her, Alice.'

Not quite understanding, Alice nodded.

'She doesn't know anything. She hasn't seen the letter or anything,' Eddie added, leaning forward. He reached for his tin of tobacco and turned it in his hands many times before speaking again. 'You've never said about it, Alice – the letter at the front of the book. What you wrote there, to me.'

Alice frowned. It all seemed a long way off. 'But that was for Florrie, Eddie not for you.

The book was for both of you, I suppose, at the wedding, but the letter, that was meant for Florrie – surely you could see that when you read it.' Her voice fell. 'Anyway, it doesn't really matter, in the end, because, well, we never...'

Eddie put the tin on his knees. He was adamant. 'That was never to Florrie, my love. It was to me. Addressed to me. You must remember. It was – you know, a love letter, Alice.'

'Eddie, I think I would know.' Alice clipped her words.

'It was a long time ago. If you don't remember...'

'Eddie, I do remember – of course I remember. Everything. But...' She puffed at him. 'Look, you've still got it? The letter?'

'Of course. Upstairs.'

'Well then. We'll read it. I'll show you,' said Alice.

Eddie flipped the tin and began to roll a cigarette. 'Not now. Not with Mags here,' he said, licking along the paper, concentrating on the folds of it.

'Oh come on, Eddie – it can't be that bad. It's not going to... she's not a child.'

Eddie shook his head and held the new cigarette between them. 'You really don't remember, do you?'

He sat back and lit the roll-up, blue smoke twirling around his fingers. Alice saw that she had let him down somehow; he was hunched and awkward, dissatisfied. If she lost him again, she knew it would be a failure. She nudged herself from the sofa and came to crouch on the floor at Eddie's feet, her arms on his knees, looking up at him in a way Florrie, with her extra height, rarely had. She was taut and strange in the growing shadows of the December afternoon, the smoke twisting over her.

'Come on, Eddie,' she said. 'I forgive you for spoiling my book.'

Eddie thought it was a pleasantry. He blew the smoke away and smiled at her. 'You were always a funny girl, Alice Craythorne.'

And then Alice took her hands from Eddie's knees and leaned forward, her weight pushing his legs apart, her lips firm. What she did next seemed to seal it, finally, between them.

Eddie's cigarette burnt through and dropped ash on the arm of the chair. After Alice had pulled away again, solemn, drawing her arm across her mouth, he flicked it off and tipped the spent dog-end into the ashtray.

'Well,' he said, prefacing something, but then they heard Maggie on the stairs and Alice sprang to her feet and went to the window, and Eddie brushed himself down and the length of Florrie's room extended between them.

Maggie pushed hard at the door. 'I thought there might be a film on,' she said, not looking at her aunt.

'I'll walk you to the bus, Alice,' said Eddie. 'I'll just get my coat.'

But Alice was sharp with him. 'There's no need. I'll be fine. You stay, Eddie. You stay with Maggie.'

Eddie went to shake his head. He had things he needed to say to her. But Maggie moved across to her father and took his hand. 'You can stay and watch with me, Dad,' she said, claiming him.

Mary came to see Eddie one Thursday afternoon on her way back from a shift at the hospital. She was still wearing her uniform, though she had a duffel coat unbuttoned over it. At first, seeing her warped by the pear-shaped window in the front door,

Eddie did not recognize her. He had not been expecting anyone. With the call of bluetits bouncing in the spring air, he was making a bird-table for the back garden and had a head full of fractions.

'Eddie, it's me. Mary Baker,' she said through the door, after she had rung the second time.

'Mary?'

The door was on its safety chain and only opened a crack. Eddie was clumsy unfastening it.

'Are you all right, Mary? Is everything all right, my love?'

Mary puffed her way through the hall and into the lounge. She did not take off her coat and she did not sit down. There was something stiff and urgent about her. Eddie was sure that a calamity had happened.

'The boys? And Charlie? They're all right?'

'They're fine,' said Mary, sharp-edged. 'Eddie, it's you I've come about. You and Alice.'

'Alice?'

The name sounded strange like that, apart from her. Eddie shuffled. He wanted to sit down, but Mary remained tight, hardly through the door, waiting.

'You found her, I heard,' she said. It was a way of starting it.

'Yes, before Christmas – by chance,' Eddie said. 'I'd given up, you see – I'd tried everything. And then there she was.'

'Eddie, it's Alice.'

'It was in the Continental of all places. She was just sitting there,' said Eddie. Still, even now, it struck him as miraculous. He thought perhaps Mary would see that too. But Mary did not seem impressed.

She stepped further into the room. 'Eddie, I've been wondering – what made you think of her, after Florrie? What made… it's not like… you didn't find… ?'

She did not move. Eddie edged past her. 'It was like I said. I bumped into her, at the Continental. Shall I take your coat, Mary?'

'But before that, Eddie? When you were looking for her? What made you look for her?'

He reached out a hand, but Mary clung to the lapel of her duffel coat and Eddie shrugged. 'Something put me in mind of her, that's all.'

'Something?' Mary's voice was brittle.

'Some poems,' he said. 'Something of Florrie's – a book. Nothing really.'

Mary knew then what she had done and seeing him in front of her, swaying from one foot to the other in front of the television, flicking the loose end of his tape measure with his thumb, puffed-up, she did not care if she offended him.

'Well, it's disgusting, Eddie. Don't you see that? Don't you see it's… it's… sick?'

Eddie said nothing. He recalculated the arithmetic for the bird-table.

'When I first heard, I thought it might be nice to have Ally back, to see her again. I was going to ring you and invite you both over, and Maggie. I was going to have a family thing. But then when they said it was something more. When they saw you kissing. *Kissing*, Eddie. At the bus station. There, in front of people, kissing Alice…'

The idea hung in the room. Eddie tried to put the knot of calculations from his head. He thought he should say something.

'I don't know that can be right, Mary.'

She huffed. 'Of course it's right.'

Eddie ran the tape measure smoothly across his palm. 'No, I don't think so. You see we've only been into Cornwall, that's all, on the bus. They can't have seen us, at the bus station, doing that – really, Mary, they can't. We didn't.'

'You haven't kissed her then?'

Eddie stepped away slightly. 'Who told you all this, Mary?'

'Never mind that. A friend of mine. It doesn't matter. What matters is... did you kiss her, Eddie?'

Mary spat the words at him, and he closed his eyes for a moment.

'It's a rumour,' he said then. 'That's all. Why would we be like that, at the bus station, at our age?'

And he might have left it at that, but Mary pressed in on him. 'You shouldn't get it in your head, Eddie, that she ever... you shouldn't think she loves you, you know.'

Eddie moved away to the bureau, lifted down the front flap and took out a stubby pencil with which he wrote his bird-table measurements on a strip of paper, to free his mind from them.

'Mary, I don't think you know about it,' he said then, suddenly sharp.

'Believe me, Eddie – I know all about it. Everything.'

'It's between us, the two of us. Between Alice and me. If I kissed her, it's just between us.'

'And did you? Did you kiss her, Eddie?'

Eddie looked straight at her, nodding slightly, stubborn. 'I might have done,' he said. 'Once. But not at the bus station, Mary – not like that.'

Mary squealed. 'Good God, Eddie, it's Florrie's sister.'

'Florrie's dead, my love.'

'Exactly. Florrie's dead. And here you are, running round like this…' She spread her arms as if that would explain it.

Eddie's voice was flat and firm. 'Look, we're doing no harm, Mary. We're just – it's something from a long time ago. I can't see it's anything to do with you.' He wanted to tell her that everything was justified by the letter, by words that had been written into his history, but Mary was desperate with him.

'Of course it's to do with me. She's my sister. And I feel responsible.'

'I know Alice is your sister—'

'And Florrie! Florrie. Have you forgotten her Eddie?'

Mary took a deep breath that swelled her duffel coat and that she did not seem to let out. Her next words came strongly.

'I'll tell Maggie,' she said. 'If you don't stop, if you go on with this, then Maggie needs to know. It's only fair on the girl. And I'll tell her, Eddie, so help me I will. If you can't stop this… this… mess.'

Eddie folded his strip of paper neatly, over and over, until it was just a tiny square, straight-edged and symmetrical.

'I'll tell Maggie myself,' he said. 'She's seen Alice here – she saw her at Christmas. She won't mind.'

'Then why haven't you told her before?'

'There's nothing to tell, Mary.' He looked up from his origami, resisting her desperation.

'No? She doesn't need to know that you and her aunt, her mother's sister, are – are, what, Eddie? In love?' Mary smiled crookedly at the thought.

Eddie put his hands flat towards her, as though preparing for a push. 'Just go, Mary. Just leave it.'

'No, Eddie. I won't just leave it. I need to know. I need to be sure you're not going on with it. If not…' She glanced vaguely in the direction of Maggie's empty bedroom. 'And she'll hate you, Eddie, when I tell her. She'll feel left out and let down. She'll think it's disgusting – it's not natural. It's weird. It'll make her sick. It makes me sick.'

Eddie pictured Maggie, as he had once imagined her, when he had been a long time at sea and she was small and undiscovered, landlocked.

'You know what I feel about Maggie. You know she's the world to me now,' he said.

'Well then.' Mary shrugged her coat higher on to her shoulders.

'You don't have the right to come in and make me choose against her, Mary. It's not like that. Alice… Alice wants us to be together,' he said, intractable.

Mary grunted a half laugh. 'Alice? Oh, and that's all right, is it, what Alice wants – it doesn't matter about Maggie and Florrie and me and… Why is it always Alice?'

'It's both of us,' said Eddie.

'Bah!'

Mary looked around her. The room appeared much as it always had done, in Florrie's time, but shabby now and suddenly old-fashioned. There were some gaudy new pictures on the wall, hung unevenly over the fireplace, freakish and creepy. But she could see no obvious sign of Alice. That, at least, was something.

'Look, this thing, with Alice,' Eddie began. He was surprised, now that he had to stand up for her, how faint Alice's face was in his head, how dingy with memories, with Florrie standing tall, away from them. But there was the covenant of the letter between them, binding them, making an irrevocable claim on him, and his words came strongly. 'Look, it's not weird,' he said. 'Not at all. You've not seen her for years. You hardly know her. You can't say.'

Mary buttoned her coat with quick hands. 'Finish it, Eddie. You can't love her. Not a woman like that.' She raised her eyebrows, damning her sister.

Eddie flicked the square of paper nimbly through his fingers, like some kind of trick. They both watched the dance of it.

'I need to catch Harper's now before they shut. I need some two-by-two,' he said, holding out the folded note as evidence.

He stepped towards her, forcing her towards the door.

'But you'll do it, Eddie? You'll finish it?'

He picked up his hat from the shelf in the hallway. 'I'll think about it,' he conceded.

'Promise me. Promise me, Eddie. I can't have this going on any longer. Not when I think of poor Florrie.'

She touched Eddie very lightly on the arm.

'I can't promise, Mary. I won't do that,' he said, fitting his hat. His face was unreadable.

They were nice to each other as they went down the front path together, although Eddie was so tight inside himself that he did not know what was being said. Nor did he see anything as they stood for a moment by the gate, Mary picking out landmarks across the river. Everything was inside him, twisted.

Beyond that there was nothing. But it happened anyway that Mary turned up the hill for her bus, pulling her coat close across her chest, and Eddie turned downhill, walking quickly, not looking back. And when she got home, Mary told her husband what had happened while she was standing up cooking tea, and he patted her on the shoulder, so that she would know she had done right. And Eddie, when he got to Harper's, argued intensely with the shop boy about what size and cut of timber was best for his job, leaving in the end with none at all, and feeling so ashamed of himself as he climbed the hill back home that he looked up at the cloud-trimmed sky and wailed.

He wanted to take Alice something. He spent the lengthening evenings in his shed making the bird-table, fixing the roof with felt so that it would be waterproof, and sanding off the edges so they were smooth. He made a little plaque out of chipboard and painted it white. Then he carefully traced the letters of her name on to it and went over them in blue paint, exact and symmetrical. He liked the shape of it. He nailed the plaque to the front of the bird-table, wrapped the whole thing in plastic, and put it carefully into a sturdy bag.

Alice was in the garden of her prefab, bending to take out the browning stems of winter-dead plants. He watched her for a moment, stooped and garden-gloved, before she saw him. When he began to explain, he did not mention Mary. He did not want Alice to think he had given in.

'I just need time, before we go on. I need to think about Maggie,' he said.

'About Maggie. What's the matter with the girl? For pity's sake, Eddie...' She stopped herself.

'But with her mother. With it being like it is, Alice...'

Alice let the stems fall from her hand into the small bucket by her feet. 'She doesn't like me I suppose,' she said, without rancour.

'I don't know. It's not that – she hasn't said.' Eddie picked up a dropped twig with his free hand and threw it into the bucket with the others. 'I think it's just – it's just Florrie.'

'Ah, Florrie.' Alice nodded. 'Come inside. We'll talk about it inside.'

'I can't – I can't come in. It wouldn't do.'

Alice laughed. 'Wouldn't do?' she prodded. 'Eddie, don't be such a fool.'

Eddie thought about Mary's friends, on a pavement somewhere, shaking their heads at his transgression, disgracing him. 'I don't want it to start up again. That's what I've come to say. I'm not coming in, Alice.'

'What do you think'll happen? What do you think I'll do to you if you come in?'

Alice leaned one foot against the tin wall of her house, shaded her eyes from the sun, and looked at Eddie. He did not answer.

'I don't know why you've come,' Alice said flatly.

'I had to.'

'To say we couldn't go on together? That Florrie wouldn't like it.'

'No. Not that. Alice, listen... I know it's what you've always wanted. I know you've been thinking of it, for ages...'

'Me!'

Eddie ignored her. 'But I have to think of Maggie. I have to be fair to her. And you know we've never really – it's been strange between us, Alice.'

Alice shrugged. 'I thought it was going pretty well.' She remembered the way he had looked at her in the sparkle of the Christmas decorations. 'I didn't think you'd give me up. I didn't think you'd still be fretting about Florrie.'

'I'm not fretting. It's not Florrie.'

'What is it then?'

Eddie felt the bag with the bird-table cutting into his palm and changed it to the other hand. 'I have a daughter, Alice – I have Maggie. And she wouldn't like it, you know she wouldn't like it.'

'But you haven't asked her?'

'No, I can't do that.'

Alice took a step towards him now. Her voice prickled. 'And what about you? What do you want? Aren't you going to stand up for me?' Eddie blinked at her. 'Ah, you're a coward. Just Florrie's sorry sop of a husband.'

She spun away, catching the bucket as she did so with her leg and toppling it. The collection of faded weeds scattered across the ground.

Eddie caught at her arm, pulling her back. 'Listen, Alice, it was you who started it. It was you who wanted it. Do you remember, all those years ago, out at the reservoir – the things you said to me, the filth. And then the letter… Blimey! What am I going to tell Maggie? What am I going to say about you? I can't tell her I fell for that.'

He held tight to her, nonetheless, and she did not pull away.

'I just wanted you for myself,' Alice said quietly.

They stood for a moment, unmoving, and then Eddie shook his head and let go of her arm. 'I don't understand. Really, I don't understand. Do you love me, Alice?'

'It's never that simple, Eddie, is it?' she said. 'Not at our age.'

'No, but if you love me, Alice. I can't believe that after what you said, even so long ago, you don't at least… but if you just tell me…' Eddie looked away.

And in that sidelong glance, Alice glimpsed the familiar twisted figures of Arthur's book. She picked up her bucket. 'You're not the man I thought you were, Eddie,' she said. But it did not sound like a criticism.

Alice went inside, leaving the front door slightly ajar, disappearing into the unlit rooms. Then there was no sign of her within and no sound. Eddie felt awkward. Moving on to the gravel path he saw that his feet had left slight dark depressions in the short turf of Alice's lawn. He had been standing very still. His bag hung loose in his hand. Beyond the small estate, the stones on the moors blinked in the sun and he could hear a curlew whooping, the call drifting away on the breeze. He didn't know what to do next.

5. Alice

FOURTEEN YEARS LATER, in a semi-detached house in a loop-backed crescent of other semi-detached houses, Maggie was watching television. She was alone. She had switched on the twirling red glow of the electric fire for comfort. It was not a particularly cold day. On the screen a man in a trim blazer was valuing antiques. The programme had been recorded earlier in the year, with the summer sun high and strong, casting few shadows across the queue of visitors waiting their turn to see the expert. The lawns of the stately Georgian house where filming was taking place were parched, and every now and again the valuer took a handkerchief from his pocket to wipe his forehead discreetly. Maggie waited. There was some discussion about hallmarking, and the difficulty of cleaning silver without causing damage. This did not interest her. But then, she knew, it would have to come, the moment she loved, when the man leaned forward, the camera steady on his face, and the bringers-in of attic goods held their breath in case they were suddenly rich.

It did not happen this time. The silver was apparently patched and stained and of more intellectual than financial interest. Maggie grinned. She went through to the kitchen where she cut some cheese precisely into cubes and set it on a small plate with some cored slices of apple. She carried her plate back to the living room, kicking the door closed behind her, and she was spreading butter on a Cornish wafer when she realized what was being said on the television. It was a different expert, greyer-haired, bespectacled, but with the same guarded enthusiasm as the first. He was wearing white cotton gloves.

'William Blake's *Songs of Innocence and Experience*. You know it's a very rare book, in this edition. Very rare,' he was saying, nodding.

The woman who had brought it to the table nodded too. Maggie turned to look at the framed picture her father had made and which she had strung by the door into the kitchen. She remembered the pile of pages in Eddie's garden shed, the discomforting sprawl of them. She held her breath, her cracker mid-air, only partly buttered.

'It just gathers dust,' said the woman. 'No one reads it.'

The valuer opened it at the first page and couldn't help smiling. 'Isn't it lovely? It's in outstanding condition, really beautiful,' he said. He rested his gloved finger lightly on the frontispiece for the camera. 'It's a piece of history.'

The woman shrugged. 'It was my husband's, my late husband's. It was given to him, I believe, by his godfather as a confirmation present. You can see, it's inscribed.'

She went to point out the faded dedication on the flyleaf, but the valuer found it first, held it for the cameras and smiled.

'Ah yes,' he said. 'Very nice. *To John, May you build Jerusalem in England's green lands*. Taken, of course, from Blake's well-known poem, "Jerusalem". It's a very erudite confirmation present if I may say so.'

He made it clear he was joking with her. He smiled directly at her, leaned forward.

'My husband was like that,' she said, and thousands of viewers heard how dreary she had found her marriage.

The valuer thought it best to press on. He started with the binding.

'It's a lovely calfskin binding, with very elaborate gilt decoration on the spine,' he said, fingering it through his gloves. 'Those of us who collect bindings would love it just for that, whatever was inside. It's really very fine.'

Maggie put her cracker down on the table. The woman on the screen was swallowing heavily.

'And it's a very fine edition too, the 1839 edition,' went on the expert. 'It's the first printed edition, by Pickering of London, and it only amounted to a relatively small number of copies. It's hard to be sure, but perhaps only a hundred in all. Blake was nowhere near as popular then as he is now. But this was a turning point, this edition. It started to get him noticed. This particularly, the *Songs*, this was what fascinated people.' He read the title again. '*Songs of Innocence and Experience, Shewing the Two Contrary States of the Human Soul*. Blake died in 1827 – very poor, unknown – but this was an attempt by the publishers to reinstate him, posthumously of course.'

The woman nodded. She had her head slightly on one side, pressing him. The valuer turned the pages and Maggie remembered the sweet, vegetable smell of the paper she had found in her father's shed.

'As to value,' the expert said, and the hum around him seemed to die. 'Well, an heirloom like this, something of your husband's, I'm sure it's not something you would sell. But for insurance purposes, you should be thinking around the five- to six-thousand-pound mark, I should think. Which is quite a lot, for a book.'

Maggie knew from the short dip of silence that the woman had hoped for more.

'Gosh,' said the woman. 'My goodness.'

Maggie too felt deflated. It had seemed like a bigger moment than it had turned out to be.

But then the expert went on. 'Of course, if this had been the *hand-painted* edition of the *Songs*, etched by William Blake himself, with beautiful, watercolour plates… Well, that would have been a lost treasure, indeed. There are only perhaps thirty known copies in the world. Every major library and museum would have been interested in that.'

His words buckled with awe. He paused, hoping the woman would ask him. She could not help herself.

'And how much would that have been worth then?'

'At auction, today, well… perhaps a hundred, even a hundred and fifty thousand pounds. Perhaps substantially more. It's impossible to say, but it's a very desirable thing, very collectable. And there's so much interest now in William Blake.'

The camera panned back to the book on the table, small and brown.

'I see,' said the woman tightly.

Maggie did not know about hand-coloured plates and limited editions. She knew very little at all about books. But she trembled anyway. She stood, brushing the crumbs from her soft trousers, and reached down the picture from the wall. The glass was dusty, smeared in one corner, and the tape on the back was so dry that it unpeeled without effort. Maggie took out the page to have a closer look at it. She turned on another light. She laid the paper on her low glass table, peering down at it. She tried to remember what the valuer had said. She tried to understand. And it looked special to her, now. She could see, she thought, the smudged outlines where the artist might have painted. But behind her, the music was playing for the end of the programme. There would be no more clues. And she could not be sure. She might be making a fool of herself. She rang Eddie.

'Did you see, Dad, that programme just now, on the telly, with the antiques?'

Eddie had been dozing. He had been retired for three weeks, since the day following his sixty-fifth birthday, and he felt he had been slumbering ever since.

'Well, er – some of it, my love.'

'Did you see the book, Dad?'

'No, I don't think so. I saw the clock. With the green face.'

Maggie didn't know what to say. 'Never mind. I just wondered, that was all… Never mind.'

'Right you are then.' And Eddie just put it down to something else that had come between them, warped by the miles, and was sorry. He dropped back in his chair.

Maggie wiped her fingers on the arm of the sofa and picked up the page again, holding it close to her face, squinting. She remembered the stiffness of the paper. It was not ordinary paper, she knew that at least. It was old, perhaps rare; the kind of paper people might collect. There was a page number at the top and of course the illustration, two figures crouched in something like a cave, recoiling from the brilliance of the light. There was nothing else. She knew this, even though she turned it over to make sure.

Maggie was surprised at the way the excitement skipped inside her; at the way the thought of the book clung to her. By the time she got off the bus in the city the next morning, with her page in a large brown envelope under her arm, she was feeling light-headed, as though she hadn't slept. She would be late for work, that was obvious, but she had not bothered to ring in. She wondered what she would say to them afterwards, when she had found out about the book. She wondered if she would tell them that she was rich, and no longer needed to type.

Usually, as she went past the library, the blue-uniformed porters were pinning back the iron gates. She had never taken much notice. There were blankets, sometimes, or boxes, left by whoever had spent the night on the wide steps, and there was a police car once parked on the pavement and an officer talking into his radio. But the shadowed red sandstone walls sank away from the traffic, and the building, despite its magnificence, seemed hidden. Maggie had only remembered at the last minute that it was a library, belonging somehow to the university, a place filled with people who made it their life's work to know about books.

Maggie climbed the long flight of stone steps that led up from the galleried entrance hall, counting them in her head and expecting any minute to be stopped and turned away. But no one came, and she climbed steadily upwards until she emerged into the corner of the reading room, a great stone hall, dim and slightly unreal in the grey light that slunk through the high windows. In front of her was a long wooden counter, imposingly tidy, and she presumed the man there would be able to help her. But he did not even allow her to open the envelope, simply asking her to take a seat on one of the low benches that hugged the walls. Maggie waited. The grand vaulted ceiling, the shivering stained glass, the rows of statues, and the dense city silence, induced in her the need to pray, but she could not conjure anyone to pray to. Feeling uneasy, she fidgeted. She slid along the bench, the cold stone stinging through her skirt. She shifted her envelope to her knees. She imagined the pomp of a white-flowered wedding in the splendid nave. She wondered about taking off her high heels, so that she did not damage the close-wedged patterns of wooden flooring. She watched the man behind the counter sharpening pencils.

The librarian, in the end, came down a twisting flight of steps in the dark corner of the library and Maggie did not see him until he paused at the counter. Then he looked in her direction, a man with a brown tie, soft shoes and white cotton gloves. She stood up. He was hurried and, although he tried to conceal it, bored.

'Won't you just come this way, to one of the alcoves,' he said.

Maggie followed him into a dim niche and he turned on a shell-shaded lamp.

'Right then,' he said, when they were seated next to each other at the heavy carved desk. 'And what is it you want to show me?'

Maggie took the sheet from the envelope. 'I want some advice,' she said. 'About this book.'

She held the page towards him, her hand flat beneath it. The tremble of the paper betrayed her. The librarian spoke first without looking at it.

'It's not a book, though, is it? It's a page.' Deliberately slowly, as if punishing her, he took the sheet from her hands. He glanced at it, to make sure that it was nothing, and then he brought it close towards him and looked at it again. He looked a long time and the texture of his face thickened.

'Where did you get this?' He was unexpectedly fierce.

'It's mine. Well, my father's really. But I have this one at home. He gave it to me.'

The librarian looked at her as though she had done some-thing wrong. 'You know what this is?'

His tone annoyed Maggie.

'No, not really. That's why I brought it to you. I thought you might know,' she said, trying not to bait him. 'I thought I saw something about it, on the television, but I wasn't sure.'

The librarian leaned back in his chair, then after a moment he got up without saying anything to Maggie and went behind to a cupboard, from which he took out a blue velvet cushion and a string of white beads. He took a long time arranging the cush-ion on the table and the page upon it, weighing down the edges with the beads, although they hardly curled. And by the time he had finished, he had forgiven Maggie for surprising him.

'It's really very beautiful,' he said softly, and for a moment, leaning over the page, he was alone with what he saw there.

Then he stepped back slightly, and made Maggie look. He talked about things she did not understand, about incunabula and folios and fugitive pigments. He showed her the way the etching had left shadow lines pressed into the paper but sheep-ishly, as though he knew she was just pretending to be ignorant. He read the lines of poetry to her, as though they were familiar to them both. He went away and came back with another book, a thick, plastic-bound catalogue of some sort, and he showed her the list of the existing known copies of Blake's masterpiece, each slightly different, each given an identifying letter and locked away in one of the world's great libraries.

'They're all complete,' he said, 'all of them. There's none of them missing an odd page like this. Your page isn't some kind of loose sheet that's gone missing. It's another book entirely, a clue to another copy that's been lost, broken up. It's a version we didn't even know existed.' He paused, but did not raise his eyes from the paper. 'There are perhaps just a few pages, like this one, remaining. But what you have here proves, at least, that it once existed. It's a page from *Songs of Experience*. Very beautiful, and very important. There'll be a lot of interest, even in this one page.'

He shook his head at the wonder of things.

'No, but you see that's just it,' said Maggie. 'We have the book. All of it. But just broken up, like this, to make pictures. They're not even very nice pictures. I don't like them really. They're too…' She couldn't explain. 'Anyway, then I saw a programme about it on television and I thought our book might be something, and I wanted to make sure.' She felt giggly.

The librarian narrowed his eyes at her, not allowing himself to understand. 'You have the whole book? Every page?'

'Yes, I think so. My dad took it to pieces years ago in his shed.'

The librarian gurgled. He shook his head again.

Maggie pressed on. 'So what should I do?' She did not dare mention value.

'Do?' It was all he could manage.

'With the book. If it's, you know, important, like you say.'

The librarian took the page from its cushion and put it back in Maggie's envelope with great tenderness. 'If you really do have all the pages—'

Maggie interrupted. 'We probably have the cover too somewhere. Dad never throws anything away.'

'Well, if you have everything, then bring it all, together, and we'll have a look,' said the librarian, not able to resist thinking about the marvel of this.

'And it would be worth something, then?'

He smiled at her. 'Each page is worth something, of course it is. But if you have everything, then the value would be greatly increased. Yes, it would be worth something.'

'Good,' said Maggie, pleased she had come.

The librarian was still tidying away his tools into the cupboard when she left. He shook her hand. The man behind the counter was still sharpening pencils. The unravelling excitement that was filling Maggie's head with thorns did not ripple the library's careful calm, and it was a relief to break out again into the dust and traffic and late rush-hour noise and whoop her joy, discreetly, into the dense hurrying crowds. When she arrived late at work, she took the plastic cover from her typewriter without stopping first to explain herself at the supervisor's office and when he called her through later to account for her uncharacteristic lack of punctuality, she could not stop smiling.

Maggie wondered how she was going to tell her father about the book. It couldn't be done, she decided, over the phone. It was too momentous. She wanted to watch his face as she told him. So she arranged to visit, but gave no reason.

'I just want to see you, Dad,' she said on the telephone.

Eddie fretted about what this could mean. In the wan night hours he conjured many unpleasant explanations, he imagined disease and bankruptcy and disgrace, but, when it came to it, he was baffled by Maggie's distress at finding the framed pages by the fireplace had disappeared.

'Where've they gone, Dad? What have you done with them?'

'I didn't like them there,' said Eddie. 'They were too… they seemed out of place.'

'But what have you done with them?'

'Nothing. They're around somewhere.' Eddie held his arms loosely in front of him, wanting to hug his daughter, but Maggie clapped her hands, puffing at the damp cold and he was put off. 'Would you like a drink? I've got some brisket in the oven, a nice piece. But it'll be an hour or so.'

It was something Florrie would have said, he knew that. It did not come from him. But he had queues of questions in his head, and Maggie had been away for so long he did not quite know what to do.

'I'm fine,' said Maggie. Her edginess kept her apart.

'Well, there's nothing much else changed. It's more or less the same, you'll find. Even your room, you see. I've not been getting rid of you.'

He laughed a little, and Maggie did, too, after a moment. Everything, she saw, was the same, except for the pictures. She would have to take her father's word on those.

'I'll get my bags,' she said.

Straight after they had eaten, Eddie turned on the television and pulled his chair closer to watch. It was not a programme he liked. Maggie went upstairs. Her boxroom seemed poky and cramped. There was nowhere to put her case. She pulled back the curtains and leaned on the shallow windowsill, stretching to see down the hill towards the dockyard. The street was still and grey and shabby. It had not changed. Maggie sucked in the view of wide-bayed semis on a broken-pavement hill, with just the hint of water beyond and in between the solid ashy docks and bridges and railways, the slightly rough children in slightly unkempt, slightly stony gardens. A song came in her head.

The framed pages Maggie had chosen from the book were hung where she remembered, in a line to the side of her bed. She took them down and sat on the counterpane to examine them. She split the dry tape on the backs of the frames with her nail file and eased out the paper, careful not to catch it on the protruding pins. Eddie had kept the curtains closed for the eleven years since she had left. There was no sun damage. She caught herself looking for the marks of etching, of hand colouring, of work to the paper and of the brown-tied librarian. She smiled at herself, embarrassed. She thought she had shaken off the defeat of arrival.

'I've found something out, Dad, about the pictures,' she said, when she came down with her hair tied back.

Eddie had not been to the cinema since he was a young man, and was not surprised to find there were things he did not know about it any more.

'I've not been for years,' he said.

'What?'

'Not been for years, to the pictures. I can't remember the last time. It would have been with your mother.'

Maggie did not laugh. 'No. No. The pictures. There.' She waved her arm vaguely. 'That used to be hung up. The ones that are in my room.'

Eddie felt a twinge of something inside him and his words came out panicky. 'You've found something out, Mags? What? What is it?'

Maggie moved forward until she was standing between him and the television. Eddie saw then that she had taken the frames in her room apart and was holding the loose pages flat on the palm of one hand.

With the excitement, Maggie did not know where to start.

'I've found out,' she said, 'about the book.'

Eddie felt his breath sink heavy within him as she started her story, as she told him what she had heard the television valuer say and what she had learned from the librarian and, finally, what kind of price the complete book might have. And when she had finished she stood waiting for him to leap at her and hug her, but Eddie was still expecting her to speak about Alice and did not know that she had told him everything she knew.

'Well?' said Maggie.

It was only then that Eddie breathed out. It sounded like a sigh.

'Well?' he echoed, waiting.

'What do you think?'

'I suppose it was bound to happen, sooner or later. You were bound to find out.'

Maggie felt her cheeks burn. 'You knew? You knew all this time what the book was, what it was worth?'

'Oh no, not that,' said Eddie. 'About Alice.'

It took them a long time to unravel it. Maggie had to explain her story again, from the start, and Eddie had to tell her something of what had happened with Alice. But she was his daughter, and he could not tell her everything, so he just put together enough of the past to make sense of the book.

'I gave Alice three more of the pages, you see, framed,' he said. 'It was one Christmas.'

'Oh my God,' Maggie breathed.

'No, but Mags, it's all right. We stopped it after that… It was just that Christmas, at the beginning—'

But Maggie was not thinking of that. She interrupted. 'Then you don't have all the pages? You don't have all the book? You've given it away?'

'It was Alice's to start with. She gave it to Florrie and me, you see, for our wedding. It meant something to her, my love.'

'And you've not seen her since?'

'No.'

'You don't know what she's done with the pages? She could have done anything. She could have burnt them. Dad! Don't you see? We need it all, if it's going to be worth what they said.'

The loose pages fluttered in Maggie's hands and because he had to find a way to comfort her, Eddie said, 'I could ask her, Mags. I could find out.'

And it was then, at last, that Maggie put down the precious papers and hugged him, and when it finally happened it was the perfume of a spring shower.

But the estate of prefabs where Alice had lived no longer existed. It had been bulldozed by the council, which was building lines of white-faced maisonettes in their place. Maggie had to stop at the edge of the building site and park the car at the barrier. They sat for a while looking up at the moors.

'It *is* the right place?' said Eddie, knowing.

Maggie just nodded.

They had had such faith in Alice.

'Then I have no idea,' said Eddie.

And though they talked for a long time about ways to track her down, Eddie, who had been through it all before, knew she would not be found.

'I don't think it's any good, Mags,' he said, as they pulled slowly up the hill to his house. 'I don't think we'll find her. Last time it was chance, that's all, you see. And that's not going to happen, is it, not again. We'll have to do without her.'

Maggie helped her father from the car back at home. His legs were stiff at the knees and he leaned on her more than she expected.

'Look, we'll think about it. There must be a way,' she said. 'She can't be that hard to find.'

'We've lost her, I warrant,' said Eddie, but Maggie thought her father was being old and defeated, incapable, and she ignored him.

She waited while he fumbled in his pockets for the key.

'It's a mess, that school,' she said, looking across the estate to the hill opposite where figures could be picked out moving around the low blocks of the campus.

'They're pulling it down. Building something new,' said Eddie, opening the door.

He let Maggie in ahead of him, as he always did, taking another glance at the school buildings while he waited. Maggie, in the hallway, had picked up the bottle of holy water still perched on the windowsill by the door, its plastic bleached yellow in the sun. She tried to turn the cap. It seemed stuck, but twisted open suddenly so that she lost her grip of it and it fell to the floor, rolling against the skirting board. She sniffed inside the bottle, but it was empty.

'Why do you keep this, Dad?' she said, following him through with the bottle held out, her voice still hard.

Eddie shrugged. 'It was Florrie's,' he said.

Maggie shook her head, surprised that this annoyed her.

The rest of the pages were as Eddie had left them, laid flat in the bottom of his wardrobe, protected by a split polythene bag. Put together with the ones Maggie had eased out of their frames, the edges tapped straight on the dining-room table, it looked like a book again and even folded down the centre where the pin-prick holes of the binding patterned their way through the paper. It was a pleasure to do this, together, and they took their time.

'It looks nice,' said Eddie.

'It'll do, until we find Alice,' said Maggie.

Before they had finished, Maggie noticed where Eddie had cut off part of a sheet and asked about it.

'It was spoilt,' was all he said at first. 'I just tidied it up, you see, that's all.'

But Maggie put down the paintbrush with which she was softly dusting the paper, and was narrowing her eyes at him.

'It's to do with Alice, isn't it?'

'It's nothing, my love,' he said.

She put her hand on his arm, and squeezed.

Eddie wanted to resist. 'Oh dear God, Maggie,' he said.

But Maggie would not let him be annoyed. 'The more pages we have,' she said evenly, 'the better it will be.'

'But Mags...'

'Do you know where it is, Dad?'

Eddie nodded.

The page, Maggie saw immediately, was different from the others. It was worn at the edges and one of its corners had a crease where it had been turned. It bore the stains of use. And she had not expected to see the scrawl of handwriting, the web of deep blue ink on the paper. The writing, when she saw it, surprised her, and what was written took her breath away.

'My God, Dad, it's disgusting,' she said. 'It's filthy. Did she write that? Alice? To you?'

Eddie nodded.

'I can't believe it. I can't believe someone would write that.'

'It was a long time ago...' he began, without at first realizing this was a mistake.

'It doesn't seem that long,' said Maggie. 'I remember her, being here. I remember that Christmas. She was very quiet. But I heard all sorts about her.' She shook her head. 'Even so, Dad, I wouldn't have thought that she could write such things.'

'No. It was before that, long before that, Mags, that it all...'

And then Eddie realized, because there was a look on Maggie's face that he had never seen.

'What do you mean, "before"? Did you meet her before? Was

there something before? Before, even, before Mum was dead?'

The 'befores' lost their meaning like that, multiplying with Maggie's panic, flattening time. She grasped hold of the sheet, looking as if she might tear it, and Eddie took it from her, fumbling. The words he needed twisted away from him.

'No, Mags.'

'No what?'

There was a moment then when anything could have been said. But the way Maggie looked at him, the pleading in her eyes and the unforgiving darkness there, behind, gave Eddie no choice.

'No, Mags, not when Florrie was here. It was nothing to do with Florrie. It was before that Christmas when you met Alice, that's all, a few months before. Nothing else. And in my mind it seems a long time, the time we spent together that autumn. But it was just a few weeks – really.'

Maggie did not reply straight away. She flicked her hair from her face and ran a hand then down one cheek. Eddie waited to see whether she would say she believed him.

'Right then,' she said. 'Sorry. It's just…'

Eddie finished it for her. He had the words now. 'It's just a lot, my love, I know that. For you to find out all at once, about the book, and then about Alice.'

'That's right,' said Maggie.

They got on with finding a way of reconnecting the letter to the rest of the book without using tape or glue or clips that might snag the paper. They worked on it as though it were like the other sheets, and Maggie did not read again what was written.

'I think all we can do is fold it in, and let them sew it or something,' said Maggie.

Eddie had presumed he would be putting the book back together himself. 'I can sew it,' he said. 'I've got tarpaulin needles in the shed, and I saw how it was done when I took it apart. It'll cost an arm and a leg to get someone else to do it, my love.'

'Dad, this thing's worth a fortune. We have to do it properly. No bodging.'

'I don't bodge.'

'No, I know. I didn't mean that. You'd do a good job, I'm sure. But we need a professional. We need to take advice.'

Eddie picked up the nearly book and turned some of the pages. 'Do you really think it needs to be there, the extra sheet, the letter?' he said.

'We'll ask someone,' said Maggie. 'They'll know. We need to keep it as complete as we can until then.'

'It seems a shame, that's all.'

'We'll ask,' Maggie said again.

The letter was still on Eddie's mind as they waited a few weeks later in the library. They were early for their appointment with the librarian, so they were sitting together on the bench by the counter. It was the afternoon and the sun was pouring through the stained-glass windows at the far end of the reading room, making the air glow warm and the crafted fittings shine. Eddie could not believe that his daughter had come here the first time, alone, unafraid. It was the kind of place the navy had kept for better men than him.

The librarian was early too. He had been waiting for his visitors for almost three hours, during which time he had done nothing but imagine what they might be bringing him. Now, as he took them up a flight of stone steps to a panelled room where he had laid out, on a long table, an immaculate white cloth, he walked with quick steps. He gave Maggie and Eddie pristine pairs of cotton gloves and swallowed firmly.

'So,' he said. 'I'm very pleased you've come back. I'm very pleased you've found it all. That *is* what you've come for? You *have* found the rest of the book?'

He leaned towards them as he asked, looking as if he might snatch their bags.

'Not quite all,' said Eddie, but Maggie nudged him. She noticed how his accent twanged.

'I'll show you what we have,' she said, and the librarian edged as close to her as he dared.

'This is the kind of thing that happens once in a lifetime,' he murmured, but Maggie presumed he was exaggerating and just smiled.

They spent a long time unpacking the sheets and laying them out in order. The librarian fussed, nudging pages so that they were not near the edge of the table, sliding overlaps apart, checking page numbers. He put the letter to one side, on a smaller table. Eddie found he wanted to stand there, near it, and moved around the room until he could feel the corner of the table sharp in his thigh.

'It's a beautiful treasure,' said the librarian, standing back from the display when all the pages were laid out and rubbing his eyes, as if to make sure of what he was seeing. 'It's beautiful. And to think you didn't know.' He chuckled. 'Isn't it funny how these things happen?'

'It's an heirloom, I suppose,' said Eddie.

'It is, sir,' said the librarian, leaning low over the table.

He had a pile of reference books on a chair at the end of the room, including the fat blue directory that Maggie recognized from her first visit. In time, reluctantly, he left the pages spread on the table and began looking things up, cross-referencing quickly, nimble with the indexes. Eddie looked across at his daughter and raised his eyebrows, impressed with such a rite of knowledge. No one spoke. Then, finally, the librarian looked up.

'I think I see it,' he said. 'If you would care to look. I think I have it.'

He held out a page to them, and Maggie tried to make sense of it, but it seemed to her a jumble of letters and dates and she gave up.

Eddie helped her. 'Would you explain?' he asked, unashamed. 'I'm not… if you could explain.'

The librarian smiled. 'Basically, every known copy of Blake's *Songs* has been assigned a letter. Here you see…' He ran his finger down the page. 'Everything from A to Z, as a means of identifying them. So, for example, copy A here, at the top, we know was printed by William Blake in 1795 and is in the British Museum; copy B is an earlier version from 1789, also in the British Museum, and so on. They're all listed.'

He looked up to be sure they were following.

'Now then, that's straightforward,' went on the librarian. 'But the trouble was, with Blake, he was printing all sorts of different versions at different times. He was always making changes: printing it sometimes one way, sometimes another; sometimes producing the complete *Songs*, sometimes just *Songs of Innocence*, sometimes just *Songs of Experience*. For a bibliophile it's fascinating, of course, but a minefield. Really, a complete minefield.'

His fingers flicked over the open page as he talked.

'So how do you know which is the right version?' asked Maggie.

'Oh no, that's not it. There isn't a *right* version. They're all versions by Blake, you see; they're all original versions in their way, just different ones. They're all equally valid.' The librarian found a mote of dust on his sleeve and brushed it down vigorously, talking still. 'And then sometimes, later, to make things worse, a collector or a dealer who already owned a copy of *Songs of Innocence* might buy someone else's copy of *Songs of Experience* and bind them both together. And so create a whole new version. You see?'

Eddie nodded again but was not sure.

'So it's unpredictable,' said the librarian. 'More than with perhaps any other book there are variables, variants. And a lot of what we know has to be conjecture; detailed, vigorous academic conjecture but still… it means there's room for surprises. Like this.' He nodded towards the table. 'This really is a surprise. An untraced version.'

'Unique,' said Maggie, pleased with the word.

'Absolutely. Unique.'

'But you know it's one of those, or like one of those?' said Eddie, waving faintly at the librarian's reference volume.

'Well, we can use this to assist us in tracking down your copy. We can piece things together, like a jigsaw, if you like, or some splendid kind of mystery. We can confirm what we *do* know and attempt to surmise the rest. Like I say – conjecture.' The librarian looked up at them. 'And what we *do* know, certainly, is that there are fifty-four plates in a complete copy. And you don't have that. There are not fifty-four plates here.'

'That'll be Alice,' hissed Maggie, 'I told you, that'll be her.'

'No, no, it's not a problem. I can see there are one or two pages missing here, but that's not what I mean. What I mean,' said the librarian, 'is that you don't have a full book of *Songs*. You never had a full book of *Songs*. You don't have *Songs of Innocence* and *Songs of Experience*. You just have *Experience*. Look.' He read quickly from the directory in his hand. It was nonsense. 'The first copies of the combined *Songs* in which the two sections were printed together were A and R in 1795. That same year, Blake printed eight sets of *Innocence* and nine sets of *Experience* impressions to form *Innocence* copy N, the "Innocence" section of combined *Songs* copy J, the "Experience" sections of combined *Songs* copies J, O and S, and both sections of combined *Songs* copies I, L, M and BB. "Innocence" of combined *Songs* copy O was once joined with "Experience" of combined *Songs* copy K, and untraced *Innocence* copy W was probably once combined with "Experience" of combined *Songs* copy N.'

He did not take a breath but Eddie blew hard through his teeth as the recital ended and then, because he couldn't help it, he laughed. Maggie thought she was annoyed with him, but found herself laughing too.

'Let's look at the pages themselves,' said the librarian.

And it was easier then, with the book in front of them, to understand. Maggie thought she grasped it.

'So what we have is just the *Songs of Experience*, from 1795, printed by Blake,' she said, her hands flat on the table to hold things tight.

'Yes, I would think so,' said the librarian.

'It doesn't matter, I suppose, which copy it is, though, precisely,' said Eddie, from his post at the edge of the room.

The librarian thought it did. 'Well, sir, it does make a difference – to know for sure,' he said.

'And it's a shame,' said Maggie, 'not to have the whole thing.'

'It *is* the whole thing, in its way,' said the librarian. 'There may once have been a *Songs of Innocence* attached to it, but we don't know that for certain. It's speculation. Quite possibly this was all there ever was. Quite possibly it's exactly what Blake intended. What you have is very special.'

'And valuable?' asked Maggie.

He nodded.

Maggie asked then what would happen about the missing pages. 'We gave them away to someone. And we can't get in touch,' she said, still not quite believing they had failed to find Alice. It seemed her father's fault.

'Well, I think you'll have to do without them. I can't see what alternative there is. It's part of the book's history, I suppose,' the librarian said, but there was regret in his voice. 'We could bind in blank pages, so that it's correctly configured, and you could write a note, explaining what happened, to create a full provenance. I think that's the best you can do. I can't see any alternative.'

Maggie felt she had disappointed him. 'I'm sorry,' she said.

He shrugged.

The librarian carefully gathered up the pages, taking a long time. Maggie picked up her bag to leave, pulling out a cardigan. Without the light from the sun the blinded room seemed colder than it was. Eddie had not moved, but he turned now slightly to reveal what they had left behind.

'And what about this one, with the writing? What'll we do with that?'

Afterwards, when he was sitting in Maggie's back room watching the cars pulling in and out of the garage forecourt opposite and thinking about things, he wondered why he had said anything at all. He did not want the letter taken away from him. He wanted to keep it. It was his. But by then it was too late.

'You're sure this is the same?' asked the librarian warily as he picked the sheet up in his gloved hands and brought it to the table.

'I am,' said Eddie. 'I cut it from the book myself, you see.'

The librarian nodded. He had read the first lines of the text. 'It does look the same, the same folio size, the same texture. I just thought, for someone to have done this…'

'It was my Aunt Alice,' said Maggie, but of course this did not mean anything.

'Well, it's just as before,' said the librarian briskly, in an effort to keep distaste from leaking into his words. 'It's a question of provenance. In a strange way it may add value. You never know.' He handed the paper to Eddie. 'It's up to you, of course, but I can only recommend that you reconstruct as much of the original book as possible, whatever the condition.'

'That's fine,' said Maggie. 'We can put it in, can't we, Dad?'

The days seemed short and melodic and Maggie tiptoed through them, waiting for the book to be finished. When it was ready she went with the librarian to the binders' workshops, a skein of concrete cabins that felt as if they might be underground and were more industrial than she had imagined. There was the dry, unromantic reek of ink and plastic, and blue-overalled men chewing gum.

When she saw the book again, there was a moment of disappointment. She had expected more. The calfskin binding that her father had unrolled from his pocket shone falsely in the strip lights and the slim brown book sitting on the binder's table, pushed up towards an uneven skyline of newly covered theses and library catalogues, looked unassuming and lifeless and unremarkable. They provided a supermarket carrier for her to take it home, and a lengthy itemized bill for the reconstruction. She doubted, then, that things would come right.

'It doesn't matter, Mags, in the end,' said Eddie, from far away.

'Oh, but Dad, all that money.'

'It's a speculation,' he said. He thought he heard the sniff of a tear. 'What comes next then? What do we do with it now?'

'We have to get it authenticated properly.'

'Hasn't he done that already – the man at the library? I thought he knew what it was.'

'He does, I hope he does. But everyone has to be sure. It has to be a world expert. That's why I'm wondering. What if we're wrong? What if he got it wrong after all?'

And the doubts stayed with Maggie, pricking through her days.

But the librarian was not wrong. His word was endorsed by a woman from an American university who travelled, first class, to the library to see the book and who, either because of jet lag or the excitement of what she found, had to sit for a long time in the corner of the room sipping a glass of British tap water. She signed a great many papers before she left, and had her photograph taken with the book, for posterity. All this too, Maggie had to pay for. And then, finally, after a much longer time than either Maggie or Eddie had envisaged, the book was put into auction.

'Why can't it happen here in Plymouth? Why does it have to be London?' moaned Eddie when he found out. 'I can't come to London.'

Maggie snapped at him. 'Of course you can come. I'll sort it out. Someone will sort it out. Dad, they'll want us to be there.'

But she found she could not discuss accommodation for her ageing father with the staff at the auction house. She also found that the train from the West Country was expensive, that Eddie had less money than she had ever imagined, and that the amorphous, slippery fear of something going wrong with the sale of the book incapacitated her.

'The book'll sell, my love, whether we're there or not,' Eddie pointed out. 'It's not like we can do anything.'

'But Dad, I want to be there. I want to see it sold. It's just I can't seem to sort it out.'

'Don't worry, Mags,' said Eddie.

'It's a big thing, Dad. We should be there.'

On the other end of the phone, Eddie cleared his throat, covering the receiver with his flat palm. 'I'm not sure it's worth going all that way for,' he said in the end, still gruff.

A photographer from the *Plymouth Herald* came to take a photograph of Eddie on the steps of his garden shed, a large pair of scissors in his hand and some sheets of rather flimsy A4 paper clasped in the other. The photographer was on his way to an under-11s netball match and could not stay when Eddie invited him in for a coffee.

'Still,' he said, as he packed away his camera, 'it's history being made, isn't it, something like this. Plymouth heritage. Like the Armada.'

Eddie could not shake the thought of this. That evening he told Maggie what the photographer had said.

'I don't think it's anything to do with Plymouth,' said Maggie, fiddling with the tight-coiled wire of the telephone. 'It's just where you live, that's all. It just happened that way.'

'Oh, I don't know – it's something to be proud of,' said Eddie, flicking open the edge of the curtains as he spoke, looking beyond. 'If I'm doing something like that, contributing to the heritage, making history…' Eddie puffed into the handpiece, a sound that reached Maggie like distant waves. 'Well, it makes everything worth while, doesn't it?' Eddie saw nothing of what passed in the bright street. He let the curtain fall back.

'I don't see, Dad,' said Maggie.

'Well, it's like everything I've done, it would be something, wouldn't it? You and Florrie, the navy, all those rules: it'd not be lost, would it? I'd be doing something that would matter; that would last. Heritage, he called it, you see, the man from the *Herald*.'

'Does this mean you want to go to London after all?'

'I think maybe I should, Mags, if you don't mind. If it's going to be a big thing, in all the papers.'

But it was unlikely that the story would have surfaced again, had not someone happened to mention to reporters that there was also the curious handwritten note, rather alarmingly erotic, the evidence of lost love. This was enough to spark things. The *Plymouth Herald* ran a spread and soon there were headlines blazing with speculation, and more photos of Eddie, taken indoors with soft lighting or with the sweeping prospect of the sea behind him. In some of these he appeared to be wearing make-up to soften the blemishes of his skin, and in one he was blowing forlorn kisses on the wind. The story was picked up for a moment by tabloids and talk shows, on local radio stations and in bulletins beating across the globe, everyone wanting to know who she was, this woman who had written so passionately.

Eddie did not give out her name. He wanted to keep Alice to himself. The clamour of public attention drew her away from him, further and further, fading, and all he was left with was his image in the newspaper photographs looking old and dazed. He could hardly remember the phrases in the letter and Alice's voice was lost in the din. It was as though he had never known her. It seemed to be just what the *Herald* had predicted, an event larger than them both, momentous, remote. He saw, too late, that this was the defeat of him. He felt the terrifying strangeness of it, travelling up to London on the train, and as he looked out at the flat land passing, smooth in the inland heat, it seemed that his substance was draining from him and only the steady rhythm of the tracks beneath was holding him together.

Maggie was bright in the void of the station, her red jacket and matching shoes beckoning to Eddie through the din of the diesel and the garbled announcements. She hugged her father with unabashed vigour.

'It'll be fine, Dad.' She touched his arm as she took his case. 'Don't worry.'

'I just hope they let us alone, Mags.'

'You could have worn a disguise.' Maggie laughed. 'A wig or something. If you had more hair they'd never recognize you.'

She seemed busy with things, his case and her purse, a slip of hair across her eyes. Eddie had to interrupt her.

'Mags, about the book... and Alice. I know you've read things in the paper, about when the letter was written...'

She kept walking, threading through the gathered travellers at the front of the station.

'I know there've been things written, about me and Alice – about how it was going on even before I married your mother...' Eddie was puffing slightly at the determined trot of her pace. 'But Mags, I don't want you to think... it's just talk, Maggie – it's nothing. I never knew – until I saw the letter, I never knew, and that was much later, after your mother had died. Mags, there was just Florrie and me.'

In the blank light between the high brick buildings, alongside the drone of the taxi rank, Maggie stopped. She turned back to him. 'Do you really want to talk about it, Dad, here?'

Eddie raised his eyes to the heavens in the hope of finding a suitable answer but saw only pigeons circling haphazardly in the hazy summer sky.

'It's nothing; a fuss about nothing,' he said.

Maggie flicked her eyebrows fiercely. 'It doesn't matter, Dad. It's good for the sale.'

Eddie could not look at her. 'Oh Mags,' he groaned.

They waited in the line for a taxi. They could hear the howl of pan pipes somewhere within the noise of the traffic.

'It was your Auntie Mary who told the papers,' Eddie said, pulling his suitcase close. 'It was her who said about the letter.'

Maggie blinked at him. 'Mary?'

'She saw the photo of me in the *Herald* and rang them up.'

Maggie edged him up the queue. 'What on earth would she do that for?'

'It's the whole idea she's never liked, the whole idea of me and Alice. It's not really anything to do with her...' Eddie shrugged. 'But still...'

'She must be jealous of all the attention. And the money. She must feel left out.'

'Charlie says the whole thing's made her cry. She's in a state. They're not talking to me,' said Eddie.

Maggie looked away to where the taxis were turning into the bay. Eddie touched her gently, on the firm ridge of her back, and she turned to him.

'It's you, Mags, that's important. That's the thing. If you don't mind...'

Maggie smiled with spare lips. 'I can't see how it's your fault,' she said.

They had lunch together, buying a sandwich and sitting on a bench in Trafalgar Square amid the spirals of birds, and then they took another taxi, when it was time, to the auctioneer's. Eddie was surprised at the speed with which things were moving.

'We'll keep out of the way,' he said as the taxi slowed. 'Just tuck in somewhere at the back.'

Maggie smiled at him. 'Don't be scared, Dad. It'll turn out fine.'

And because they had arrived early, they were shown to seats quite near the front of the saleroom, but no one took any notice of them and Eddie sat quietly with his hands folded. He was grateful for the air conditioning.

In time the esteemed and portly Mr Theodore Wilcox PhD, auctioneer, shook their hands, slightly sweaty, and wished them luck. They were given a complimentary catalogue and a glass of wine each. Eddie put his wine under his pink-plush chair and, much later, found his glass had tipped and a puddle of chardonnay was leaking into the fine pile of the carpet. They felt as if they should whisper, even though the crowd that was gathering slowly around them was full of crisp voices, and when the auctioneer climbed on to his dais and began to shuffle papers, Eddie took Maggie's hand and squeezed it. Everything was bustle and noise and not quite identifiable.

'There're a lot of bow ties,' whispered Maggie, and they both laughed at this because it was so obvious.

It was a relief when the librarian, unequivocally plain and familiar, tucked through the row of chairs in front of them and reached across to shake their hands. He, too, kept his voice low and was pink in the cheek and chin. He wiped his brow with a handkerchief before he spoke, but did not mention the heat swelling outside the room.

'It's rather a mêlée, isn't it?' He smiled. 'Lots of American interest, I hear. And Japanese. We'll do well to keep it. But it should be good for you; it'll push up the price. There are silly prices being paid at the moment. Nothing the libraries can compete with.' He remembered the hours he had spent alone with the book in the cool quiet, studying it with a magnifying glass, and the days on which the thought of it had sustained him.

'Still,' he added, before he moved away.

Eddie, turning to watch the librarian make his way down the side of the room, was not quite sure about what he saw next. Maggie had her eyes fixed on the auctioneer who, having arranged his papers was, in turn, intent on following the hands on the wide-faced clock as they ticked around the final minutes. She thought Eddie had nudged her by accident and did not respond. But Eddie prodded her again, hard in the ribs, because he could not be sure by himself, among the perfumed swarm of buyers and their consorts, among the tweeds and silks, among the excitable smart set of the arts sales market, whether the woman in a summer suit of bright florals and with her metallic hair cut short was indeed who he thought.

'Mags,' he whispered urgently. 'Look!'

But Maggie still did not turn.

Alice stood for a moment at the back of the room to catch her breath. She felt her new skirt stiff around her waist. The murky heat of the city lay heavy on her lungs and she was disorientated by the bustle of the saleroom. Around her, people were taking the last seats, even the hard-bottomed chairs pushed against the wall, but she did not try for a place. She watched as the auctioneer, taking his final position on the podium, raised his hand for quiet, and then she walked swiftly down to the front, banging her large document case against chairs, knees and outstretched ankles as she passed.

'Excuse me, madam, could you take a seat? The auction is starting.'

It was not Mr Wilcox himself who spoke, because he had not yet noticed Alice and because he had been planning in his head, for many days, the exact phrasing and intonation of the first public words he would utter on this significant occasion. It was a younger man who appeared from the side. He sounded offended by her being there.

'I need to talk to the auctioneer,' said Alice firmly, without looking at him, rapping her fist instead on the edge of the podium.

Alice was somehow unignorable, and Mr Wilcox looked straight at her now, from his height. He did not speak. He glanced instead at his colleague who this time took Alice by the arm.

'Madam, please. This is not the time.'

Alice shook him off.

'I want to talk to you about the rest of the book,' she said, not quietly, and it was heard all around her, in the first few rows of the saleroom, as far back as to where Eddie and Maggie were each calculating a changed future. 'I need to know what has happened to the rest of the book.'

Maggie was panicking. 'Oh my God, Dad, she's going to say it's hers. She's going to take it out of the sale. There's going to be all sorts of... can you prove she gave it to you? Can you prove it, Dad?'

Eddie put a hand on her arm. He was noticing how the back of Alice was so neat this time, her hair perfectly trimmed and flat, her jacket hanging full, her skirt uncreased.

'I suppose there's just the letter,' he said. 'If that's proof.'

Maggie covered her eyes with the heels of her hands, pressed hard, and groaned.

Alice unzipped the top of her document case, just far enough to prise it open so that the edges of the pages inside could be seen. The auctioneer bent, despite his better judgement, peering over the top of his stand at her. He presumed the interruption would be brief and eccentric. But then he saw quite clearly the swirl of Blake's colours, the truncated lines of text, the thick edges of old folios, and looking over Alice's head he raised his hand again, this time to signal a delay. The man at Alice's arm stepped back, and a deep hum burst into the hall as though someone had let a swarm of hornets through the window. Only Eddie and Maggie, it seemed, were quiet, trying to listen.

'You are, I presume,' said Alice, 'missing some pages. And I have some of them – here. A few.' She swung the document case in a wide arc. 'But the rest?'

If there was more, neither Eddie nor Maggie heard it. Because the saleroom crowd was swelling forward, noisy, and because there was an announcement about something from the dais, and because Eddie was pushing his way along the row of people seated alongside him, desperate to see Alice, having no idea of what he would say, and hearing nothing except the bellow of an ocean gale.

Theodore Wilcox stepped down. He shook hands with Alice neatly, and then led her away beyond the cameras and micro- phones to a door behind, through which they disappeared. Music was piped then into the saleroom and a woman with fiercely blonde hair apologized to everyone for the unforeseen delay. More wine was served. No one seemed to mind. Eddie was awk- ward in the aisle. He looked back to Maggie, but she still had her face covered and her head bowed.

The door behind the auctioneer's dais led into a short corridor. There was a small, clean office through another door on the far right, and this is where Theodore Wilcox took Alice now. He offered her a seat and a drink, but she remained standing, asking just for a glass of water. This never arrived.

Alice laid the document case carefully on the table.

'I have three pages,' she said. 'All from *Experience*. But you know, when I last saw the book it was the whole thing: *Innocence and Experience*. Exactly as it should be.' Alice was calm but her voice was heavy with accusation and lapsed anger. 'I knew he'd taken it apart – that's how I got these – but he told me he'd kept everything. Everything. But now, I need to know what's happened. Who's got the rest of my book?'

Mr Wilcox was cautious. 'Now, before we begin, madam, Mrs… ?'

'Alice Craythorne.'

'Oh,' he said. 'Alice. From the letter? That Alice?'

He seemed to peer at her. Alice glared. 'Shall we talk about that later?' she said. 'Shall we sort this out first?'

Mr Wilcox summoned the words he had read at the front of the book and couldn't help them repeating in his head. He found it hard to concentrate.

'Right, Ms Craythorne, well, now – yes. But before we begin, I have to say, I'm not in a position to offer any kind of official authentication today. It's very specialist, this kind of expertise. There are only a few people in the world… you have to understand.'

'Never mind, never mind that.' Alice was impatient. 'These here, these are genuine pages. You can take my word for that.'

Mr Wilcox huffed quietly. 'But that's not important, not really. It's the rest that's important. What have you done with it? Did you know there was more? Is it a sales thing? Does it get you more money?'

The questions stacked up between them. The auctioneer tried not to let his face give away his confusion.

'I don't quite understand,' he said. 'Obviously you know this book very well, Ms Craythorne, but…'

'It was mine to start with,' Alice said reasonably, and then, more quietly, 'it came to me from my father.'

Theodore Wilcox was conscious, all at once, of the heat in the room pressing in on him. He thought he could hear the drone of expectant voices in the hall. He wiped his face with his hand and came close to Alice.

'Look, Ms Craythorne, this is, I know, a tricky, one might even say a sensitive situation. I appreciate that it must be upsetting, to find out, like this, that a favourite family item is being sold. But if you're wanting to make a claim on it—'

'To find out *half* of it's being sold. To find out it's been butchered,' snapped Alice. 'And through the papers – to find out everything through the papers.'

'Yes, well, of course, a sale of this nature is a significant event. There's a great deal of public interest, as you might imagine,' went on Mr Wilcox.

'I never imagined anything like this.'

'No, of course, but a sale of this nature, as I say, and with the added personal interest of the book's history, Ms Craythorne – it's the kind of sale that captures the imagination.'

He beamed. Alice was wishing the glass of water would come.

'But it's not right; none of it's right,' she said, not quite knowing where to begin. 'It's not just a book for sale. It shouldn't be for sale at all, not like this. It's not the right book at all.'

Mr Wilcox pursed his lips. 'Ah. I see. Ms Craythorne, it's the new binding that alarms you, the reconstitution of the book, the metamorphosis.' He smiled. 'But you see it's not a problem. It's all correctly recorded. It's in the catalogue. If you would like to come with me, back to the saleroom, I can show you exactly.'

The auctioneer moved to the door, opening his arm to Alice as though to usher her through. Alice pulled a chair from the table and sat down. She sighed.

'It's not that,' she said.

When Eddie and Alice met again it was in the auctioneer's office, with its barred-window view of bricked London yards and its stale scent. It was with Theodore Wilcox dry-mouthed and stiff, Maggie near to disappointed tears, and a bevy now of other staff pushing in through the door to see for themselves what had caused the interruption. Eddie was fretful, and Alice's disappointment had drained her colour, making her seem grey. They said nothing to each other. Separated by the table and its display of pages and the people they did not know, they did not come close. But there was a longing they each acknowledged, written deep and old, uniting them.

'I need to know what you've done to the book,' said Alice.

'We couldn't find you,' said Maggie, breathless.

Alice did not smile at her niece. 'And this letter malarkey, too;

this, what is it, a publicity stunt? Oh good Lord… I didn't know you would do this.'

Conscious of his responsibility, Theodore Wilcox felt obliged to step in and take charge. 'So, Ms Craythorne, now that everyone is here we can straighten out everything, I'm sure. Bearing in mind that we are here today, all of us, to sell this beautiful copy of William Blake's *Songs of Experience*.' He looked around firmly, not letting them speak. 'And I needn't remind you that there's a packed saleroom out there, waiting. People from all over the world, respectable buyers. Not to mention the press.'

'We just need a minute,' said Maggie. 'Then it'll be fine, I'm sure.'

'Well, I can't put this thing off for ever.'

Alice put her hands on the table and looked ahead of her to where the staff were crammed into the narrow doorway. 'I want answers to my questions,' she said. 'I need to know about the book.'

Theodore Wilcox drew himself up to speak but Alice turned to Eddie.

'This is what I need to know,' she said, and she hauled a breath from deep within. 'Simple things, Eddie.'

'Alice, I don't know if I can… here… I don't know what to say,' said Eddie. He felt Maggie take his hand.

But Alice went on evenly. 'Let me see then, if I've got it right. So far. What I've read in the papers, what I've pieced together, what I know. First, that after Florrie died you went through her things and you found a book. Then, after a while, you found me. And then when you took the book apart – God only knows why you would take it apart, for pictures or trinkets or whatever, but anyway – when you took the book apart you gave me three pages. Here.' She tapped the top of her document case. 'Here, all three of them are here. Take them and see.'

She thrust the case towards Theodore Wilcox. He unzipped it with clumsy hands and took out the sheets, laying them flat on the table. There was a push forward as everyone tried to get a view.

'They appear authentic,' he said, nodding. 'They look like Blake. But of course, as I've said before, I can't, myself—'

Alice didn't let him finish. 'And really, that's not too bad. Three pages, that's all, and they came back to me. It's all right, Eddie, that. I knew about all that. But then, some time later someone must have told you there was money in it, and you—'

'It was on the television,' interrupted Maggie.

Alice glared at her. 'You found out there was money in it,' she continued. 'And Eddie, what did you do then?'

There were people between them, and Eddie could move no closer to Alice. The clutch of Maggie's fingers was tight on his hand.

'Is it a question of title?' suggested Mr Wilcox. 'Of ownership? Because—'

'It's a question of what you've done with half of my book and why you've cooked up this stupid sordid letter idea,' spat Alice.

There was a shuffle in the room, a slice of conversation from people passing in the corridor and then a wail. It was Eddie.

'I don't understand,' he moaned, and seeing that Alice looked away from him, he moaned again.

Theodore Wilcox, also, did not understand, but he did not

expose his confusion. Instead he asked measured questions, many of them, and it took a long time. Twice someone came through from the auction room to ask what to tell the gathered buyers, and twice the gathered buyers were asked to wait just a few more moments while the unforeseen difficulty was resolved. Mr Wilcox tried not to show his impatience. He tried to stay calm. But Maggie, in the end, was desperate.

'Look,' she said, 'Dad. Just tell her. It's our book. We can do what we like. We can sell it. She gave it to you.'

Mr Wilcox had already ascertained the basic truth of this, and nodded. 'I'm quite satisfied of that,' he said. 'The provenance is hereditary, clearly, as stated in the catalogue. You don't contest that you gave the book away, Ms Craythorne, as a gift?'

Alice shook her head. 'But I gave them the *whole* book,' she said.

'I've just said that,' hissed Maggie, through clenched teeth.

'I gave nothing to you, missie, so don't you start,' Alice snapped. 'It was Florrie's – Florrie's and Eddie's – and it was the whole thing, every word. *Innocence and Experience* – not just this.' She threw an open hand towards the saleroom.

Again there was confusion. But the auctioneer was beginning to see, at least in part.

'Ms Craythorne,' he said, wiping his face with the yellow handkerchief from his breast pocket. 'Do you mean…?'

The plot of things was coming to him. He wiped his face again. 'Yes, yes – let me intervene. Let me imagine this. Just for a moment.'

He raised an authoritative plump finger and the room was quiet. Eddie had his eyes fixed on Alice. The sun was shining through the barred window making the tips of her hair molten.

'Let me suggest this,' went on Theodore Wilcox, 'as a possible scenario: that you gave to your sister and her husband, as a wedding present, a volume of William Blake's *Songs of Innocence and Experience*, complete. A long time ago, we should note. And for many years subsequently, we should also note, the volume remained in storage. As far as we know, neither your sister nor her husband read it, nor even opened it.'

Eddie nodded at this. It was as though he had called out. Everyone turned to him.

The auctioneer continued. 'And then on the death of Florence, you, sir, you found the book with other of your wife's effects, and with your daughter you proceeded to make pictures – and so on and so forth as we have established.' His finger waggled broadly across the table, ushering away the inconsequence of this. 'Until the book comes here, no longer both sets of *Songs* but just the latter half. Half the original book.'

He spoke slowly, his voice ringing even in the little office. He knew he had it now. He opened his arms expansively, taking in the room.

'Yes, and let me imagine this also. That in the intervening period, in that time when neither of you had the book, *someone else divided it*. Someone else took it away, had it rebound in two parts, and returned one part, the *Songs of Experience* to you, sir. Leaving you, Ms Craythorne, none the wiser, and you, sir, with what still amounts to a very valuable object. In my sale.'

He was proud of the pause that followed.

'That can't be right,' said Alice at last, but quietly. 'Who would do such a thing? Why would anyone divide the book?'

She looked at Eddie, the sunlight slipping on to her face as she turned her head.

'It wasn't me, Alice. Really. I've kept everything that ever came to me, every page. It wasn't me.'

Maggie was relieved. 'It must have been Mum. If it's like you say, Mr Wilcox, it must have been her. She must have found out it was worth something and sold it, half of it. That must be it.'

The auctioneer brought his hands down so firmly on the table that Alice's document case jumped. 'Exactly,' he said.

'It fits all the facts,' said Maggie.

But Eddie shook his head. 'I don't think she'd do that. I don't think Florrie would do that, Mags. And I would have known.'

'Not if it was before, Dad, when you were away. Not then. She might have done it without you knowing. She might have needed money for things.'

Theodore Wilcox was putting Alice's pages back into her case. He looked up at Eddie. 'It happens all the time, sir, all the time. We hear of it a lot. Sales are frequently made – how shall we say – discreetly.'

Eddie could not let this be true. He shook his head again. 'It's not right. I know she wouldn't… Alice you don't think Florrie sold it, do you, half of it?'

Alice's voice was dull. 'No,' she said, and then, 'I don't know.' She sat back in the chair. Some of the staff had drifted away from the table now that the mystery was solved, and in the corridor a young man was flipping a coin.

'But if I could return your attention to the sale,' insisted the auctioneer. 'Perhaps we could continue. There seems to me no

reason not to continue. Now that the confusion has been…
allayed.' He rested his hand on Alice's document case. 'And these
other pages, Ms Craythorne. Obviously we can't sell them today.
That would be most unwise. They are subject, of course, to
authentication. But if we could perhaps display them with the
rest of the book; make it known that they are available; that they
could be sewn back into the volume by the buyer, then it would,
I'm sure, only be to everyone's advantage. A prospective buyer
would be reassured, I am certain, at the prospect of acquiring,
sooner or later, the complete volume.'

He picked up the case. The noise from the saleroom rumbled towards them as the door through was propped open to
allow everyone to pass quickly. Maggie now let go of her father's
hand.

'It's not the complete volume,' said Alice firmly, standing up.

The auctioneer made himself very large. 'Madam, the book
out there in the auction has been authenticated. As far as anyone
is aware – anyone outside this room – there was never more to
it. There is conjecture that at one time it might have been differently bound, perhaps with a now lost copy of *Songs of Innocence*,
but this is conjecture, academic conjecture. We do not need to
concern ourselves with it today. All we need to know is that the
book out there, in the auction, is now richer by three very beautiful pages.'

It felt as if everything was resolved.

Maggie moved towards her aunt and sighed. 'We thought,'
she said, 'that perhaps you wanted the book back, the whole
thing. That you were going to say it was yours. And stop the
sale. It's a relief.'

Alice pursed her lips, biting slightly on the lower one. Theodore Wilcox offered her his arm magisterially.

'It was all just rather unexpected,' he said, the noise of the saleroom luring him. 'Rather exceptional. But we are unambiguous now, we are agreed, and that is the main thing.'

In a moment the mechanics of the auction were moving inexorably along again. The office was cleared, the auctioneer was refolding his pocket handkerchief in preparation for the show, and Maggie's cheeks were flushing red with the excitement of promised wealth. There was a scraping of distant chairs, a slight draught of cool air and the light in the room suddenly sharp and slightly green. But then Alice looked across at Eddie, still sitting in the corner, smoothing the creases in his trousers meticulously with troubled hands.

'It's no good,' she said. 'I need to settle things.'

The auctioneer puffed. 'Really, Ms Craythorne. We need to be quick.'

'Eddie, I need to settle things,' said Alice, ignoring him.

Eddie looked at her blankly, as though he did not recognize her, and it was Maggie who answered.

'I'll stay, Alice. I'll go through it again with you.'

'Oh, for goodness sake, Maggie, it's nothing to do with you,' said Alice, and when Maggie looked at her father, he nodded.

'She's right, Mags,' said Eddie.

The auctioneer closed the door to the hall behind him and it was quiet. There was just the hum of things. The click of Maggie's heels on the tiled floor receded from them. Eddie got up and held out his hand to Alice, low down, unobtrusive.

'We'll find out about it, one way or another, one day,' said

Eddie. 'We'll find out properly, if you like. I can't believe Florrie would do that.'

Alice stepped away. 'Ripped it apart, in the end – sold bits of it on – to pay for what? Stockings? Prayer cards? Perhaps she gave it to the priest, to save her soul.' She was somewhere distant, almost laughing. 'I didn't think she had it in her,' she marvelled.

'Look, Alice—'

The determination of Eddie brought her back. 'Oh, but Eddie – for pity's sake! The letter! The rest of it we could've… but the letter – that was the thing. Why did you do that?'

'I wanted to keep it back,' he said. 'I wished I had, really I did. But you see, it was the librarian and everyone, saying it had to go in. Saying it was part of its history. I'm sorry.'

There were long years between them that they would never navigate. But Alice tried. 'And what did you do with what I'd written? To Florrie?' she asked.

Eddie thought she was confused. 'No, you wrote to me, Alice. That's what they've put in the book. The letter – the love letter – you wrote to me.'

He held out his hand again. Alice looked at the white of it against the worn blue of the office.

'I never wrote to you, Eddie,' she said, frowning. 'Why would I write to you? I told you that before. It's not my letter.'

Eddie was stubborn. 'But I was sure…'

'Why on earth would I give you a wedding present like that? Think about it.'

Eddie was rubbing his face hard, his eyes tight shut, his skin creased. He thought of all the things he had heard about Alice, but they would not settle, he could not stack them into any kind of order; everything about her was confused.

His words were smothered. 'But if you never wrote it, Alice; if you never said those things...'

Alice was scornful. 'Eddie, I saw it in the newspaper. It was trash. I'd never write something like that.'

'But Alice, that's what started it all.' His hands dropped away and his voice came clearer. 'When I read that – when I thought...'

'That? You read that – that rubbish – and you thought...' Alice laughed through tight teeth. 'Oh Eddie! It's been a mess. For a long time.'

Eddie was getting up to come towards her when he thought of something else. He sank back. 'Do you want the book back then, Alice?'

'You can't sell it.'

'But everyone's waiting. It's all arranged.'

'Just take it home, Eddie. They can't stop you.'

Eddie shook his head. 'Maggie's banking on it,' he said.

Alice stepped towards him. 'You can't sell it, Eddie,' she said firmly. 'Not after everything.'

Eddie ran his hand over the case on the table. 'Look, we won't sell your pages, Alice. They're yours. If you want to keep them, they're yours.'

Alice had her hands too now on the case, to support herself, but still she did not touch Eddie. A heavy tear dropped on to the plastic cover and ran away towards the zip.

'Oh Alice, look, don't you see, it's Maggie's as much as mine. And she's set her heart on it, on selling it.'

Alice knew she only had the words for one appeal.

'Eddie, listen to me. The book is mine. It's always been mine. It was never Florrie's or yours. It was certainly never Maggie's. It's mine. It's all there is of me. You'll betray me, Eddie, if you sell it.'

He could never understand this. He was cross with her for spoiling things. 'Don't be stupid, Alice – it's just a book. And if you didn't write the letter, even – if you never even thought you might love me …'

Alice shook away his dismay. 'I only said I didn't write the letter, Eddie. I only said that. The rest of it …' She looked at him. 'I don't know. I can't remember. It's all so long ago, with Florrie being there and …'

Eddie put a hand up and brushed the hair gently from Alice's cheek, feeling the coolness of her tears. She did not move away.

'I'm getting to be an old man, Alice. I don't work any more. If Maggie had the money… if the sale went ahead …'

Alice touched her hand on his. 'I think there'd be too much lost,' she said.

'No, Alice, listen to me. There'd be nothing lost. You'd have the money – you can have some of the money, of course you can… and we can do something. It'd be a new start.'

'I don't think I could,' said Alice, decided. 'I think perhaps it's too late for all that.'

Maggie turned the bend in the corridor back towards the sale-room. She could see Alice and her father still in the office, close, their faces almost touching, their eyes on the table, not seeing. Their voices were low, but she could hear the rumble of passion in them. When she passed the open door, they did not see her; did not even raise their heads. She walked more quickly. For a moment, at the end of the corridor, she paused, but then she pushed open the door to the saleroom and Mr Wilcox, relieved, beckoned to her from the dais. She felt the buzz of noise around her.

Alice and Eddie were slow together, tangled. It was some time before they made their way out of the office, the document case swinging metrically between them. They pushed open the door to the saleroom and Eddie stood back for Alice to pass, but they both stopped abruptly in the silence beyond, in the catch of breath before Theodore Wilcox, in full voice and imperious, called another figure.

'Eighty-eight thousand, five hundred, on my right.'

There was nothing around Alice suddenly but the dark, and apart from it all, the book, a beautiful thing, resting on a midnight velvet, lit from above, glistening almost, drawing her. Alice knew the place at which it was open for display. It was the song of 'A Little Girl Lost', with a tree sucking at the text of the poem, golds and weeping crimsons like bruises at the bottom of the page. She could hear the words of it in her head, Arthur's voice knotted within them, and she felt herself trembling. There was too much now, shrieking at her from the poem, obliterating everything. She reached for the book, quivering, seeing everything now as it had once been, the blossoming love of it and the weariness. Around her was nothing but dim curtains. She was completely alone.

A hand rested gently on her arm. Alice started. There was the dazzle of the display lights and an eddying mist of colour beyond that would not resolve itself. And then Eddie.

'Eddie, stop him. He can't do that. He can't sell the book.'

But Eddie had seen Maggie already, seated to one side, her eyes fixed on the auctioneer, leaning into the weight of the numbers he was calling.

'I'm sorry, Alice,' he said. And he took her tightly in his arms, drawing her back again to the edge of the saleroom, holding her firm across the shoulders, the unyielding plastic of the document case stiff and pungent between them.

The bidding was measured but brisk, the auctioneer's timbre steady. The price continued to mount magnificently. At three hundred thousand pounds Theodore Wilcox paused to take a sip of water from the glass at his side and to glance discreetly at the clock. At four hundred thousand pounds there was a fleeting lull while the bidders considered their limits. Eddie could not look at Alice. He unwrapped his arms from her, taking her instead by the hand. She twisted her little finger between two of his and they held on tight, unsteady. The light in the hall became metallic and brittle as the sun faded outside, and somewhere a siren sounded. Still the sale continued. Then there was a silence, a glimpsed moment when anything was possible, before the auctioneer dropped his gavel ceremonially at slightly more than half a million pounds, and the book was summoned across the Atlantic to be locked in a private library cabinet. There was a shuffle in the hall as people began to stand.

Maggie was defiant. 'He had our instructions,' she said, fidgeting from foot to foot in front of them. 'We'd signed everything. I suppose he got tired of waiting. I suppose there was a schedule.'

Eddie nodded and for a moment put out a hand on Maggie's fluttering arm. Then he looked at Alice. Her face was flushed pink with the shock of it, her lips parted in surprise.

'It doesn't matter, Alice,' he said. 'Does it?'

He saw the lines deep in the corners of her eyes, the shadows of tears there still, the whisper of Florrie in the turn of her mouth. He waited for her to say something. Maggie peeled away, buoyant in the crowd, and Eddie saw her with the auctioneer, embracing him. Then there was just the two of them, quiet.

'Alice, it doesn't matter?' Eddie asked again. But he was afraid. Her mournful stillness was beyond him.

Alice did not know what to say. The words she was used to were in the book and now they had been taken away, the lines of verse spluttering like broken prophesies at the limits of her vision. She would have to begin again with a whole new language, and she did not know yet if she could. But she took Eddie's hand, and led him through the clustered crowd and out on to the street where a sudden summer shower had split the sky with rust and marbled the pavements with rainbow damp. The noise of the traffic swelled like a January sea. They stood outside, along from the saleroom door, waiting. In the blank glass of the office window behind them, Alice knew she should be able to see herself, but the dust and the rain and the city grease obscured the reflection, the sharp light of the late sun breaking through the gap in the buildings opposite and making everything flat. Alice brushed her hair from her face.

Ahead of them, caught in the slow traffic, a bus pulled to a halt, the conductor leaning out to look up the street and its open doorway beckoning. It pulled forward a few paces and stopped again, puthering dark fumes from its exhaust. The conductor disappeared inside. And all of a sudden there was something irresistible about the way the narrow metal stairway wound up into the dark of the top deck. Alice began to run, her document case flapping as she called to Eddie, her arms splayed, her shoes splashing up the rain on to her skirt, her eyes fixed on the red of the bus staining the line of traffic, and just as it moved again, faster now, purposeful, Eddie caught up with her and they skipped together on to the low platform where they hung for a moment side by side. And as they clung to the metal pole, surprised at themselves, the bus turned a corner into unfamiliar streets, gathering speed now as it moved away, and Alice looked steadily across at Eddie then, ready to answer him.

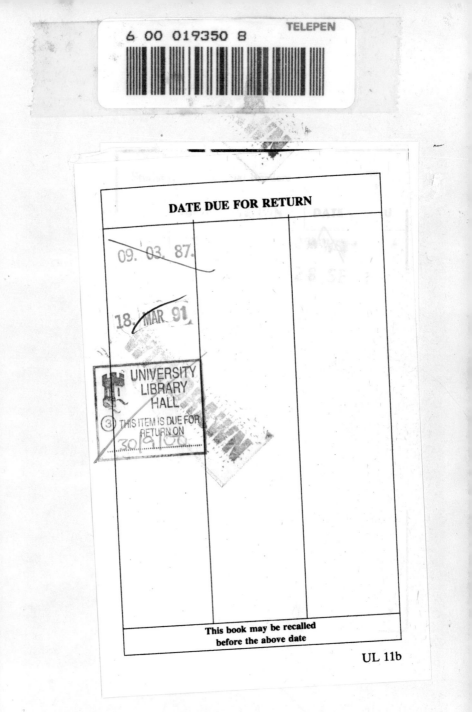

THE BRITISH POLITICAL FRINGE